THE SECRET OF DUNHAVEN CASTLE

THE SECRET OF DUNHAVEN CASTLE

A CATE KENSIE MYSTERY

NELLIE H. STEELE

A Novel Idea Publishing

For my mom, Stephanie
Happy Birthday!

ACKNOWLEDGMENTS

A very special thank you to everyone who made this book possible! Special shout outs to: Stephanie Sovak, Paul Sovak, Michelle Cheplic, Mark D'Angelo and Lori D'Angelo.

Finally, a HUGE thank you to you, the reader!

MacKenzie Family Tree

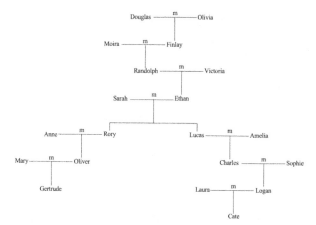

CHAPTER 1

"And so despite all the stories you've heard, Paul Revere never shouted 'The British are coming!' in his famous ride," Dr. Catherine Kensie said concluding her final lecture for the week. Cate was one of a handful of history instructors in the tiny and declining Department of History and Classics at Aberdeen College, a small liberal arts institution in the central United States. She had been at the college for the past few years after finishing her doctorate in history. In her early thirties, she looked little older than some of her students and was often mistaken for one. The effect was most apparent when she appeared in class after hours spent researching in the library. Like many female students, her dark hair was swept into a haphazard bun held by a pencil, a few pieces escaping to frame her blue eyes, glasses pushed on top of her head and sporting a pair of jeans and boots.

"We'll end there today remember that you have your final term paper due on the American Revolution next Thursday!" she shouted over the rustling of students packing laptops and notebooks into their bags in a mad dash to scramble out of the lecture hall.

"Please see me in my office hours if you need to discuss this further..." Her voice trailed off as it became clear that no one was listening. It was late on a Friday afternoon and students were in a rush to end their week and start their weekend.

She sighed as she began stuffing her notes into a folder and packing all her materials into her tote bag. Once she had everything collected, she started up the steps toward the back entrance of the lecture hall. A quarter of the way up she paused, sighing again. She returned to the lectern and picked up her keys, which she often forgot as her mind swirled with her lecture ideas and research topics, and pocketed them. "I'd forget my head if it wasn't attached," she mumbled before beginning the climb up to the exit again.

Once at the top, she pushed open the door to the waning warmth of a bright spring day. Despite the late afternoon hour, the sunlight was still bright, almost blinding after being in the darkened lecture hall. She shielded her eyes against it as she fumbled in her bag for a pair of sunglasses. Pushing them onto her face she started her walk across campus to the History Department's main office. She enjoyed the heat of the warm spring sun on her face and the sound of newly grown leaves rustling in the gentle breeze. Aberdeen's campus, with its central manicured lawn that connected its various buildings, was most beautiful in the spring.

The campus was a collection of neo-classically designed buildings, giving it an "old college" air. While compact rather than sprawling, it had plenty of green space which contrasted the light tan stone of the buildings. Cate headed toward one of the smaller buildings across the lawn, which housed several of the liberal arts departments, including hers. On a late Friday afternoon, Cate was almost alone as she made her way across campus. She saw a few students heading to cars or dorm rooms after a late class, but many were already gone for the weekend.

When Cate arrived at the History department's main office, she found the door locked. Given that it was after 5 p.m., most others, including the department secretary and other office staff, were long gone. Cate was used to it; she often taught the early and late classes that other faculty preferred not to teach. A perk of being a tenured or tenure-tracked faculty member was to be more selective of the courses one taught including their scheduled time, the course material or the general makeup of the students expected to take the course. Since she was only an instructor without tenure, nor was she tenure-tracked, she was on the bottom rung for schedule selection so she got whatever was left over. She didn't mind much. She loved her job teaching history and didn't mind being alone in the office. Cate dug into her pocket for her keys and rooted around for a moment trying to find the right one. A voice startled her from behind. "Still here, huh?"

"Oh!" She grabbed her chest, shutting her eyes for a moment before turning around. "Brian, you startled me. Yes, I'm just finishing up for the week."

Brian, the building's custodian, was pushing a vacuum toward her. "Was just about to vacuum in the main office, here, let me get that door for you. I'll wait 'til you're done in there!" He unlocked the door and pushed it open, holding it for her to enter.

"Oh, thanks," she said, "you don't have to wait, I'm just going to grab my mail and be out of your way!"

"No problem, have a great weekend, Cate!"

"You too!"

The afternoon sun shone through the back windows warming the office and illuminating it enough to find her way to her mailbox without needing the overhead lights. Collecting her mail, she glanced through it, discarding a few unneeded items like book advertisements and conference announcements. An envelope marked with the Dean's office return address peeked out from the rest of the mail. She stared at it a moment then decided to open it at home and shoved it into her tote bag. It most likely was a response to her request to transition her full-time instructor position to a tenure-tracked position. With the recent retirement of a tenured colleague, she hoped they would grant her request. She had been here several years, with an unwritten understanding that she could transfer to a tenure-tracked position as soon as one became available. While the tenure process was demanding, the promise of job security made it worth it. Her current position meant that she required a renewal letter annually. The stress of waiting to find out if you had a job from year to year was taxing.

After clearing out her mailbox she left the office, waving another goodbye to Brian as he vacuumed. She walked across the parking lot in front of the building heading toward the back of the lot where her car was parked.

Throwing her bag into the backseat, she climbed into the car. She turned the key and there was nothing. Great, she thought, come on! The car refused to start even after jiggling the key and trying again. As she slumped back in her seat, she sighed. "Okay," she said after a moment, "I know you can do it, come on now." The third time was the charm, the car sputtered then came to life. "Oh, thank you!" she said exasperated. She buckled her seat belt before pulling out of her space and onto the road. She didn't have far to drive; she lived on the outskirts of Aberdeen.

Aberdeen was a college town with Aberdeen College at the heart of it. She had grown up in the Midwest, so Aberdeen had a familiar vibe because of its Midwest location. However, small town living was new to her, since she had grown up living much closer to a mid-sized city. Her apartment was not within walking distance but she picked it because it allowed pets and she needed a place where her beloved Riley was welcome. Riley was her little black and white dog, her best friend and the only family she had in the world. She had found Riley shortly after she had moved to Aberdeen when she needed a friend the most. Her parents had died in a car accident only a few months after she graduated, leaving her alone in the world and reeling with grief. Always an introvert, Cate became even more so after the death of her parents. She had found the little fluffy ball of fur in a local shelter after the tiny puppy had been abandoned on its front door. She had fallen in love with him the moment she saw him and adopted him that day. The two had been inseparable ever since. She smiled as she pictured his little black face with its white streak up the middle waiting for her at home.

A five-story rectangle with no distinguishing features faced her as she turned onto her street and glanced up at her building. It wasn't glamorous, but it was home. Her apartment was average and nondescript, just a hallway with a kitchen to the left, living room to the right, and her bedroom and bathroom straight ahead. She pulled into the parking lot and headed to the back of the building. Luck was on her side and she found a space near the building, pulled into it and climbed out of the car. She grabbed her bag from the backseat, locked the car and walked through the back door into the building.

Her four-room apartment was on the third floor and she preferred the stairs on most days, so she began her two-story hike up. After pulling open the door she found the hallway deserted. Good, she thought, I can make it straight in with no interruptions. After her long day, which began with an early morning class and ended with a late one, peppered with meetings, research and student appointments in between, she was exhausted.

She didn't get farther than a few steps down the hall toward her door when she heard another door being unlocked. She closed her eyes as though that would stop the inevitable from happening. Taking a deep breath, she opened them and continued down the hallway. As she predicted, the unlocking door noise belonged to an elderly neighbor of hers. The door popped open the moment Cate was near it. Cate smiled at the woman but said nothing, trying to hint to her she didn't intend to stop for a conversation. It didn't work.

"Katie, oh, Katie, just the person I wanted to run into!" Mrs. Kline said, standing in her door way.

Cate loved the way she pretended that this was a chance meeting. It was one that happened nearly every other day at the same time. "Hi, Mrs. Kline," Cate answered. She bit her tongue, resisting reminding her that her name was Cate, not Katie.

"How are you?" Before Cate could answer, she continued, "I hope your day was better than Wiley's, he barked all day, dear. I think he's just frustrated being stuck in that apartment."

Cate sighed to herself. "Riley. His name is Riley. You know, sometimes he just barks at his toys when he plays, he thinks it's fun," Cate said, explaining Riley's supposed barking for the umpteenth time. Riley wasn't much of a barker so she figured Mrs. Kline's description of Riley's constant daily barking might be a stretch.

"Oh, no, dear, no, this isn't playful barking. That dog of yours just barks and barks, sometimes I'm ready to call the police! Oh, but I would never do that, I know you take good care of Wiley."

Cate wrinkled her nose at the last comment but let it slide, particularly the incorrect reference of Riley's name. "Well, at least it sounds like he's quieted down now, I don't hear any barking."

"No, he's been quiet now for hours, I think he tired himself out."

Cate held back from rolling her eyes. She was tired and wanted to get home but she knew the conversation wasn't finished. Mrs. Kline wanted something, and it wasn't just to complain about "Wiley".

"Well, I guess I should go check on him," Cate said, attempting to end the conversation.

"Oh, before you go, dear," Mrs. Kline began. Finally, let's get to the point, Cate thought. "I was wondering if I could trouble you for twenty dollars. It's just until my daughter can get to the ATM for me, I've run out of cash. I'll get it back to you just as soon as she can replenish my slush fund."

"Sure," Cate said, digging into her bag for her purse. It wasn't the first time Mrs. Kline had asked to borrow money, it probably would not be the last. Cate felt a bit sorry for the older woman. She knew that her daughter rarely came by to visit, let alone replenish her so-called slush fund, and she thought the woman probably didn't have much money to begin with. Cate didn't mind helping her out, even if she complained about Riley all the time. "Here you go, Mrs. Kline, why don't you take forty dollars just in case your daughter doesn't come by soon."

"Oh, oh no, dear, I wouldn't want to short you... but, well, I mean if you are offering." She took both bills from Cate's hand, then added, "you know I'm good for it."

"Of course, Mrs. Kline, I know you are," Cate fibbed as she couldn't remember ever being paid back before.

"Well, I had better let you get to Wiley, dear. Have a good night!" Mrs. Kline was already closing her door. Cate gave her a tight-lipped smile and a nod. She continued down the hall to her apartment.

She arrived at her door with no further interruptions, shoved her key into the lock and opened it. She rushed inside and immediately shut it behind her. As usual, Riley was standing in the hall ready to greet her, his feather-like tail wagging excitedly. "RILEY!" she exclaimed as he rushed over to her. She dropped her bag on the floor near the door and bent down to grab him. "I missed you, buddy!" she said, scooping him up into her arms and giving the fur on his head a quick tousle as he licked her face.

She carried him down the hall and into the bedroom while he snuggled against her. It seemed Riley missed her as much as she missed him. "Let me just change my clothes, buddy, and we'll go for a quick walk," she promised him as she set him down on her bed. Riley, knowing the routine, laid down to watch her as she changed from her work clothes to a pair of sweats, t-shirt and hoodie. Riley sat up just as she was pulling on her tennis shoes, knowing it was almost time for his walk. Riley loved his walks, especially on warm sunny days like today. Unfortunately, there wasn't a lot of green space around the apartment building to walk in and he had to wait all day for it, but he loved it just the same.

"Okay, buddy!" she said as she stood up, "let's get your harness, leash and go!" Riley jumped down off the bed and raced over to the doorway, heading straight for the entry table where Cate kept his collar and leash. Cate fastened his harness around him, attached his leash and scooped him into her arms to carry him down to the small green space outside.

The sun was already beginning to lower in the sky but was still warm and bright on her face as she watched Riley frolicking around on the grass. He smelled every blade as if it were the first time he'd ever set his nose to it. She let him explore for about twenty minutes before she collected him to return to the apartment. While sad to leave all the wonderful smells of the outside, she knew Riley was more excited to eat his dinner.

Pushing through the door of her apartment again, she set Riley down and locked the door behind her. The little dog sat as she removed his leash and harness while saying, "Ready to go get your dish, Riley?" He danced on his hind legs. "Come on, buddy!" she said and headed to the kitchen.

Riley danced behind her watching for his little blue bowl to appear in her hands. When it did he stood on his hind legs in anticipation as Cate shook some kibble into the bowl from a bag. "Hungry today, huh, buddy?" she said as she filled the bowl and set it in front of him. He made short work of the food and was soon at her side again as she prepared her own dinner.

"I got a letter from the Dean today, Riley, we can read it after dinner. I hope it's good news!" she said, looking down at the little pup. Since she lived alone, she was used to talking to him as though he could understand everything. He stared upwards at her as she cooked a scrambled egg at the stove. "If it's good news, maybe we can find a place of our own! We'll get a big yard for you to play in and a little dog house for shade in the back!" Riley's eyes gleamed as he listened, tilting his head from side to side.

She finished her cooking and sat down to eat. Riley curled up near her feet, waiting for her to finish her dinner. She forced herself to eat slowly as she contemplated the contents of the letter that was burning a hole through her tote bag. If administration had granted her request she would have a lot of work ahead of her to achieve tenure but she would finally be on her way to a permanent position. She could settle, no longer having to wonder if she would have a job from year to year. As she had promised Riley earlier, they could buy that permanent place to live. And she could begin to feel like she belonged somewhere after feeling so lost following her parents' deaths. She imagined a small house with a big lawn and a picket fence, Riley running around in the front yard, his floppy ears flying in the wind as he romped. It brought a smile to her face and as she finished her last bite she reached down and gave his furry head a scratch. "I hope," she murmured and picked up her plate and utensils, clearing the table.

As she cleaned up her dinner dishes, she noticed her answering machine blinking, showing a new message. She hadn't noticed it earlier; she pressed play to hear the message.

An unfamiliar voice filled the air, a man with a British accent. "Dr. Kensie," he began, "this is William Smythe from Smythe, Smith and Smithton. I apologize for the departure in the plans detailed in my letter; however, my connecting flight has been delayed at JFK so I will arrive later than expected in Aberdeen and cannot meet you at your office as planned. Unfortunately, as I mentioned in the letter, my return flight leaves tomorrow morning, so I will still need to meet with you tonight. I apologize for the lateness of the hour that I will arrive, around 8:30 p.m. I plan to come straight to your residence unless you'd prefer to meet else-where, in which case, please leave a voicemail on my cell phone." The man left his number as a perplexed Cate stared at the machine.

"What in the world is that about, Riley? What letter?" Cate thought she had better check before reading her letter from the Dean. Someone named William Smythe would soon appear at her home and she had no idea who he was or what he could want. She checked the time, it was around 6:30 p.m., she had about two hours before his expected arrival.

She scooped up Riley and headed to the couch, grabbing

the letter from the Dean and her laptop out of her bag on the way in. Once settled on the couch, with Riley curled up next to her, she opened her laptop. "Let's see who this William Smythe guy is, Riley," she said, typing his name and company name into the search bar. She got a list of results. Clicking on the first one, she saw that Smythe, Smith and Smithton was a large law firm in London. That would explain the British accent, Cate thought. William Smythe was at the top of the page that listed the firm's attorneys. He was an older man, standing straight as a rail in his expensive suit. He had a pale, chiseled face with an aquiline nose ending in a small mouth that seemed set in a perpetual scowl.

"Well, there he is, Riley. William Smythe. We know who he is and what he does, but I have no idea what he could want. Maybe a case of mistaken identity. Whatever it is, it must be important to have a British attorney coming all the way to Aberdeen on a Friday night. And what letter? We didn't get any letter from William Smythe, Riley. I guess time will tell. Speaking of letters, let's see what this one says."

After closing her laptop, she picked up her letter from the Dean. She studied the envelope for a moment, as if trying to read the contents without opening it. Cate sighed, "Moment of truth, buddy, let's see what it says." She flipped the envelope over and slid her finger under the flap and popped it open. Her hands shook as she pulled the letter out, unfolded it, and scanned it. Her heart sank as she saw the words "unfortunately", "sorry" and "regret". She let the letter fall onto the coffee table as she sunk her head into her hands. After a moment, she retrieved it and gave it a thorough read.

Dr. Kensie:

The Dean's office has received your request to change your current position of Instructor to a tenure-tracked position. Unfortunately, we regret to inform you that this is not possible at this time. We are sorry that we cannot accommodate your request and acknowledge and appreciate your work for Aberdeen College. We encourage you to continue your hard work and apply at a later date.

It was signed by the Dean of the college, or rather, as she took a closer look, the signature had been stamped by her secretary. She sighed again, setting the letter down on the coffee table and reached over to stroke Riley. He looked at her quizzically with dark eyes. "Sorry, buddy," she said deflated, "looks like I got your hopes up for nothing. No house yet, but hopefully we won't have to move." I think I'll get my contract renewed, I hope anyway, she thought to herself.

Cate sighed, rubbing her temples as she set the letter down. Sometimes she wondered why she continued to stay at Aberdeen College. Despite all her efforts, Aberdeen never felt like home to her. She could answer that question quickly though. There weren't that many tenure-track academic positions in her field and despite the number of applications she flooded the limited market with, she hadn't been offered anything better. She had been told many times from her department chair that a tenure-track position was in the cards for her at Aberdeen, but at each opportunity, there had been some reason it never happened.

No matter how much she tried to convince herself that things weren't that bad, she couldn't help but be depressed. The retirement of her colleague was the break she thought she needed to convince administration to offer her a permanent position. She didn't see when they would ever grant her request if not under these circumstances.

Cate flipped on the television and navigated around on Netflix to find a distraction. There wasn't anything that she would solve tonight, although she'd most likely lay awake trying. With the spring term nearly over and summer right around the corner and no confirmation of a summer or fall schedule she would have to do some fast thinking on what to do to pay her bills.

After a while she settled on watching re-runs of an old favorite TV show, The Office, and settled back to begin her weekend. She absentmindedly stroked the fur down Riley's back. It soothed her as much as it soothed him. "We'll figure something out, Riley," she said as she stroked him and let the TV show numb her mind.

After a few episodes, she started to doze off. An early morning class paired with a late afternoon class was taking its usual toll and sending her off to an early bedtime. She checked the clock across the room, 8:15 p.m. What an exciting life I lead, she thought to herself, here I am falling asleep on my couch before 8:30 p.m. on a Friday night. "I'll be lucky if I'm awake when this guy shows up, Riley," she joked. At hearing his name, the little dog next to her roused from his sleep.

"Well, Riley," she said, "let's go take a quick walk before our visitor arrives!" Riley followed her into the hallway by the door while she fitted his harness and leash onto him.

"Okay, let's do it!" she said as she opened the door. With her attention focused on Riley, she nearly ran straight into the man who had been standing outside her door. Stifling a startled scream, she jumped back as Riley began barking at the stranger looming outside the door.

CHAPTER 2

"*O*h my gosh," she stammered, "I'm so sorry, I didn't see you there! Riley, shh, shh, no barking!"

"Not a problem," he said rather disingenuously in a crisp British accent as he smoothed out his black, well-tailored suit. "Are you Dr. Catherine Kensie?" He glanced at Cate then focused his energy on frowning at the small dog barking at his feet.

"Yeah, I'm Cate, eh, Catherine. Yes, I'm Dr. Kensie," she continued to stammer while picking Riley up to quiet him. Cate recognized the man as William Smythe.

"Please allow me to introduce myself." He produced a business card. "My name is William H. Smythe, Esquire, I am an attorney with Smythe, Smith and Smithton, LLC in London. As I stated in my letter, I represent the estate of Lady Gertrude MacKenzie."

She took the business card and gave it a cursory glance, her mind trying to focus out of its startled daze and into the situation at hand. "Yes, I got your call, but I never received the letter you mentioned. You're a little far from home, aren't you?" she said half serious and half joking.

"Oh, my apologies if you did not receive the letter. We sent it to your business address; your personal address was a bit harder to track down and Lady MacKenzie did want the matter taken care of in a timely fashion. Also, again, I apologize for the lateness of the hour, but I've come straight from the airport and given my early flight tomorrow morning, I'm unable to meet at any other time. As I said, I am here representing the estate of Lady Gertude MacKenzie. May I come in to speak with you further in a setting offering us more privacy?" He motioned toward the interior of the apartment.

"Ah, I'm sorry, I don't have any knowledge of a Lady Gertude Mackenzie or anyone from London, what does this have to do with me?" Cate asked, still not fully understanding what was going on and how it pertained to her. Riley continued to offer protective growls and as menacing of a stare as he could muster for a ten pound dog.

"Actually, Lady MacKenzie was from Scotland, I am from London. As I've stated several times, Dr. Kensie, I would like to discuss Lady MacKenzie's last will and testament with you. Although, I would prefer to do so in private."

"Sure, but I still don't know Lady Mackenzie from Scotland or from anywhere. I really don't see why you'd need to discuss this with me, I'm not even acquainted with this person. Oh, or did you have a history-type of question? I have done some consulting in the past, I could help with that if that's what you need." Cate was rambling, it was her tendency when she was nervous. She had no idea what this man wanted from her, she assumed that perhaps he had made some sort of mistake, but he clearly knew her, so perhaps he hadn't.

The man seemed to be impatient. "Dr. Kensie, please, if you wouldn't mind, I would prefer that we discuss the business in private." He motioned again into the apartment as he glanced around the hallway. Cate remembered her "chance" encounter earlier with Mrs. Kline. She pictured her standing at her peephole with a glass pressed against the door, trying to make out every word. Maybe it was best to move the conversation inside.

"Oh right, yes, come in, please. Sorry, I didn't mean to keep you waiting in the hall, sorry," Cate rambled again, nervously tucking her hair behind her ears with one hand, while holding Riley with the other. She motioned to the inside of her apartment and stood back from the door. She glanced into the hallway before shutting her door. Now Mrs. Kline was probably judging her for inviting a man into her apartment on a Friday night. She shut her door from any prying eyes. Riley gave a protective growl as the man crossed the threshold. Cate shushed him.

"We can head into the living room if you'd like, please make yourself comfortable," she said, motioning to the couch. Mr. Smythe sat down rather stiffly on the couch, teetering on the edge as though he hated to touch it. Cate positioned herself in an armchair adjacent to the couch with Riley still in her arms. "Can you tell me what this is about now, Mr. Smythe?"

He removed some file folders and a small bag from his well-polished briefcase and set it on the coffee table. "Yes, as I said earlier and in the letter which you did not receive, my firm and I represent the interests of Lady Gertrude MacKenzie of Dunhaven, Scotland. Specifically, I am the executor of the late Lady MacKenzie's will."

"I have no idea what this is about. I'm not aware of any Mackenzies so unless I'm being sued by one or you need me to provide a consult on something, I have no idea what's going on," Cate answered, still confused.

"Immediately following the death of Lady MacKenzie, I was to track down her closest living relative in order to execute the instructions within her last will and testament," he continued, while pulling several papers out of a crisp manila folder. He paused and looked at her directly.

Cate's eyes darted around the room, as if searching for an answer. Not finding one, Cate answered, "Okay..." prompting him to continue speaking.

"You are Lady MacKenzie's closest living relative and therefore her heir," he said, as if annoyed that she hadn't grasped the concept yet.

"What?!" Cate exclaimed. "You must be joking. No, I think you may have made a mistake. I don't... I don't think I have any relatives, or at least none in Scotland." No, this couldn't be real, Cate mused, me, the heiress to a Scottish lady?

"I'm quite sure no mistake has been made, Dr. Kensie. We will, of course, verify your identity with a DNA sample, but I am confident that will be a mere formality."

He continued, "Subject to the DNA verification, you will inherit the bulk of Lady MacKenzie's estate which includes her title, Dunhaven Castle, the grounds on which it resides, its contents, a sizable sum of money to maintain the estate, and one gold timepiece. One of the stipulations of the inheritance is that you must live at the estate on a permanent basis, it is not to be sold."

Cate was speechless. She tried to make sense of it but her head was still spinning. This must be a mistake; she didn't have any relatives. Her parents never mentioned any relatives, certainly none in Scotland that lived in a castle. "Uh, um, uh," she stammered, "Castle? Is this a joke, am I on camera?" She glanced around the room, half expecting to see someone filming this for a reality television show.

"I can assure you this is no joke," he said, his face straight. It didn't look like this man could even tell a joke, Cate thought, remembering her earlier attempt to joke had fallen flat.

She swallowed hard, trying to collect her thoughts. "O-okay, so, this Lady MacKenzie, she was a relative, MY relative, and she left ME everything she owns?"

"Outside of a few odds and ends, yes. She was a distant relative, an only child, and she never married, nor had any children. You were identified as her closest living relative to whom the bulk of the estate along with her title was left, pending a DNA verification, as I've already said."

"The details," he continued, matter-of-factly, "are here in this folder along with information about and pictures of the estate for you to review. As you can see," he said opening the folder and producing a few photographs, "the property is in excellent condition and has been quite well maintained. Additionally," he shuffled through to grab another piece of paper, "the current estimated sum is sufficiently large enough to continue to maintain the estate with ease for several generations." He pointed discreetly to a large number marked near the bottom of the page.

Cate's eyes widened. "Whoa, is that dollars?" she said, surprised. The amount seemed to Cate as though it would support more than a few generations.

"No," he said stiffly, "it's in pounds."

"Oh, right," she replied, sheepishly.

"Along with the property, you'll inherit the title carried with the estate, Countess of Dunhavenshire. And, lastly, the gold timepiece which can only be imparted to you directly from myself once your DNA has been verified. If you wouldn't mind, I would like to collect the sample and leave you to enjoy the remainder of your evening."

"Wait, wait, wait just a second," Cate shook her head as she responded, "how do I know you are legitimate and not going to use my DNA for, well, something else."

He set his jaw. "I'm not in the habit of collecting DNA samples from nearly unemployed history professors."

"How did you..." she began before being cut off by Mr. Smythe.

"The letter you left on the table. My apologies that your request didn't work out the way you hoped but if you wouldn't mind, I would like to finish my job and retire for the evening."

"I don't mean to hold you up, really I don't, I just, I think, that is, I can't, well, to be honest, I'm just really in shock," Cate stammered. "I've never heard of Dunhaven, or a castle, or a Scottish relative and I'm just a little stunned that this woman would make it a point that you search me out so that I could inherit her... house, I mean, her castle and estate." Cate rambled on, letting her thoughts spill directly from her brain to her mouth.

"Dr. Kensie, I can understand your surprise," he said, sounding as though he had never been surprised in his life, "but I can assure you my only intention is to execute the last will and testament as specified by Lady MacKenzie. That execution has led me to you after an extensive investigation into the MacKenzie lineage. Of course, a DNA test will confirm easily that which we believe to be true. If you will allow me to collect the sample, I can be on my way."

"Oh, right, sure, yes, of course. Gee, you must be working overtime on triple rate to collect this on a Friday night as it is." Cate made another attempt at humor to help ease the tension. He ignored it again, intent on the task at hand. She watched him open the small bag and remove a tube and a cotton swab. He handed it to her and watched her swab the inside of her cheek. Handing it back, he deposited it into the plastic vial and returned the vial to the bag. He stowed it in his briefcase and began to close it.

"So, I can't get the watch of all things before my DNA is verified, that's funny," she again tried to joke.

He gave her a stern look. "It was quite an important item

to Lady MacKenzie and comes with careful stipulations to be given only to her closest living relative, so, no, you cannot."

She pinched her lips together, this guy really had no sense of humor at all. "Of course, sorry," she finally answered, after her embarrassment passed. He stood up as did she, setting Riley down on the chair behind her.

"The DNA results should be returned within two weeks. Once verified, I will contact you again to discuss the details and finalize paperwork. Should you need to contact me, I am staying at the Marriott tonight and will be back in the office on Monday." He stuck his hand out.

She accepted and shook his hand a little slowly. "Okay, well, thank you, I think. And you'll let me know either way?"

"Yes, good day."

"Right, good day or night or whatever."

She walked him to the door and closed it as he left. Returning to the living room she sunk onto the couch. Riley looked on curiously from his perch on the armchair.

"Ooooof." She let air slip out of her mouth. "Riley, what in the world is this about? It looks like we may have a bit of a mystery on our hands!"

CHAPTER 3

The bright morning sun shone through Cate's bedroom window. Since it was Saturday, Cate hadn't set an alarm clock, instead relying upon her trusty pal, Riley, to wake her early. True to form, Riley had bounded onto the bed and began to shower Cate with kisses in the form of licks to her face. Cate opened her eyes and blinked a few times while they adjusted to the bright morning light.

Cate yawned. "Good morning, buddy," she said sleepily. She rubbed Riley's head as she turned to look at the clock. It was ten minutes to seven; Riley was right on time.

She lay in bed for a few more minutes before getting up to begin her day. As she lay there, she contemplated the events of the night before, wondering if she had maybe dreamt it all in the haze of a long week. The folder on her night table confirmed that it was real. The thought of how strange it all was struck her. Before she let her mind slip further into pondering it, she decided she had better get up.

With a sigh, she got out of bed and headed straight into the bathroom for a quick shower before pulling on a pair of jeans, a t-shirt, and a pair of tennis shoes. After taking Riley for a short trip outside, she headed for the kitchen, making a quick bowl of instant oatmeal for breakfast and giving Riley a bowl of kibble.

She tidied the apartment then ran some errands, returning around 9 a.m. "Let me put the groceries away, Riley, then we'll head to the park," she said cheerfully.

With her morning routine out of the way, it was time to enjoy her weekend. The first stop was the Saturday morning trip to the park with Riley. Aberdeen boasted a large park near a pond as one of its amenities. Cate and Riley enjoyed visiting it almost every Saturday, regardless of the weather. Today the weather was on their side. The bright sun had no plans of being shut out by clouds and promised to send temperatures soaring into the high seventies.

As Cate unpacked her supplies, Riley ran into the hall to wait by the door for his weekly trip. Cate found him guarding the door so she couldn't leave without him. After securing Riley's harness and leash, she pulled on a ball cap and hoodie for the cool morning air. She grabbed her keys, headed out the door and down to her car.

Within ten minutes, she was pulling into the Aberdeen park's parking area. Riley stood at the window, tail wagging furiously. "Who's excited to go to the park?" she asked as she slid her car into an empty spot. Riley glanced to her then back out the window, tail still wagging. His eyes darted around watching people, birds, and other animals. Cate scooped him up and exited the car. Still carrying him, she walked to the gravel pathway leading from the parking lot further into the park before setting him down on the ground. His nose was immediately glued to it, taking in all the scents. They walked together down the path for about ten minutes before they came to their favorite spot near the pond. Aberdeen College stood in the distance. The picturesque campus stood tall on a hill behind the pond, adding to the beauty of the pond and its landscaping. Cate stopped there, leaving the path and making her way onto the grassy area with Riley in tow.

Riley bounded through the grass next to her. As she slowed to a stop he also stopped beside her, staring up at her expectantly. She glanced down at him, "Yes, I brought it," she said, smiling. She removed his leash then stood up and produced a small, blue ball from her pocket. Riley danced on his hind legs, daring her to throw it. "Ready?" she asked. Riley offered a small bark in response. Cate threw the ball into the distance, Riley bounded after it. When he found it, he snatched it up and raced back to Cate, dropping it at her feet. She picked it up and threw it again, watching Riley race off after it. They played for about twenty minutes until Riley brought the ball back and laid down in the grass rather than bark to demand another toss. Cate settled onto the lawn next to him. "Tired out, buddy?" she asked him. He responded by laying his head on his front paws with a big sigh.

Cate stretched her legs out in front of her and lay back on her elbows. She stared at the silhouettes of the buildings of Aberdeen College in the distance wondering, as she had so many times before, if she would have a job there in the upcoming term. Suddenly the thought struck her she may not need a job there in the upcoming term. Her thoughts turned to her curious visit the night before. She had trouble believing that she would actually inherit a Scottish castle and all its trappings. Still she couldn't help but imagine what it would be like if she did. No more worrying about being able to pay bills from term to term, a permanent place to live, an incredible yard for Riley to play in, it all seemed too good to be true. She pictured Riley romping around the gardens shown on the estate pictures or roaming through the gigantic house with her, exploring it. "What do you think, Riley?" she asked the small dog, "would you like to live in a castle?" Riley looked quizzically at her before setting his head back down on his paws. She smiled then sighed; it was a nice dream, but just a dream. She couldn't imagine the DNA test confirming her as the heir. Surely if this was legitimate someone would have told her before that she had relatives; relatives with a castle; relatives with a castle in Scotland! She pushed the thought from her mind, no sense dwelling on it when it was likely never going to materialize. "Come on, buddy, let's finish our walk around the pond," Cate said, as she reattached Riley's leash.

She climbed to her feet and Riley did the same. They made their way back to the gravel path and continued their journey at a leisurely pace, allowing plenty of time for Riley to stop and explore. The rest of the walk took an hour and a half. Back at the car, Cate opened the passenger door, allowing Riley to climb in. After securing his seatbelt to his harness she made her way around to the driver's side and climbed in. "Should we get some lunch, Riley?" she asked.

They stopped at one of their favorite roadside shops. Cate ordered a hot dog and nachos and ordered Riley a doggie dish of ice cream to enjoy while she ate. They found a shaded picnic table near a grassy area and sat down to eat. Cate's mind kept returning to the strange visit from last night, wondering if it could be true. She didn't know much about her family, but she thought there wasn't much to know. Her parents hadn't talked about relatives much, but she thought that was because she didn't have any living relatives. If there was a connection between her and this Gertrude MacKenzie, wouldn't someone had told her? It seemed like a large detail for her parents to conceal. Had there been a family fight resulting in a rift? She couldn't answer any of these questions. If there were any information available, it would be in the box of her parents' things that she had in her closet. She resolved to check there when she returned home. She hoped to find a clue to point to a potential resolution.

Cate's mind focused almost continuously on her potential inheritance despite her reluctance to get too excited before anything was confirmed. It would be a long two weeks.

Cate's thoughts turned from wondering if she was the heir to what she would do if she inherited this property. Moving to a foreign country, even one where the customs may not be that different like Scotland, was a big step. Would she like it there? Would Riley? What if it was sheer misery living in the Scottish countryside? Or what if the castle was drafty and musty and she and Riley had to walk around bundled in sweaters and coats all the time to keep the chill off? Thoughts about the horrors of living in a rural castle shot through her mind faster than she could process. She shook her head and took a deep breath. She was panicking, possibly over nothing. First, it probably would turn out she was not the actual relative and second, someone had lived there for her whole life and had survived it into a ripe old age so it couldn't be THAT bad.

Still, Cate wasn't so sure she would just move. She looked around her. Aberdeen was familiar to her; she had lived there for a few years. Although it never felt like home, she figured this would always be her perception no matter where she lived after her parents' deaths. What did she have holding her here, she wondered? A job going nowhere, a small apartment with a lonely, pesty neighbor and, her eyes fixed onto the small dog next to her, Riley. Riley was the only thing of importance to her and he would move with her. Maybe she would move if she had the chance, she thought, it would solve a number of her problems.

Cate finished her meal and cleaned up after herself, stacking Riley's little plastic bowl and her cardboard hot dog container onto the nacho plate and dumping them all in the trash. She took a few last sips of her soda and pitched the cup. "Okay, Riley, let's head home!" She fastened Riley's seatbelt to his harness and climbed into the driver's seat. "Let's see if we can solve some of this mystery when we get home, Riley."

Despite her curiosity, she took the long way home, enjoying a little more of the spring day. By the time they arrived in her building's lot, Riley's big morning was catching up to him and Cate carried him up to the apartment. Her hallway was quiet, Mrs. Kline would avoid her for a few days, having gotten what she needed to tide her over until the next request. After entering her apartment, she removed his harness and set him on the couch. He nestled into the cushion, his eyes heavy. Cate made her way to her bedroom and over to her closet. She pulled the chain to turn on the light and reached for the small box containing what she had kept of her parents' things. On her tiptoes she teetered trying to pull the box down. Inch by inch she worked it until it nearly toppled onto her. A few items toppled over the top of the box and onto the floor. She bent over to retrieve them, a wave of sadness washing over her as she saw the picture of her with her parents at her college graduation. She stared at the two smiling faces on either side of her. No matter how much time passed, the grief sometimes still hit her like a brick wall. She looked at the photo for a moment more, this time with fresh eyes. Were you hiding something from me, Mom and Dad, she pondered? Not getting a response from the photo, she put it down, picked up the box and headed to the living room to join Riley on the couch.

She placed the box on the coffee table and, settling herself next to Riley, she opened it. The next few items included death certificates, a few news clippings about the crash, and a select few other family photos. After setting those aside she dug deeper, finding a few other personal effects from her parents including her mom's jewelry box and her dad's wallet. She went over each with a fine-tooth comb, pulling out every item, searching for any clue linking her to anything even remotely related to Scotland or any Scottish relatives. She found nothing. The last item in the box was an old photo album, one from her childhood. She took it out and began to page through it. She searched every photo for clues, people who she couldn't identify, locations that might have been a relative's house. Again, she found nothing that gave her any insight. Closing the book she set it down beside her, sighing. The search yielded nothing because there was nothing to find. Lost in thought, she let her head fall back onto the couch behind her.

Afraid of falling asleep, she pushed everything aside, picking up her laptop. Cate decided some work on her current research project might help clear her mind. With the journal article she was working on open on her screen, she lost herself, as she always did, in her work.

After a time, Riley stirred next to her and climbed up, standing on his hind legs to reach her face. He nudged her with his nose then gave her a lick. She laid her head back and stroked his fur, her thoughts turning from her work to Riley romping around a grassy yard in Scotland. "Well, Riley, you may not get to live in a Scottish castle, but at least it should provide us with an interesting two weeks!" she joked. Riley wagged his tail and gave her another lap with his tongue. She picked her head up to look at the little dog, stroking his fur again. For the first time in hours she noticed the time. "My goodness, Riley, it's nearly six o'clock!" she exclaimed. "I bet you are hungry!" Riley wagged his tail at her.

"Let's head in for your dish!" At the sound of the "d-word" Riley leapt from the couch and dashed into the kitchen. Cate followed, retrieved his bowl and, filling it with kibble, fed the little guy. Likewise, it was time for her to eat so she opened a cupboard and pulled down a bowl. In another cupboard, she reached for a box of cereal and poured a hearty amount into the bowl. With a small splash of milk over top, she got a spoon and dug in. "Another wild Saturday night, Riley!" she said to the pup.

After dinner she cleaned up her parents' things, placing them back in the box as melancholy washed over her. She returned the photo to the box and placed it back on the shelf in her closet. As she was returning to the living room, she spotted the folder from William Smythe on her night table. She grabbed it and took it with her. Opening it, she picked up the photographs of the property, studying them for a moment. Riley peeked over her arm at the photograph then at her. He spent a moment studying her face then decided another nap was in order and stretched out next to her on the couch. Cate picked up the business card William Smythe had given her. She considered calling him and asking if he had any news. Patience was not her virtue. She decided against it, figuring he would have let her know if he had any updates. He didn't seem like the type of person who let things sit. She was going to have to wait until he contacted her. She replaced the business card and photographs and closed the folder, choosing to watch a little television before heading to bed.

Sunday rolled around bringing a dreary day with rain falling most of the time. Cate spent the better part of the gloomy day grading papers from her European History course. Riley contented himself chewing on one of his favorite bones or chasing one of his balls around the apartment. She finished the day off with an evening of reading, cuddled with Riley in her favorite armchair by the window. Although her book was an excellent read, she stared out at the rainy day, daydreaming of a life in Scotland.

CHAPTER 4

*M*onday morning came before Cate was ready. Her alarm screamed its arrival, ripping Cate from a pleasant sleep to the reality of an early morning class. She drowsily rose from her warm nest, showered, ate, and walked Riley before heading to campus and delivering a lecture on the Elizabethan era. After wrapping up her first class, Cate headed back to her office. Sitting down at her desk, she flipped the page of her calendar to show this week's events. Outside of a few student appointments, it looked like she had an easy week. This meant she could catch up on some end-of-semester work and maybe some sleep, she felt exhausted. She pulled her laptop out of her bag and opened it on her desk, preparing to record the grades she had worked on yesterday.

As she entered the first grade, she heard a knock on her door. Assuming it was a student, she shouted "Come on in!" in a loud voice, not looking up from her laptop.

"Got a minute?" a voice answered her. She recognized the southern drawl of her department chair, Dr. Jeffrey Goldstone.

Startled, she looked up. The tall man stood in her doorway, leaning against the doorjamb. His tan suit was a little rumpled, as though he had slept in it. The color matched his hair except the parts around the temples, which were graying. His dark brown eyes were fixed on Cate. "Jeff, oh, yeah, sure, I was just entering some grades, come on in."

He entered the office and took a seat across from her desk. "How have you been?" he asked.

"Good, how about you, Jeff?"

"I can't complain. How's the little mutt?"

"He's doing good, enjoying the nice weather." Cate knew Jeff wasn't here to inquire about Riley.

"That's great, that's great." He smiled at her and paused before continuing. "Hey, I have a question for you."

"Sure," Cate answered, glad to get to the heart of what Jeff wanted.

"We have an event coming up this Saturday, I need someone to cover it. There is nobody better than you, Cate. You're a great representative for the department. You up for it?"

Cate considered the request. Was there no one better than her or hadn't anyone else volunteered, Cate wondered? Saturdays were sacred time for her and Riley. The Saturday events were open houses for prospective students. They occurred about four times per semester. Cate had already represented the department on three of those four occasions, she felt as though she had put her time in. If she was such a great representative for the department, it would be nice if they committed to her in the form of a permanent position. The recent request denial still stung her, and she wasn't in the mood to do any favors for a department that wouldn't recognize her worth after years of service. Still, she would like to continue to be employed, so she felt badly turning down the request without more consideration. She hedged. "Let me look at my calendar and get back to you."

"Sure," Jeff said. "Yeah, just let me know. Like I said, we'd love to have you represent us." He got up to leave. He headed for the door and as he reached it he turned back around. "Oh, I almost forgot. I think," he added a stress to the word as though struggling to get it out, "I may be able to get you some summer classes. I'm still working on fall, nothing definite yet but I'm doing my best." He waited for her response.

She was annoyed. He didn't get the answer he wanted so he would dangle the employment carrot in front of her nose. Cate knew this song and dance well, they did it every year. Though they rarely got rid of their untenured employees because they were more economically efficient. She struggled to keep her composure as she answered, "Thanks, Jeff. I appreciate that. I assume they copied you on that letter from the Dean about my permanent position request."

"Yeah, I saw that. Tough break, kiddo. I was behind you all the way, I don't know what they were thinking. Anyway, I hope to get you something in the fall and you can put your request in again."

"Yeah, thanks, Jeff. I appreciate that," she said without meaning it.

"Hey, no problem," he answered. "Let me know about this Saturday as soon as you can, okay? Have a good one!" He rapped his knuckles on her doorjamb as he left and disappeared down the hall.

Cate breathed deeply as she sat back in her chair. This was the third time they had turned her down for a permanent position. She was beyond frustrated, she did as much work as everyone else in the department if not more but did not receive the same perks. They were taking advantage of her. Her position was being held over her head to eke more work out of her than was fair, work that no one else wanted to do. It was a job, and it paid her bills, she thought, as she took another deep breath. She spent a moment more weighing the pros and cons of her situation then resolved to make a final decision later about the Saturday work request and continued with entering her grades.

By the time her next lecture rolled around, she had only gotten about halfway through the stack. After finishing that class, she grabbed some lunch at the campus food court and took it back to her office to finish recording grades before her afternoon classes began. She finished them all before giving her two afternoon lectures. After finishing her last class, she gathered her things and opted to go straight to her car rather than stop at her office. She wanted to avoid another run-in with Jeff while she continued to consider giving in to his request.

When she arrived home she dumped her stuff, changed clothes and took Riley out for his walk. As she watched him frolicking in the small patch of grass, she replayed her conversation with Jeff from this morning. The more she reflected on it, the madder she became. She had already given up three Saturdays earlier to cover department events for a department that didn't want to make her a permanent member. But they had no issue asking her to chip in like a permanent member and then some. Most other departments on campus did not use their non-permanent faculty to cover events unless there was an emergency. And after three denials for permanent status, she began to realize the position they had more or less promised her would never materialize. She felt like a horse in a race trying to catch the dangling carrot. A carrot they may never let her catch because it was cheaper for them if she remained untenured. Her reluctance on putting her foot down was the steady income and the chance of becoming permanent, even though that chance seemed to be becoming more and more remote. Although grateful to have a job, she was upset about being used by the department. She elected to make the decision later after she had time to let her emotions run their course.

The remainder of her evening was quiet. After feeding Riley and herself, she settled in for the night by streaming a few episodes of her favorite comedy show and, after taking Riley out one more time for the night, headed to bed.

When she awoke the next morning she still didn't have a clear idea on a final decision about the weekend work so she decided to avoid work colleagues to the best of her ability for the day. She packed herself a lunch and spent her free time doing research in the library.

After finishing her morning lecture, she headed straight to the library. She settled at a table near the back. Cate was surprised at how empty the library was considering how close to the end of the term they were. Students must not have been fully committed to studying for finals yet. It also helped that it was a warm, sunny spring day with temperatures set to rise into the low eighties. Most students were taking advantage of the nice weather before hitting the books. Opening her bag, she removed her notepad and spread out the research she had already done. In need of additional resources, she went in search of more materials.

She found the books she had intended to study next and returned to her table. Cracking open the first book she leaned in, pen in hand, preparing to take notes. After glossing over a sentence or two, she found herself lost in thought, ruminating about whether the library held any answers to the history of a certain Scottish castle. She pulled out her laptop and decided a simple Internet search might give her a start. Connecting to the library's Wi-Fi, she ran a search on Dunhaven Castle. She found a limited Wikipedia article on Dunhaven Castle featuring a picture of the castle itself along with some basic information about when it was built and other details. It offered no clues on how she was connected to it.

Pushing back from the table, she headed for a computer that could help pinpoint materials for her search. She ran the name Dunhaven Castle, Lady Gertrude MacKenzie, Dunhaven and a few similar related searches. They turned up little to nothing other than a one line reference in a text called *Scottish Castles: The Complete List* and a brief mention in a text called *The Mysteries of Scotland*. The second reference seemed intriguing even if it didn't provide her with much information but the library did not have access to the text. Cate considered asking for an inter-library loan but she figured by the time she got it she would no longer need it having already determined her connection or lack thereof to the castle. She checked her watch and found it to be shortly after noon. The rumblings in her abdomen further confirmed the hour. She headed back to her table to eat her lunch while continuing her research.

After finishing her lunch, she continued her readings and note-taking for another hour before cleaning up her area, returning the books to the book cart and gathering her notes, packing everything into her bag. She took a quick look around to be sure she had collected everything and headed toward the library entrance. When she exited, she found the air had warmed up several degrees. Students dotted the lawn connecting the campus buildings while they enjoyed the weather by studying, relaxing or playing Frisbee. Cate made her way from the library to Smith Hall for her single after-noon lecture. After delivering it she called it a day and headed home to retrieve Riley for a quick trip to the park, sure that he would also like to enjoy the warm weather.

As she suspected, Riley was thrilled to take a long walk around the pond at the park, prancing down the path with Cate and stopping now and again to explore something that caught his eye, or more specifically his nose. After the walk, Cate grabbed something to eat rather than have to make dinner. After a quick bite, she headed back home and spent the evening organizing her research notes. It was a mindless task that allowed her to focus on what she would have to tell Jeff when she saw him tomorrow. She knew she couldn't avoid seeing him for another day so she had to make her final decision. After an hour of work, she still wasn't sure how she would answer. She decided to sleep on it for another night. Stretching and yawning, she left her notes sprawled on the table, took Riley for one last trip outside and headed to bed.

Wednesday morning brought a cool rain. The crisp smell of rain and fresh flowers permeated the campus as Cate made her way to her early morning class. As she finished her lecture, she faced the reality that she would have to speak with Jeff. An idea crossed her mind, and she decided she would go with it so she made her way to the department's main office.

As she entered, she saw Molly, the department secretary, had not arrived yet but Jeff's door was already open. He was in his office as she suspected. Perfect, she thought to herself, time to enact my plan. Cate made her way over to the open door and knocked on it, popping her head into the office. "Hey, Jeff, got a minute?" she said, smiling.

"Oh hey, sure, kiddo, come on in," Jeff answered after looking up from his laptop. "To what do I owe the pleasure?"

"Mind if I sit?" she asked, taking a seat before he could answer. "Hey, we're getting really close to the summer term, have you made any progress with getting a commitment from administration on summer courses for me?"

She watched Jeff as he hesitated for a moment before answering her. He stared at her, trying to read her face. She tried to keep her expression as blank as possible. She noticed how he weighed the answer he was about to give, suspecting she was up to something. "No," he said, "I haven't locked them down yet but I'm trying, kiddo, I'm trying." He winked.

"Really?" Cate played surprised. "Wow, the term is nearly upon us and they still haven't made final decisions, how frustrating."

"Yeah, yeah it is," he answered, thinking his answer had sufficed. "But you know how it is."

"Yeah, I'm beginning to understand," she laughed. "Well, let me know as soon as you have an answer if you could." She stood to leave.

"Oh, I will, kiddo."

"Thanks!" Cate took two steps toward the door.

"Oh, ah, Cate..." Jeff began. Cate stopped, a small smile spreading on her face before she regained her blank expression and turned around to face him.

"Yeah?"

"Did you check on your availability Saturday? I meant to ask you yesterday, but I didn't have the chance."

And here it goes, Cate thought. "Yeah, I did, sorry, I'm not available." Cate had decided just before the conversation that if they couldn't commit to her for another semester, she couldn't commit to them. If this Saturday event was the deciding factor between her continued employment or lack thereof, then so be it. She would not continue to do more than her share of work only for them to hold her hostage at the end of every term.

"Aww, shucks," Jeff said, "that's too bad. Well, thanks for checking anyway."

"Sure, Jeff. Anytime!" Cate turned on a heel to leave but was stopped again.

"Oh, ah, Cate?" Jeff said as she turned around again, "I wouldn't count on the summer term courses. I mean I'll fight like hell for you but I think it's a losing battle."

"Thanks for the heads up," Cate said, not surprised. Of course he would make her feel as bad as he could. He hadn't gotten his way so now she would suffer right along with him. It made her sad that her colleagues would treat her this way, but she had expected this.

A mix of emotions coursed through her as she made her way back to her office. She was proud for having stood up for herself but saddened and frustrated that she had spent years trying to be a good faculty member within the department and had never gained much respect from her coworkers. In the end, she was happy with her decision, concluding that if she would have caved in, she would have felt worse than she did right now.

She looked around her office. Maybe I should spend some of my office hours cleaning out my stuff, she thought to herself. She concluded that she didn't have to just yet. While Jeff wanted to play hardball and make her sweat, he would have at least a class or two that no one in the department wanted because it was at a bad time or bad location or freshman only or some other point of contention that most other faculty members were unwilling to accept and that he'd need her to cover. With that settled, she cracked open her laptop to do some work.

The rest of her day was uneventful with just a few student appointments, two lectures and a quiet evening at home. The remainder of the week was the same. She didn't see or hear from Jeff; he was great at avoiding her when he didn't need something.

When Saturday rolled around, Cate took pleasure spending the morning hours at the park with Riley knowing she had this time because she had refused to take on the extra work. Celebrating her independence and what she hoped was not the end of her career, she spent part of Sunday at the park, ending her weekend with some quiet reading at home as she watched the sunset from her armchair while Riley cuddled with her.

CHAPTER 5

*C*ate groaned as her alarm went off Monday morning. The dreaded finals week was here. Mountains of grading, sobbing students begging for another chance, late nights, early mornings, endless emails, it was the week of the semester that every faculty member hated. "Can't get it finished if I don't get it started," Cate said to herself as she climbed out of bed.

She showered, made breakfast, walked Riley, and headed to the office. Her cell phone rang just as she sat down at her desk. Not recognizing the number, she answered it anyway, figuring it wasn't a telemarketer calling at 8:12 a.m.

"Hello?"

"Dr. Kensie," a voice answered her in a crisp British accent. "This is William Smythe. We spoke ten days ago regarding the estate of Lady Gertrude MacKenzie."

"Mr. Smythe, yes, I remember." How could she forget?

"The results of the DNA test are in and confirmed by a second party. I am back in the States. Would it be possible to meet for lunch today? I can come to you."

"Uh…" Despite ten days of wondering, Cate was dumbfounded by the request. "Sure, sure. Today around noon is fine. I'm at work, Aberdeen College. We can meet in the Terrier Café's faculty lounge. It should be quiet there and we'll be able to talk."

"Perfect, I will see you at noon, Dr. Kensie."

"Great. I'll see you then. And, oh, please, call me Cate."

"Goodbye, Cate." The phone clicked. Cate ended the call and set her cell phone down. The DNA results were in and confirmed, she assumed they confirmed that she was the heir to the MacKenzie estate. But how could that be? It made little sense, her parents wouldn't have kept this from her. Did they not know? That seemed improbable. Still, William Smythe did not seem like the type of man who would make a lunch date with a professor at a local liberal arts college to break the news gently that she wasn't inheriting a castle. It still didn't seem true. But if it was, what was she going to do? She had to decide what to do about this castle. Perhaps Mr. Smythe would have some instructions or suggestions. Maybe it was left to her to dispose of, perhaps they didn't even want her moving there. But the will stipulated that she must live there. So, if it wasn't left to her to sell she'd have a big decision on her hands. She checked her clock. It was 8:24 a.m., less than four hours until the meeting. She'd have to wait until then for more answers.

She worked through the morning, trying to keep her mind focused, preparing grade books for dispatching grades, organizing paperwork from the semester, tying up loose ends on her course websites. Peppered in were a few student appointments. Time seemed to drag. It didn't help that, on average, she checked her watch every five minutes. Finally, it was 11:30 a.m. Close enough. By the time I walk over and get us a table, well, I'll still have to wait fifteen minutes, but oh well, she thought.

Cate made her way to the café, it was a buffet style cafeteria with many unique options. Cate paid for two meals telling the clerk at the front that she was expecting a guest. She left his name with the clerk, asking her to send him back to the faculty lounge when he arrived. "He'll be easy to spot," Cate said, "he has a British accent."

Cate entered the faculty lounge at the back of the cafeteria and found it deserted. She selected a table in the back corner to give them privacy in case someone joined them. Setting her keys down on the table, she exited into the main café, made herself a hearty salad, grabbed a glass of water and headed back to her table. Still finding herself alone, she made a start on her salad. She had gotten about two bites in when the door to the faculty dining area opened. She recognized William Smythe, wearing another crisp black suit, he looked out of place against the backdrop of students in sweats and yoga pants. He carried his impeccably polished briefcase. Scanning the room, he caught site of Cate. Still, Cate waved as though he might not see her. He strode across the room taking a seat across from Cate. "Dr. Kensie," he began.

"Cate, please," Cate interrupted him. "You can help yourself to some lunch, the food here is rather good!"

"Thank you," he said. "Perhaps I'll make a salad, if you don't mind my doing so before we conduct our business."

"No, not at all, please help yourself." He was so formal. He left the dining area and returned with a small salad and a glass of water. Unfolding his napkin across his lap, he took a small bite of food then set his fork down.

"Let's get down to business," he said flatly. "As I mentioned during our phone conversation, we have confirmed your identity through two separate DNA tests, you are the heir to the MacKenzie estate, as I suspected."

"Mr. Smythe, I have to tell you I'm really surprised by

this. No one told me anything about any Scottish relative before."

"I can assure you, whether or not you heard about it, you are Lady Gertrude MacKenzie's closest living relative and her rightful heir. There are stacks of paperwork to complete; my firm will handle most everything outside of a few signatures needed from you. I'll collect some of those from you today, the rest when you arrive in London and the final few when we make the trip to Scotland. I assume you'll need some time to get your affairs stateside in order. Do you have an estimate on when you expect that you'll be able to move? I assume you have a valid passport and my firm will complete any paperwork needed for you to live in Scotland."

He said it all so matter-of-factly, as though he had discussed this with Cate before. Cate paused before answering, not sure where to begin. This was a huge life change, moving to another country, giving up her career, it was all so overwhelming. The man stared at her, waiting for her reply. He took another small bite of food as he waited. "Um," Cate began, buying herself some time, "again, I'm sorry, I'm just a little overwhelmed. Ten days ago I hadn't even thought of moving, let alone to another country. I'm just catching up with you here." Although she had been over it so many times in her head, it still seemed overwhelming.

The man seemed to soften a bit. "Please take all the time you need, however, I would like to begin the paperwork on my end if you wouldn't mind signing the forms I have for you today. I assume that you will take up residence at Dunhaven Castle as required by the terms of the will?"

"Yes, of course," Cate blurted out without thinking. Within an instant, her second-guessing set in and she followed up with, "Well, I mean, I think so." While it was a big step, quitting her job and moving to a new country, what was holding her here, she thought.

"Perfect, at the conclusion of our lunch, I'll just need your signature on a few forms."

"Sure, absolutely. I don't want to hold you up at all, I just need a day or so to get things in order. I should be able to give you a better estimate then."

"Of course, Cate." He said her name in a forced, awkward way. "I plan on traveling back to London this evening, but you have my contact information, please let me know when you have an idea so we can prepare for your arrival."

They finished their salads while discussing a few minor details about the will. As they finished, Mr. Smythe dabbed the corners of his mouth with his napkin before setting it aside on his plate and pushing both aside. He snapped open his briefcase and drew out a tidy green folder. Opening it he pulled out several papers, each with flags showing where signatures were required.

"If you don't mind, I'd like to wrap up the signatures I mentioned earlier," he said as he paged to the first signature flag on the top document. "There are several documents here, the first retaining my law firm as your legal counsel in this matter. Please review the document and sign where indicated when you are ready." He handed her the first paper along with a very nice pen that he withdrew from his suit jacket pocket.

"Mr. Smythe, I have one question."

"Of course."

"How sure are you that this will pan out?" Cate's panic was resettling in her mind. She didn't want to go through this just to be left jobless and homeless.

"Very. We have the verification that you are the legal heir, Lady MacKenzie had no other, closer relatives. Even if someone filed a challenge, I am certain that it would have no merit."

"And it's not a conflict of interest that you were Lady MacKenzie's executor and legal counsel as well as mine?"

"Absolutely none. The document there states that you would retain my firm only for this matter, although we hope to continue our representation of the MacKenzie family at your discretion, of course. My firm has represented the MacKenzie family for generations. Lady Gertrude was not only a top client but also a very dear friend. We handle most of the day-to-day business of the estate along with accounts payable. We kept Lady Gertrude apprised of the estate affairs quarterly. We can adjust that to a schedule of your liking."

Cate took a moment to look over the form. It looked like standard legalese and seemed to state that the firm of Smythe, Smith and Smithton would represent her in only the matter of resolving Lady Gertrude MacKenzie's estate and would resolve all issues relating to this matter. She wondered if she should have another attorney look over the paperwork before she agreed to sign but she couldn't see what she had to lose as the terms set forth in the contract seemed to be standard, including the fee for the work. Taking a deep breath and pushing the last remnants of panic from her mind, Cate signed the document.

"Excellent. This second one allows me to act as your agent in all matters regarding the estate including, but not limited to filing motions on your behalf to retain ownership of accounts, property, and handling the transfer of titles." Cate scanned the document then signed.

"Finally, this document stating that I have provided you with a current copy of Lady MacKenzie's final will and testament for your records." As he spoke he slid a copy of the document over to Cate. Cate read the final form, glanced through the document he had given her and signed.

"Excellent," he said flatly, as he gathered the signed papers off the table and stacked them neatly in the folder. Closing it, he placed it into his briefcase. "Well, that will conclude our business for today. I expect you have many details to attend to, if you have questions or need assistance with any arrangements, please reach out. I will pass on your contact information to my assistant, Gayle Pearson. She will also reach out to you via email within the next few days, I'm sure. When you have an estimated arrival in London, please let us know so we can prepare."

"Yes, I will, thank you. I hope to have that information for you soon."

"Thank you. I look forward to hearing from you. Good day, Cate." Again, he spoke her name as though he hated to use it, although he sounded sincere in wanting to hear from her again. She watched him cross the room and disappear through the door. It closed, slowly shutting out the din of the cafeteria. Cate sat for a moment trying to process what had just happened. It felt as though it wasn't real. If the document had not been sitting in front of her, she would have wondered if she had dreamt the whole thing. She sat for another moment before gathering her things and leaving. Back in her office, she found herself unable to concentrate on much work. With no pending student appointments and nothing keeping her there, she called it an early day.

She remained lost in thought while she walked to her car. Random items that needed done ran through her mind along with the incredibility of the entire situation. She was still numb with shock. She drove home with her head still some-what in the clouds. When she arrived at her apartment, she set down her bag. Riley greeted her in the hallway, happy to see her as always. Bending down to pet him she held his little head in her hands and exclaimed, "Riley, it looks like you'll get that yard after all!"

CHAPTER 6

*T*he next few weeks will be a whirlwind, Cate surmised. Her alarm had gone off a few minutes earlier. As if on autopilot, she turned it off and sat up, prepared to start her daily routine when the thought struck her that she was an heiress. It hit her like a bolt of lightning and she sat dumbfounded for an extra minute before climbing out of bed to begin her day. She still couldn't believe it was happening; it still didn't seem real. Regardless, it was happening and was real and details needed to be worked out. Cate never imagined she would move to be honest. She expected to stay at Aberdeen College for quite a while, if not for the duration of her career. She never expected that she would relocate to another country!

Cate didn't have any obligations on campus until noon when she was scheduled to proctor a final, so she took the morning to create a list of things that needed attended to before her move. The prospect of an international move was overwhelming to her, but Cate was a meticulous organizer, so she used those skills to calm her nerves. After she finished jotting down the things that came to mind she had her work cut out for her. Her lease on the apartment was up at the end of the month, making the decision on when to move easy. Given that timeline, she had about three weeks to get everything together. Glancing through the list, it was a tall order, but she figured she could pull it off.

Cate got a jump-start on a few things before heading to campus. She grabbed her laptop, setting it on the kitchen table, opened it, and began checking her email. She found a few emails waiting for her, most of them unimportant. A few were student emails that she answered. As she was about to close her laptop and move to another task, she saw a new email pop into her inbox. It wasn't from a name she recognized and she was about to leave it for later when she noticed the subject line read MacKenzie Estate.

Cate clicked to open the email and scanned through it.

Dear Dr. Kensie,

Please allow me to introduce myself; my name is Gayle Pearson. Please call me Gayle! I am the administrative assistant for Mr. William Smythe, Esq. Having spoken with Mr. Smythe earlier this morning, I understand that you will be joining us on this side of the pond! I wanted to reach out and discuss your arrival plans whenever you may have them. I will assist you with any plans to help make your move easier. Also, I can help you with setting up your travel arrangements. Once you have a more concrete idea of your schedule, please let me know and I will be happy to take care of the details. You can contact me via email or my office phone: 044 1901 456789. I look forward to hearing from you, Dr. Kensie!

Sincerely,
    Gayle Pearson
    Administrative Assistant to William Smythe, Esq.

Law Firm of Smythe, Smith and Smithton

The email cemented in Cate's mind the reality of her situation. What was like a dream was becoming her reality. Cate suddenly became anxious. What was she doing? In three weeks, she was moving to a foreign country having never even traveled outside of her own country before. What if she was making a terrible mistake? A sense of unease swept over her, she had made such a snap decision yesterday in the café; it was unlike her. Cate took a deep breath and pushed aside her rambling thoughts. She was panicking, plain and simple, because she felt overwhelmed by everything she had to do. She had made a decision, and she planned to stick to it. Besides, she didn't have a lot of choice, if she wanted the inheritance, she had to move. And who wouldn't want to inherit a Scottish castle? It provided her with the security of a home and the means to maintain it for a lifetime. Settling her mind, Cate read the email again. Unlike the straight-laced, uptight Mr. Smythe, Gayle seemed warm and inviting. Cate sent a quick response before heading to campus.

Hi Gayle,

Thank you for the email. Please call me Cate! I hope to have some solid dates for you soon but my rough plan is to travel near the end of the month. This will coordinate well with my lease expiration and give me some time to wrap up some affairs on my end. Once I have some specific dates in mind, I can let you know. Mr. Smythe said that I would first come to London to complete some paperwork and then on to Scotland. Do you know how long I would spend in

*London before going on to Scotland? The information would help
in planning my arrival.*

Thanks so much!
   Cate

Cate gave it a quick re-read and sent it on its way before
closing her laptop. She checked the time; it was around 9
a.m. With the six hour time difference, that would make it
around 3 p.m. in London. Cate hoped Gayle would receive it
before leaving the office.

Cate decided she would get ready to head in to give her
final. After a quick shower, she tossed on a pair of jeans, a
striped top and a blazer. She took Riley for a short walk
before gathering her things and heading to campus. On her
way, she stopped at the local home improvement store to
pick up some boxes and packing tape. She bought about two
dozen to start with and stowed most of them in the trunk of
her car. The others she put in her backseat, intending to use
them for some things in her office.

She arrived at campus with about an hour to spare before
the final exam commenced. She headed to her office, boxes
in tow. Looking around she mentally started cataloging what
she needed to do before she left. Although her office wasn't
large, she had several things to clean out and box up. Since
she had some time before the final, she started organizing
some materials. She began by gathering some of her personal
effects, packing them into a box together and marking its
contents on a paper that she stuffed into the top. Thankfully,
she didn't have many personal effects. What she had a lot of
was books. She looked at the stuffed bookshelf and
wondered if the four remaining boxes were enough. Most

likely not, she concluded, but she could get a start. She thought packing them by topic might make the most sense but she soon gave up on that idea and resorted to packing them by what would fit together and what, when combined, wouldn't make the box too heavy for her to carry. Two boxes in and it was like she was playing a live game of Tetris.

Cate checked her watch, it was twenty minutes to noon. She figured she better get to the lecture hall to give her final. Leaving the boxes behind, she gathered her tote bag and the stack of finals and left the office. After making her way across campus, she entered the lecture hall and found it filled. She hadn't seen this many students in the room since the first day. A nervous tension filled the air as she made her way to the front, setting the stack of finals down along with her bag.

"Good afternoon, everyone," Cate said loudly. "Is everyone ready?" A few groans answered her. "Remember, no text books, notes, cell phones, copying neighbor's papers allowed. If you have questions during the exam, please raise your hand. Once you have completed the exam, please bring it to the front of the room and then you are free to leave and begin your summer break." This elicited a chuckle from a few students. She began passing out the exam papers. "Just relax and think everything through, you'll be fine. Good luck!"

When she had finished passing out all the papers, she made her way back to the instructor's desk at the front. Before sitting down, she scanned the room. She pulled out her laptop and her list from this morning, prepared to busy herself with planning until she could begin grading the papers as they were turned in.

As she waited for her wi-fi to connect, she scanned the list. She decided to knock off a little shopping for items that she and Riley would need for the trip. Turning to her laptop, she checked her email first, finding an email from Gayle waiting for her.

Hi Cate! The end of the month would work nicely for us and we will plan for that. Again, once you have determined specific dates, please let me know and I can make the exact arrangements. You'll need to spend a few nights with us (2-3) in London before moving on to your new home! Mr. Smythe and I will accompany you to Dunhaven. If you have any other questions, please reach out.

Best,

Gayle

Gayle seemed to be very on top of it, although she figured she would have to be working for William Smythe. He didn't seem like the kind of man who suffered incompetence. Cate had another question for Gayle but she didn't want to bombard the poor woman's email so she thought she would wait to see if any additional questions popped into her head and send them all at once.

Cate did another scan of the room; everyone was hard at work. Turning her attention back to her laptop, Cate browsed around a few retail sites, deciding that Riley needed a new carrier for the trip along with a new bed for his new house. She picked out a new coat and ball for him, too. She didn't get any further before she heard a rustling of papers. A few students were packing their things having finished their exam already. She checked her watch, about fifty minutes in with an hour to go. The students made their way to the front of the room, handing her their papers and saying their goodbyes before disappearing out the door. Cate began to grade the exams as they were handled in, shoving her laptop aside. She wanted to finish up anything she could so she could focus on her move. Taking out her answer key she began to mark each first page before moving on to the next. As she worked a few more students turned in their papers. She added these to the stack and made it through the first page of each before anyone else turned in their exams.

The remaining time in the exam flew by. Cate continued to grade all the papers she had received, going back to the first few pages a few times to mark new submissions. With ten minutes remaining, she announced the time left to the remaining students. This prompted a few more to finish their answers and pack up. She waited to continue any grading since the exam was almost over. At 1:50 p.m. she announced that time was up and students should complete their answers and turn their papers in. A few students hastily selected their final few answers, collected their things and brought their papers to Cate. After stowing her laptop and to-do list in her tote, she collected all the papers and headed back to her office. She planned on finishing the grades for the final and the course overall before heading home for the evening.

After finishing all the final exam grades, she input all the grades into her grade book, made final grade calculations and posted her grades to the online grading system. "One class finished, three to go," she mused. Checking the time, she figured she could pack one more box. When she finished, she stacked the boxes in the corner near the door, gathered her tote and headed for her car.

A few minutes later, she pulled into the parking lot of her building. She gathered her packing supplies and headed in. Piling the flattened boxes in the hall, she bent down to greet Riley. He was his usual excited self. "Hey, buddy! How was your day? After dinner, I want to show you all the new things

I've got in my cart for you!" Riley gave her a lap to the face as though he agreed.

After changing her clothes and making some dinner, Cate spent the rest of the evening showing Riley his new things and completing her purchases for him. He seemed to approve them all. The purchase seemed another way of cementing the reality of Cate's new circumstances.

The next day Cate spent in her office finishing grades for two more classes and packing the remainder of her things. Before she left the apartment, she sent a quick email off to Gayle asking where she should ship the boxes with her personal effects. The ever-efficient Gayle had already responded with the address, indicating that she would arrange for everything to be put in an "obvious but unobtrusive space" in Cate's new home so she could deal with them at the time of her choosing. It seemed so strange for Cate to think of it being her new home, of leaving Aberdeen behind. She couldn't imagine what it would be like, but she was experiencing a mix of emotions about it.

When Cate arrived at the office, she decided that she would do her grading first then finish with whatever packing she could. She hoped to finish with all grading and packing by the end of finals week, allowing her to shift her focus to what she needed to do at home to prepare for the move. She spread out the papers on her desk and started reading the final papers of each student group from her American History class. It took her just under two hours to read each group's papers and input their grades into the grade book. She completed all course grades and entered them into the system. "Halfway done!" she thought.

Glancing at her watch she saw that it was about 10:30 a.m., so she moved on to her next course's final projects. This course, in European History, had a similar final project to her American History course in which groups submitted final papers. She had about thirteen groups to grade so she dug in. She made it through about two-thirds of the papers when her stomach started to rumble. Checking her watch she saw that it was now close to noon. She grabbed a to-go salad at the cafeteria and returned straight to work. She finished the last of the papers while she ate her lunch. By the time she completed all the grades for this course it was just before 1:30 p.m. She had finished all the work she had planned for the day, leaving only one class' grades to finish. Those grades she decided to complete tomorrow and spent the rest of her afternoon packing.

Cate stood up and stretched then started building and filling boxes. She cleared nearly two more shelves of books when there was a knock at her door. "Come on in," she yelled as she taped up another box and marked the address that Gayle had given her in bold letters with a Sharpie.

She turned as Jeff was walking through the door; he looked around, genuine surprise on his face. "Hey, when I said not to count on summer, kiddo, I didn't mean you had to start packing yet!"

Cate gave him a small laugh in response. "About the summer, Jeff," Cate began.

Jeff interrupted her. "Yeah, I've got great news. I managed to get you a few classes," he grinned as though he had just done her the world's biggest favor.

"Thanks, Jeff. I appreciate what you've done but I need to decline."

"Decline? Cate, are you serious?" His face expressed genuine shock.

"Yes, I am serious. I need to decline. I've had some… developments on my end." She chose her words carefully. She didn't want to offer much information, she was sure it would sound crazy if she said it out loud. And, despite her excitement, she felt a momentary sadness in leaving behind something that had become so familiar.

"Developments?" he said, almost to himself, "Were you offered another position?"

Cate smiled to herself a bit. "Yes, in a way I was. Anyway, what it boils down to is I don't need the summer classes or a contract for the next academic year. I'm sorry about the late notice, Jeff, if I had known, I would have told you sooner but I only just found out myself."

"Well, ah…" Jeff was clearly at a loss for words. "Ah," he struggled, rubbing his chin with his hand, "I guess congratulations are in order!"

"Oh, thanks!" Cate said.

He slowly extended his hand to shake hers as if trying to grasp the reality of the situation at the same time. She took it and gave his hand a big shake. "Well, ah, it looks like you've got moving under control and there's nothing I can do to change your mind."

"Nope, sorry, it's too good an opportunity to pass up." She wasn't lying.

"Well, ah, okay, I guess I'll leave you to it. Good luck with… ah, well, everything!"

"Thanks, again, Jeff! I'll pop in before I leave at the end of the week to say goodbye."

"Yeah, great, thanks." Jeff left her office, but not before taking one last glance over his shoulder as if to confirm that what had just happened really did happen. Then he looked her in the eyes again, "You're sure there's nothing I can do to change your mind? I think a permanent position is in the cards for you here, eventually."

"Sorry, Jeff, there's nothing."

"Well, okay, can't blame a guy for trying!" With that he disappeared down the hall.

Despite a twinge of sadness, a smile crept across Cate's

face. She was content not to live contract-to-contract. Taking a deep breath, she began building another box to clear off her final shelf. After packing the final box, she emptied her file cabinet, marking files that the department needed to keep and discarding those that were no longer needed. A quick scan of the office showed nothing left to pack. She checked all her drawers one final time. Satisfied that she had everything packed, she began carrying boxes one by one to her car, stacking them in the backseat. After making several trips back and forth to get all the boxes, she was spent. She made one final trek to her office to retrieve her laptop and bag. Not wanting to haul the boxes in and out again she stopped at the post office on her way home and shipped this set of boxes to their new destination.

When Cate arrived home, she was exhausted physically and mentally. After a short walk with Riley, she settled on the couch with a bowl of cereal and relaxed for the evening.

As Thursday morning arrived, Cate was all too aware that this was the last she would see of Aberdeen College. She headed to campus with mixed emotions. Despite being glad that she was moving on and not subject to the whim of the department, its chair, or administration, it had been familiar to her. It was the only home she had known since she was on her own so it was bittersweet in many ways for her. Her plan was to finish the grading for her last course, double-check that she had packed everything from her office and turn in her keys. As she readied herself for the day, she promised Riley she wouldn't be late today. She headed to her office, shutting the door behind her. There shouldn't be anyone looking for her today, finals week was almost complete, all papers and projects had been turned in and she had given her notice to Jeff so she should be on her own. She looked at the stack of papers on her desk, twenty-one final reports stood between her and the end of the semester. No sense in delaying, she concluded, and, taking the first paper from the stack, she dove in. It took her the better part of the morning to read and grade all the papers. Digging her laptop out of her bag, she started it up to put all the grades in and finish grading for the course. After completing this, she added the pile of papers to the "keep" pile for the department. As she was just about to close her laptop, she thought it might be a good idea to write a quick letter of resignation for the department so they had it both in writing and verbally.

She pulled up her word editor and typed a brief letter stating that was she resigning effective the end of the spring semester, adding that she had enjoyed her time at Aberdeen College and had experienced a good amount of growth as a faculty member while there. Digitally signing it, she sent it via email to Jeff carbon copying the department secretary.

Closing her laptop, she glanced around the room. It looked barren, like the day she came. She checked all the drawers, finding them empty. Nothing on the bookshelves, nothing hiding under her desk, nothing on the bulletin board. Satisfied, she stowed her laptop, grabbed her keys and worked on removing her office keys from her key ring.

She took one last look around; she had pleasant memories of her first moments in this office at her first real job and some difficult moments that she had rode out in this office. It wasn't easy to leave but, as she reminded herself, she had never truly felt at home here. Sighing away her nostalgia, she tossed her keys into her bag, grabbed the two removed keys, shut off the lights and closed the door on her office for the last time. She lingered a moment with her hand on the doorknob but before she could let any more doubt set in, she forced herself to make her way down the hall. She took the stairs down a flight to the department office. As she expected, she found the door open and Molly, the department's secretary, behind her desk.

"Hey, Cate," she said brightly as Cate entered.

"Hi, Molly," Cate answered. "I have my keys to return to you." She set them down on the desk in front of Molly.

"Keys? Are you moving to a new office?" Molly seemed confused.

"No, sorry. I thought maybe you had heard from Jeff or saw the email I sent a few minutes ago. I've resigned my position, I won't be returning to Aberdeen."

"What?" Molly exclaimed. Lowering her voice, she leaned in to Cate and said, "Is this because of the tenure situation? To be honest, I think Jeff could have done more, but I'd try to hang in there and keep pushing, honey."

"Oh, thanks, Molly, but that's not it entirely. I'm actually moving."

"Moving? To where?!"

"Scotland," Cate said as matter-of-factly as she could.

"SCOTLAND?! Are you kidding me? What prompted this, if you don't mind my asking? Did you get a job offer there?"

"Oh, I just found out I have family there." Cate twisted the truth a bit.

"Oh, that's great, honey, I can understand you wanting to move for your family." Molly said nodding her head as though it all made sense now.

Happy with being able to dodge any further explanations, Cate smiled and said, "So, I guess this is goodbye! I left all the current student paperwork in my office with dates marked showing when they are no longer current and can be disposed of and again, here are my keys, so that's it!"

"Just like you, Cate, always so organized!" she paused a moment, waving a hand in front of her face, tearing up a bit, "And now just a minute, this can't be goodbye just yet. Let me take you to lunch!"

"Oh, you don't have to do that, Molly!"

"Nonsense, come on, then you can tell me all about this move to Scotland!"

Cate considered it for a moment. Molly was always her strongest supporter in the department. She thought it was kind of her to offer, but Cate had one demand for the lunch, "Okay, but only if it's my treat."

"Now, Cate…" Molly began.

"I insist or the lunch is off!" Cate grinned.

"Okay, okay, I give in!" Molly said, holding both hands up to admit defeat. "How about tomorrow? I know you will be getting busier the closer your move gets!"

"Works great for me! Should we meet in the café here?"

"Blah, no, let's go off campus for a change! How about that new Italian place that just opened on Third Street? You can try it before you leave, at least!"

"Sounds good, I'll see you there, around noon?"

"See you there!" Molly answered.

Smiling, Cate retreated from the office and headed straight for her car, hoping to avoid any more attempts to say goodbye. Luck was on her side, she made it through unscathed and headed home. She got back to her apartment around 12:30 p.m., early, just as she had promised. Given that it was her last day of the semester and of work at Aberdeen she celebrated by taking Riley to the park.

On her way, she grabbed some lunch. Making their way down the gravel path from the parking area, she and Riley found their favorite spot overlooking the pond and sat down to eat their lunch. She had treated Riley to a cup of peanut butter ice cream while she ate a hamburger and fries. She gazed off into the distance. Aberdeen College stood behind the pond. Thinking of the last few glances of her office, she felt sadness to leave behind the familiarity of her current life but she couldn't deny the excitement building for her new adventure. And despite there being no actual family there, the connection to her family heritage felt very real to her.

As she finished her lunch, she pulled out Riley's favorite ball. He jumped to attention, ready to play. She tossed the ball and watched Riley race after it. She imagined playing with him on the lawns of Dunhaven Castle. Riley would love the open spaces there. No more cramped apartment, no more tiny patch of grass!

When Riley had grown tired of playing fetch, he collapsed in a heap next to Cate, content to watch life pass them by as he caught his breath. Cate rubbed his head gently as she watched life unfolding. She stared off toward Aberdeen College. Turning to Riley, she said, "So, what do you think, Riley? Should we leave Aberdeen behind and go on an adventure?" Picking his head up, Riley looked inquisitively at Cate. "We can live in a castle with a nice big lawn and you can go on walks every day! You can play ball every day, Riley!" Riley's dark, almond eyes gleamed back at her. "Well buddy, I guess we had better get packed and ready to go. We're leaving in just a few short weeks!" Riley jumped to his feet. Cate laughed, "Relax, buddy, let's enjoy our day today and get at it fresh tomorrow morning." Riley sat down, still looking intently at Cate. "Okay, okay, let's finish the walk around the pond before dinner, sound good?" Riley jumped to his feet again, excited to go.

Cate climbed to her feet and started toward the path after cleaning up from their lunch. As she walked with Riley, she wondered if they would find a pond or lake to walk around and enjoy in Scotland. She hoped they would, but even if they didn't, she decided they would still have a great time and find wonderful places to walk.

After concluding their walk, Cate and Riley climbed into the car and headed home for some dinner. Cate fed Riley his kibble, which he ate with enthusiasm after his big day while she opted for a peanut butter and jelly sandwich. She turned in early, planning to get an early start tomorrow on her to-do list before moving. A part of one chapter in her life had closed today; the prologue to another was about to start tomorrow.

CHAPTER 7

*E*ven with the early night, the alarm woke her sooner than she would have liked. She slept lightly, her nervous energy to get started kept her tossing and turning. The clock read 5 a.m. She turned over to lie on her back, tempted to sleep in. The length of her to-do list convinced her otherwise. Forcing herself out of bed, she slipped out of her pajamas and straight into clothes, opting to skip the shower until after she had gotten some work done. She fixed breakfast for both Riley and herself, deciding to make scrambled eggs to give her a hearty start for her day.

After cleaning up her breakfast dishes, she grabbed her laptop out of her bag and opened it, navigating to her email. There were a few emails already awaiting her, most of them were advertisements or other solicitations that she deleted. There were two student emails that required brief responses. After she finished with those, Cate dropped a line to Gayle and passed along her personal email address. Since she was no longer employed with the university, she did not want to continue to use her university email account since she expected it would be deleted and she was not sure how long she would have access to it.

After emailing the updated contact information, Cate said aloud, "Well, I guess I can't put it off any longer, time to start." Closing her laptop, she pushed herself back from the table and stood up. She was overwhelmed as she looked around the room. So many things needed to be dealt with; it appeared she accumulated a lot over the years. Most of her things would be donated; she doubted she'd need the furniture, dishes, silverware and other household things. She tried to picture her shabby couch in the middle of a grand castle's sitting room or her cheap silverware adorning the massive dining table in the dining room. Yeah, she thought, I just need to box things and send them to charity!

Cate decided the best place to start was the living room. There weren't many small items; the work went quickly. She had a few personal items and keepsakes in the living room that she boxed for shipping along with some of Riley's toys. Riley watched Cate curiously as she packed his prized possessions, sniffing gloomily at the box as though he'd lost old friends.

Each box packed, each item sorted made things more and more real. As she boxed keepsakes, she wondered if she would find a place for them in her new home. There wouldn't be a lack of space, but trying to imagine them somewhere else seemed foreign to her. She couldn't help but feel unsettled, but she assured herself that things would be fine and finished in that room. Next, she tackled the hall and its closet, boxing any winter items and anything extraneous of Riley's that he wouldn't need within the next ten days or for the trip. After finishing that, she looked at her watch, it was just after nine. Now that it was a decent hour, she took a quick break to make some phone calls.

Starting with her landlord, she left a message on his

voicemail that she did not plan on renewing her lease and would have the apartment cleared out by the end of the month. Also, she requested that he meet her sometime next week to go over the apartment to make sure there were no issues with its condition. Her next call was to a local charity that provided donation pickup to arrange for a day to have all her furniture and other donated items retrieved. She scheduled them to come out the following Thursday for everything. With that settled, she called a few of her utility companies to cancel her service at month's end. When she finished with all her calls, she took immense satisfaction in crossing these items off her to-do list. While the list was still long, she had made a good dent. Her next project would be to tackle packing the kitchen. This would leave her with no dishes, cookware or silverware, so she decided the best thing to do would be to hit the local supermarket for some paper products and easy meals for the next week.

Checking her watch, she could just make the trip before her lunch with Molly. She took a shower and put on fresh clothes then made the quick trip to the store. She returned with a variety of paper plates, bowls, and plastic cutlery and a few microwavable meals. Still in bags, she set everything in the hallway so she didn't clutter her next workspace in the kitchen. Peering in at her next job, she was relieved to have scheduled the lunch so she could put it off a little longer.

If she left now, she could arrive earlier than Molly and request a table outdoors to accommodate Riley. Scooping up Riley, she fitted his harness and leash on him and carried him outside. The restaurant wasn't far, so Cate walked, enjoying the weather and allowing Riley to stretch his legs. She arrived at the eatery with ten minutes to spare and they seated her at an outdoor table near the front corner of the building.

Molly was only a few minutes behind her, pulling into the

parking area just after Cate was seated. She spotted Cate, giving her a big wave as she made her way over.

"Hi Riley!" she said, sitting down. "How are you, little guy? Oh, he's too cute, Cate."

"Thanks," Cate said, wholeheartedly agreeing, "I hope you don't mind outdoor seating, I didn't want to leave him alone with half the apartment packed. I thought he might be anxious."

"Not at all, I'm cooped up in the office all day just looking at the sunshine through the window, it's nice to bask in it!" Molly opened her menu to look at the choices, "So, what looks good to you, Cate?"

Cate perused the menu, despite already having made her selection after visiting the restaurant's website the night before. "I will go with the gnocchi with butter sauce."

"Don't you always order that when you eat Italian?"

"You know me, I'm not very adventurous." Cate laughed. "What about you?"

"I'm going to have the spicy Risotto. I am adventurous! And, hey, speaking of not being adventurous, I beg to differ, Miss 'I'm moving to another country in a few weeks'," Molly chuckled.

Cate giggled, but didn't get to answer since the waitress approached to take their order and deliver a basket of home-made bread. After the waitress left, Molly grabbed a slice of bread and said, "So, tell me about Scotland. How did this happen? When? Where? Give me all the juicy details!"

"It was quite sudden and unexpected," Cate said, also diving into the bread basket. "The Friday before last I got this strange message on my machine from this attorney saying his flight was delayed and he'd have to meet me later than expected. He said he sent a letter to me, but I never received the letter. I had no idea what he was talking about, but I was taking Riley out for one last walk before he said he would arrive, opened the door and ran right into him. I still had no idea what any of this was about or why he was coming to see me. Turns out, he was an attorney for an estate of someone who is a distant relative of mine. Recently, she passed away and I am her closest living relative. So I inherit her estate. The stipulation is I have to move to Scotland to maintain it, so here we are!"

Molly listened intently as Cate outlined the story. "Oh my gosh, I have so many questions, I don't know where to begin. So this guy just shows up and what? Tells you you're inheriting some property in Scotland but only if you move there?"

"Yep." Molly seemed at a loss for words, so Cate continued to fill the silence. "I mean I had to have a DNA test to make sure I was Lady MacKenzie's relative. I just found out a few days ago that the test showed that I was. No one ever told me about any relatives, even distant."

"Wait," Molly stopped her, "LADY MacKenzie? What are you inheriting a castle or something?" She laughed.

"Yes, that's what I'm inheriting."

Flabbergasted, Molly exclaimed, "Cate! Are you serious?!?!"

"Yes." Cate had brought the picture that Mr. Smythe gave her in her purse to show Molly. She took it out and placed it on the table.

Molly picked up the picture just as their food arrived. The woman looked as though she was ready to burst as she waited for the waitress to serve the food. "CATE! Please tell me you'll let me visit!" she exclaimed as the waitress walked away.

Cate laughed, "Of course, Molly. I'd love to have you visit! You're the only friend I've had in Aberdeen. I mean, I know I'm not the most outgoing person, but, I never made many friends after my parents' deaths."

"Oh, your offer is so accepted, Cate. I will hold you to

that! I'd LOVE to see Scotland, and I'd love it even more to stay in a CASTLE while I'm there! Well, at least I think I would."

"You think?"

"Yeah, I'll let you try it out first, make sure it's not haunted."

"Haunted? Are you serious?"

"Yeah, haunted. You know, like on all the movies, those castles are always haunted! All those generations living there, some of them dying there. You go make sure it's not haunted before I come over."

"Okay, deal. Once we can verify that there are no ghosts, I'll send your invitation."

"Deal! So now it all makes sense on why you are moving all of a sudden. I'd have moved too, once I made sure it wasn't haunted, of course." Molly winked.

"Yes, but I didn't ask about it being haunted. I didn't have any offers here yet, so I decided to just go with it. It's a beautiful property, I've not made it very far with my career here, I had nothing holding me back."

"You don't have to explain it to me. You'd be crazy not to move regardless of your career, although, they gave you a raw deal AGAIN. Don't even get me started on that tenure-track denial!"

Cate smiled at her, silently thanking her for her support. Molly continued, despite Cate not prompting her, "Jeff did NOTHING to help you. It serves him right to be scrambling this late for the summer. The contracts went out three weeks ago."

"Three weeks ago?" Cate asked, remembering that Jeff just told her this week.

"Oh, don't tell me. He didn't offer you anything until late," Molly groaned.

"He told me he had a few classes for me earlier this week, that's when I told him I was resigning."

"Well, that's divine providence if you ask me, Cate. You were MEANT to go to Scotland and Jeff was meant to get stuck for playing his games. It serves him right. Finally caught up to him."

"Well, I can't say that I'm complaining with the outcome, that's for sure! Maybe it worked out just the way it was supposed to."

Cate and Molly finished their lunch, chatting about Cate's move and plans once she reached Scotland. Molly offered to help Cate with any last-minute details but Cate declined, figuring she had things under control given her timeline.

"Well, I guess this is goodbye then," Cate said as they stood up from the table.

"Goodbye FOR NOW," Molly corrected her. Reaching out to give her a hug, Molly said, "Promise you'll keep in touch!"

"I promise!" Cate said. Another bittersweet moment, Cate held back a tear that threatened to escape from her eye.

"And you, Riley, have fun playing in that HUGE yard!" Riley looked curiously at Molly.

Cate laughed, "I'm sure he will enjoy that! Well, back to packing for me! Next time you hear from me, I'll be in Scotland!"

"Thank you for lunch, Cate, and I can't wait to hear that you're settled!" After another few moments of chitchat, the women parted ways, with Cate heading back to her apartment.

After her heavy lunch, Cate didn't want to do much of anything else. She wrinkled her nose, staring in at the kitchen. "How about you clean this room out, Riley?" He looked at her, tilting his head as though considering the idea. In the end, he found one of his toy bones still left out and chewed it in the hallway. "I guess I have my answer. Well, I'll start fresh tomorrow. Instead, let's spend some time watching those haunted castle movies Molly mentioned," Cate said to Riley.

Cate spent the next two days packing the remaining rooms in the house and clearing the apartment. While on a break from the work, Cate saw that, following their lunch, Molly had sent an announcement to the department stating that she regretted to inform everyone of the departure of Dr. Cate Kensie, who was leaving the university at the end of this semester and wishing Cate the best of luck in her "NEW SCOTTISH CASTLE". Cate smiled to herself, Molly had a flair for the dramatic, but out of everyone at the university, she had been a true friend to Cate. Leave it to her to send out a goodbye message and leave it up to the rest of her department to ignore it.

Cate sent Molly her personal email account information so they could keep in touch. She doubted Molly would check her email on the weekend, but she would find it there on Monday morning.

She also answered an email from Gayle that confirmed her new email account and that she would use it for communication going forward. She wanted to give her as much notice as possible about her travel plans. Clicking reply, she typed a brief response saying that she was making good progress on her end wrapping up all her loose ends and preparing to move. She estimated that she would have everything finished within a week so she would be prepared to travel one week from today. Given that paperwork needed to be completed, Cate indicated that perhaps traveling on Sunday or Monday might be best if that worked for Mr. Smythe's schedule.

Cate had not expected to receive a response on the weekend from Gayle, but, upon checking her email just a few hours later, she was stunned to find a response from her.

This woman was quite the worker! Gayle had listed several flights on the days in question, asking Cate to select the one that worked best for her. She also stated that once the flight was arranged, she would schedule a car to pick Cate up at the airport and transfer her to the hotel that Gayle had recommended, unless Cate preferred another hotel. Gayle indicated that Mr. Smythe's schedule allowed him to meet with Cate on Monday and Tuesday. She had held open the rest of the days that week so he could travel with Cate to Dunhaven to complete the remainder of the paperwork.

Cate scanned the list of flights, it seemed Gayle had selected various departure times throughout the day and had minimized layovers and connections, a fact that didn't escape Cate and that she appreciated very much. Cate selected an early morning flight, so she arrived in London at a decent hour. After thanking Gayle for handling the arrangements, Cate listed her flight selection. With regard to the hotel, Cate said that she was fine with whatever recommendation Gayle made but informed her she was traveling with Riley in case the hotel did not permit dogs.

Within minutes of Cate responding, Gayle sent another email. She would secure the flight of Cate's choice, arrange a car, arrange for luggage service so she did not have to handle her bags at the airport, and yes, she knew that Riley was Cate's traveling companion and had selected a hotel that would accommodate both guests. She stated that she couldn't wait to meet Riley in ten short days and would send all confirmations to Cate as soon as she had them.

The woman's work ethic was impressive! Ten short days, Cate thought, as Gayle's statement rattled around in her head. That wasn't very long, possibly not long enough for her to finish packing her closet. Amazingly, she finished it all and got the boxes to the shipping store before it closed on Monday.

When she returned, she looked around the half-empty apartment. Even with the furnishings still left and several boxes decorating the space, it had no personal touches, making it seem more than half-empty to her. She spent the rest of the day relaxing, feeling like she had been hit by a truck after hauling all those boxes over the last several days. She couldn't believe in less than a week she was moving to another country so in addition to relaxing, she spent the down-time trying to wrap her head around that by reading up on all things Scotland.

Tuesday and Wednesday were uneventful. Riley's new items arrived on Tuesday and, after receiving the Riley seal of approval, Cate packed them for the trip. Cate spent her remaining time in Aberdeen enjoying the days with Riley at the park and researching some things about her new town. Dunhaven seemed to be a charming small town. She was excited to experience it in person.

About halfway through the day Wednesday, Cate realized that she would soon donate her furniture and therefore would have nowhere to sit or sleep. She decided the best course of action was to head to a hotel for her last few days in town. Around mid-afternoon, there was a knock on Cate's door. She saw it was one of the student workers from her department through the peephole and opened the door. The student greeted her, handing her a letter. "Hi, Dr. Kensie. Molly sent me with this for you. She said it was important."

"Thank you," Cate said, accepting the envelope. After the student left, she glanced at it and saw the return address was from Smythe, Smith, and Smithton, LLC. It must be the letter that William Smythe had sent her; it had arrived through campus mail, finally. It did detailed his plans to travel to meet with her to discuss Lady MacKenzie's will, collect a DNA sample, and gave his itinerary. "Well, better late than never I guess, Riley, but this would have been

71

helpful a few weeks back," Cate joked. "We're on our way now, almost time for us to move!"

The pickup truck for her donations pulled into the parking lot around 10 a.m. on Thursday bringing two able-bodied men with it to move furniture. Cate helped carry boxes and odds and ends while the two men handled the larger items. Even with her help it took about three hours to clear the apartment of all its belongings. Cate thanked the men and gave them both a generous tip. On her way back to the apartment, Mrs. Kline waylaid Cate.

"Oh, Katie, Katie, I'm so glad I ran into you." It was like listening to a broken record. Even so, she might miss the older woman.

"Hi, Mrs. Kline."

"I couldn't help but notice you've been quite, eh, active, in the last few days."

"Yes, I'm sorry, I hope I haven't been disturbing you with noise."

"Oh, no, not at all, but I have seen you making trips with boxes and furniture. You wouldn't be disappearing on me now, would you, Katie?"

"Yes, Mrs. Kline, I am. I'm moving."

"Moving? Really? You? Katie, I thought you'd be my neighbor until I died. You and that barky little mutt, Wiley."

No, cancel the earlier thought, Cate would not miss her. "Sorry to disappoint, Mrs. Kline, but I am moving, leaving today."

"Today? You don't say. And, ah, where in the world are you moving to? Did you finally find a nice young man to settle down with? I haven't seen anyone at the apartment, just that older gentleman the other night. Oh, are you marrying an older man?" she asked, eyes wide with curiosity.

So many presumptions made in such a short time, Cate

thought. "No, I'm not marrying anyone. I found some relatives and I am moving there to live."

"And where exactly is 'there'?"

"Scotland. Dunhaven, Scotland."

"You're moving to Scotland?" Mrs. Kline was dumbfounded and speechless. With a break in the line of questioning, Cate made her get-away.

"Yes, and if you'll excuse me, Mrs. Kline, I have so much to do before I leave. Sorry to be abrupt, but I do need to get going." Cate began inching toward her apartment.

She turned to make her break for it as she heard Mrs. Kline call after her, "Oh, ah, promise me you'll write!"

"Of course!" Cate called as she pushed through her door.

Returning to the apartment, Cate found a lonely Riley sitting in the middle of the hall. The apartment looked so bare. There was nothing left to do, the list was complete, the apartment was empty, the landlord had signed off on the condition. Cate took a deep breath, taking it all in, the end of a chapter. She had a slight sense of melancholy, but she did her best to push it aside and fill the space with excitement for her upcoming life change.

"We made a lot of good memories here, Riley. But let's go make some new ones!" she said. "Time to throw the last few things into the suitcase and go!" She packed away the few things she had left out from this morning for herself and Riley into her suitcases, transferred them to the car then retrieved Riley. They headed for a quick trip to the park before grabbing some takeout and settling into the hotel room she had rented.

The next few days seemed to drag. Cate filled the time by keeping busy with Riley in the warm weather, enjoying the last few trips to Aberdeen's park they would ever take. The waiting was driving Cate insane, but time passed and Saturday evening was upon them.

Cate lay in bed, unable to sleep. Riley snuggled in his bed, sleeping like a baby. Lucky, she thought. Nervous anticipation kept Cate from being able to rest. She worried about her new life, her flight, if her boxes made it to their destination and a thousand other small things. Several times throughout the night, she got up to pace the floor, get a drink of water, look out the window, or anything else to settle her mind. None of it worked, but eventually she dozed off. It seemed like she had just fallen asleep when her alarm woke her. She had an early call for her flight. She jumped from her bed, racing around to get dressed. In actuality, she left herself plenty of time and had a twenty minute wait for the cab to take her to the airport.

She opted to keep Riley with her during the flight so she tucked him in his carrier, although she planned on walking him before heading through security and into the waiting area.

Riley was none too pleased to be back into his carrier after his short walk at the airport so after Cate checked her bags, passed through security and had a comfortable spot in the corner of the waiting area, she took him out of the carrier and held him. He was understandably nervous, looking to Cate for reassurances. He enjoyed a bit of attention from a child sitting near them but not enough to make him any happier to get into his carrier for the flight when boarding began.

Gayle had booked Cate in first class; it was her first time traveling this way. Too much of this and she would be spoiled. Seated on the plane, Cate felt butterflies in her stomach. The moment was here; she couldn't believe it. A nervous excitement filled her. Still in shock about the turn of events, it still didn't seem real to her, but it was becoming more real by the second.

Within twenty minutes, the passengers had boarded and

the flight attendants closed the doors. While the flight attendants gave their flight safety presentation, Cate felt the plane move, being pushed back toward the runway. The moment was finally here. Cate leaned over to Riley, "Here we go, buddy!" "Next stop: London, England!"

CHAPTER 8

*W*hile Cate may have fibbed to Riley since they had a layover in New York, they made it to Heathrow. It was about half-past nine, but it seemed like early evening to Cate. "We made it, buddy!" Cate exclaimed as they exited the plane. Even at this hour, the airport was bustling. Everything was so foreign to her already. She heard a mix of accents and languages. It seemed like the airport had more people than Aberdeen had in the entire town. Cate held tight to Riley's carrier, pressing it as close to her as she could while she followed the signs toward the exit.

As she approached the exterior, she saw a small, blonde man in a black suit holding a sign with her name. He watched as people passed him. Cate approached him; he seemed to recognize her. "Excuse me," she began, "I'm Cate, Cate Kensie."

"Ah, Dr. Kensie, a pleasure to meet you. I'm Sam. It's my understanding that your luggage is being delivered to the hotel for you," the man answered in a bit of a muddled British accent.

"Yes, that's correct," Cate answered. "Is it always this busy here?" she asked.

"I don't rightly know but I'd bet on it, yes. Would you like me to carry the dog for you?" Sam asked.

"Oh, no, no thanks. I like to keep him close."

"Of course! If you'll follow me, I'll take you to the car."

"Thank you, Sam. And please, call me Cate."

Nodding his head at her comment, he began guiding Cate toward the car. A light rain or mist seemed to have settled over the city, she could smell the dampness, an acute change from her sunny hometown. The weather was cool and drizzly, Cate shrugged her sweater tighter around her as she followed Sam to the car. She felt as though she may never get warm, the dampness chilled her to the bone.

They reached the car, a black Town Car, very typical for a private driver. Cate, intending to enter the car on the passenger side, awkwardly headed toward the driver side of the car before realizing that cars were in the opposite configuration on this side of the pond. She and Sam shared an awkward laugh before he guided her to the correct side and made sure she was seated in the backseat with Riley. "THAT will take a bit of getting used to," Cate said, laughing as she climbed into the car. After offering her water and snacks, he closed the door for her then slid behind the wheel.

"Okay, Cate," Sam said, turning to face her, "are there any stops you'd like to make before going to the hotel?"

"Uh, no, I don't think so, the hotel will be fine, thanks!"

"Right-o. Let's get you to your hotel then!"

As they drove toward the hotel, Cate marveled at the size of the city and how foreign it seemed to her as they made their way through the crowded streets. Cate surmised if she had to retrace her steps, she'd never find her way back to the airport on her own. After a short while, Sam pulled into a very prestigious looking hotel called the Langham. Sam pulled the car to the front where a bellhop met them and opened Cate's door, offering his hand as she exited the car. Cate accepted it and climbed out, looking up at the hotel. The hotel was most impressive. Built in the 1860s, Cate had never stayed in a hotel this old. It looked like a church to her. She retrieved Riley's carrier from the back.

Approaching Cate, Sam said, "I'll see you in the morning at nine thirty sharp, Cate, to drive you to Mr. Smythe's office. Enjoy your evening!" With that, Sam disappeared back into the car and pulled away. The bellhop who introduced himself as William, guided Cate inside the hotel and to the front desk. The lobby was amazing to Cate. Columns of black-and-white marble held the ceiling at bay while a marble staircase with wrought-iron and gold railings led upwards to the main lobby. A massive crystal chandelier hung in the middle of the room. This was pure luxury, Cate thought.

Cate approached the desk and a chic-looking woman greeted her with a smile. "Welcome to the Langham. How may I help you?"

Cate was still not used to being greeted by a British accent. "Yes, I'm Dr. Catherine Kensie, that's K-E-N-S-I-E. I believe there is a reservation for me."

"Welcome, Dr. Kensie. I'll retrieve your reservation now," the woman, whose name tag read, Elise, said, graciously. After a short moment she replied, "Yes, I have the reservation here. We have you with us for three nights, checking out on Wednesday morning. Is that correct?"

She glanced to Cate, waiting for an answer. "Yes, that's right," Cate answered. "I also have my dog, Riley, with me."

"Yes, Dr. Kensie, there is a note attached about Riley. Is there anything that you would require for Riley during your stay with us? Perhaps grooming services or dog walking?"

"Um, no, thanks. I think we'll be ok."

"Certainly, Dr. Kensie. I have your key ready and if I could have your signature on this paper, you will be all set!"

Cate signed the paper and retrieved the keycard. "Thank you!"

"You are most welcome, Dr. Kensie. And when you are ready, William can assist you in finding your room and getting settled. Thank YOU, Dr. Kensie and I hope you enjoy your stay."

Cate turned toward an already approaching William. "Dr. Kensie," he said as he approached, "would you like to walk your dog before heading to your room?"

"Yes, thank you," Cate answered.

"Excellent, I can show you to an appropriate area before we go to your room." William navigated through the hotel and drew Cate through a set of doors, walking her a short distance to a small grassy area. She set the carrier down and unzipped it, grabbing hold of the leash she had left attached to Riley during the trip. She gently coaxed Riley from the carrier. He was curious but a little nervous given all the new smells, sights and sounds but eventually he found the grass to be just as interesting as it was in Aberdeen. It didn't take him long to search out a good spot to leave his mark. After having done so, Cate put him back into the carrier, and zipped it shut, much to Riley's dismay.

"All ready?" William asked.

"Yes, thank you."

They headed back into the hotel and toward a bank of elevators. "May I see your room key, please, Dr. Kensie?" William asked as they entered the elevator. Cate handed him the key, he glanced at it and pressed the button for the fourth floor. The elevator sprang to life, pulling them upwards until it chimed its arrival and the doors whisked open. Stepping out, William headed to the left, until he arrived in front of Cate's room. He inserted the keycard and opened the door, standing aside to allow Cate to enter first. Cate stepped into the room; it was luxurious and elegant. It included a sitting room, separate from the bedroom. It surprised Cate that the hotel room was not that much smaller than her apartment. "Dr. Kensie, as soon as we have received your luggage, we'll have it sent up. Is there anything else you may require?"

"No, I don't think so!" Cate said. She dug into her purse and removed a few American bills. Passing it over to William, she said, "Sorry, I haven't changed currency yet, I hope this is okay!"

"Most acceptable, thank you, Dr. Kensie," William said, accepting the tip. "If there is anything else that you should need, please contact the front desk."

"Thank you!" Cate said as the young man left the room.

Alone at last, Cate set down the carrier and opened it. Riley bounded out, excited to be free. He leapt onto Cate, demanding to be in her arms and showering her with kisses once she picked him up. He looked around, recognizing nothing. "Where are we, buddy?" Cate asked him, also glancing around the room.

Cate noticed a plate on the coffee table near the sofa along with a note. Walking toward it, she noticed it was a fruit and cheese plate and a bottle of wine. Next to it was a small plate with dog bones. Cate picked up the note. Printed in crisp block letters was the message *"Please enjoy some refreshments after your long trip. See you tomorrow! Gayle."*

Gayle was extremely thoughtful and on top of things!

After setting him down, Riley set to work smelling around the room excitedly. He came close to the dog biscuits. When he got a whiff of those, he tried to snatch one off the table by standing on his hind legs. Cate laughed and picked up a biscuit, handing it to him. He chomped on it eagerly. Cate nibbled on the cheese and fruit. Opening the bottle of wine, she poured herself a glass to enjoy while she continued to feed Riley the biscuits. "It was nice of Gayle to send us some snacks, wasn't it, Riley?"

In the middle of their snack, Cate's luggage arrived, brought to the room by William and set in the bedroom. After Cate polished off the cheese plate and Riley his biscuits, she checked the clock. It was almost 11 p.m., but to Cate it was only 6 p.m. Still, given the late hour in her new time zone, she figured she had better try to get some sleep. Cate appreciated that Gayle had made her appointment with Mr. Smythe the next morning at 10 a.m. so she could have a leisurely morning after traveling if jet lag made it impossible for her to sleep.

After gathering Riley into her arms, she made her way to the bedroom. She found her luggage neatly placed on luggage racks near the wardrobe in the room. Setting Riley on the bed, Cate unlocked her luggage and found her pajamas. Removing her toiletry bag, she made her way to the bathroom where she completed her nightly routine and changed her clothes.

Riley followed her into the bathroom, unsettled by the new place and reluctant to be without her. He followed her back into the bedroom, unwilling to let Cate out of his sight. She folded her clothes from the day and placed them back in her suitcase before heading to bed. Feeling sorry for the little guy, Cate scooped him up into her arms and climbed into bed. With a few pillows propped behind her, she cuddled him into her arms. As she laid her head back against the pillow, it surprised her how tired she was despite it only feeling like mid-evening to her. Riley had already let his head loll back, falling asleep almost as soon as Cate had ceased moving. Cate looked down at the little dog and smiled before drifting off to sleep.

CHAPTER 9

*T*he next morning Cate elected to sleep in, hitting the snooze button twice before climbing out of bed. Riley had found a spot on the bed next to Cate to finish out his night and was also content to lounge in bed for the extra time. After arising, Cate ran Riley out for a quick morning walk, still in her pajamas, before returning to her room to get dressed and have breakfast. She opted for room service, not adventurous enough to explore the city or even the hotel's restaurant this morning. While she ate, Cate glanced through the newspaper delivered by room service with her meal. It looked like Cate had a lot to learn about the different culture she was about to immerse herself in based on what she read.

After breakfast, Cate rummaged through her luggage and selected a red sheath dress for her meeting with William Smythe. She added a red and black striped sweater over top to account for the cooler-than-she-was-used-to weather and finished with a pair of black t-strap pumps. She also had brought a light jacket, having checked ahead of time and determined that the weather would require it.

Cate glanced at her watch; it was quarter after nine. She gathered up her purse and the manila folder Mr. Smythe had left with her when they first met. She suited Riley in his harness and attached his leash, then gathered him up to carry him downstairs. Opting for the elevator, she rode down to the lobby level and took Riley for one more walk prior to meeting Sam.

True to his word, Sam appeared at 9:30 a.m. Cate was waiting for him in the lobby. She went outside to meet him as he emerged from the car to open the back door for her.

"Good morning, Cate," he said, brightly. "I hope your first night in London went swimmingly."

"Yes, thank you, to be honest though, I didn't do much other than have a snack and go to bed," Cate answered as she climbed into the car.

Sam slid in behind the wheel and responded, "Well, if you ate and you slept, I'd say it was a success in my book!"

Cate laughed, "Yes, it was a good night!"

"Let's get you to your appointment then," he said, pulling into traffic.

Cate watched the buildings and people pass by through the window as they drove. London seemed so large compared to little Aberdeen. She was glad she was not navigating it herself and mentally thanked Gayle for arranging her transportation.

Their ride was not long before Sam pulled to a stop in front of a large building. He hopped out of the car and ran around to open her door, offering his hand to assist her out of the car. Then he raced ahead of her to open the door into the building.

"The office is on the twelfth floor," he said as she walked through the door.

"Thank you, Sam." Cate called as the door closed, separating them.

Cate headed over to the bank of elevators and pressed the call button. One elevator eased open. Cate stepped in and pressed the button for the twelfth floor. The doors slid closed, and the elevator whisked Cate and Riley upwards. Again, Cate felt like she should pinch herself to see if she was dreaming, still struggling to believe that she was in London to meet with an attorney to inherit a castle.

Before she had time to think about it more, the elevator doors opened and she exited into the hallway. At the end of the hall, two large glass doors were adorned with large black block letters stating

SMYTHE, SMITH AND SMITHTON
SOLICITORS

Cate headed toward the door and opened it to find a large and luxurious reception area. Behind a large desk sat a small woman with her brown hair pulled into a low bun, wearing a navy blazer over a crisp white blouse. She had a Bluetooth earpiece in her ear, ready to answer any calls to the law firm in an instant. Cate approached the desk.

"Good morning," the woman said, "may I help you?"

"Good morning," Cate answered, "I'm Dr. Cate Kensie. I have an appointment with Mr. William Smythe."

"Yes, good morning, Dr. Kensie." The woman scanned a list of the day's appointments. "I see you have a 10 a.m. appointment with Solicitor Smythe. If you'll have a seat, I will let Gayle know you are here."

"Okay, great, thank you!" Cate said before finding a seat on a large leather armchair positioned on the side of the room.

The woman behind the desk pressed a few numbers on her keypad then spoke into her Bluetooth device, "Gayle, I have Dr. Kensie for Mr. Smythe." She promptly disconnected the call and returned to clicking around with her mouse.

It couldn't have been more than a moment until a short blonde woman appeared hurrying down the hall toward the reception area. Her hair was pulled neatly into a French twist, with a few tendrils framing her face. She wore a blue skirt suit, with the hemline falling just below her knee and navy pumps in a fashionable but sensible heel. She had a pair of glasses dangling around her neck on a chain. Her clothes were as crisp as Mr. Smythe's had been. She had a kind face, Cate thought.

As she approached Cate she extended her hand, saying, "Cate, so nice to meet you, finally. I'm Gayle Pearson. And this must be little Riley."

Cate shook her hand. "Nice to meet you, Gayle. Yes, this is Riley!" Gayle extended her hand to allow Riley to sniff it, and then gave him a gentle scratch on his head.

"Riley, can you shake hands?" Cate said. Riley extended his small, white paw toward Gayle, who accepted it for a shake.

"What a clever little pup you are, Riley! If you'll follow me, I'll get you situated for your meeting with Mr. Smythe," Gayle said, turning to walk back down the hall.

Cate followed her down the hall and took the opportunity to thank her in person for making all her travel arrangements.

"Oh, it was nothing, Cate, my pleasure. I hope you are finding your stay pleasant. Everything is satisfactory with your room, I hope?"

"Oh, yes, everything is great!" Cate said as they entered a small conference room. "And thank you for the snack, it hit the spot after the long flight!"

"Wonderful to hear. May I take your coat?"

"Yes, thank you," Cate said, setting Riley on the nearby chair and removing her jacket.

"And can I interest you in a cup of tea?"

"Oh, no, thank you, I don't want to put you to any trouble," Cate answered.

"No trouble at all, Cate!"

"Well, then yes, if you don't mind, I would love a cup of tea, thank you! Something warm would be great, it is much cooler than I'm used to here!"

"Coming right up!" Gayle said, leaving the room.

Cate took a seat at the table, retrieving Riley to sit him on her lap. A few moments later, Gayle returned carrying a tray with tea, cookies, and a few dog bones. She set the tea and cookies down near Cate. "Here, this will take the chill out of you! Do you take sugar and milk, Cate?" she asked.

"Just sugar, no milk."

"Ah, very American of you," Gayle replied, handing the sugar to Cate. "And, Riley, I have a special treat for you if your Mummy will allow you." She produced a bone-shaped dog biscuit.

Riley's tail wagged furiously. "Yes, he's allowed, thank you!"

Gayle gave the biscuit to Riley, who ate it in a few bites. "And now, I will spoil you and give you a second one whether or not your Mummy likes it!" Gayle teased, handing Riley another which he ate as quickly as he ate the first.

"I think you've made a friend for life," Cate joked as Riley stared at Gayle as though she were an automatic treat dispenser.

"And what a cute friend to have! If you need anything, just give me a shout, I'm just outside. Mr. Smythe will be in shortly."

"Thank you!" With that, Gayle left, pulling the door slightly closed behind her. Cate took a sip of the warm, sweet tea. It helped to take the chill off from the damp weather. As she set the cup back down, William Smythe entered the room with Gayle trailing behind him, carrying several folders. Mr. Smythe also had a folder in his hands.

He approached the table, taking a seat at the head of it with Gayle setting her folders down across from Cate. She spread them out in an orderly fashion before leaving the room and pulling the door slightly shut again.

"Hello, Cate, good to see you again. I hope your trip was pleasant and your accommodations agreeable." He paused awaiting an answer from Cate.

"Oh, yes, everything is excellent, thank you!"

Nodding, he opened his folder. "There are several things that we need to go over and some paperwork that needs taken care of over the next few days. We'll finish everything that we need to here before traveling to Scotland on Wednesday. I'll stay on with you until Friday to finish all the details there."

"Okay, that sounds like a plan!"

The next few hours before lunch contained loads of paperwork, signatures, and legalese. It all started to blur together after a while. They wrapped up just before lunch. Gayle had come in to retrieve the signed forms so they could file and process them that afternoon. She informed them that she had planned for lunch to be delivered and asked if Cate would like her to walk Riley or, if she preferred, Gayle could show her where to walk him.

Cate opted to stay with Riley and followed Gayle to the outdoor spot, making some small talk along the way, mainly about the changes in weather compared to Aberdeen. Gayle had ordered soup and salad for lunch, which was set up in the conference room by the time they returned. Lunch was enjoyable and Gayle offered Riley a few more biscuits as they ate.

"Careful," Cate warned jokingly, "you will spoil him more than he already is!" Cate thought it was considerate of Gayle to have brought biscuits for Riley. They both seemed so attentive; it was making her adjustment much easier so far.

After lunch, Mr. Smythe had arranged for them to travel to the bank used by Lady MacKenzie to complete paperwork to transfer accounts from the late Lady MacKenzie's name to Cate's. While there, he also showed Cate the contents of Lady MacKenzie's safe deposit box. One item was the gold timepiece that Mr. Smythe had mentioned when first meeting Cate.

"Ah, the infamous gold timepiece!" Cate exclaimed.

"Yes," he answered. "This is the timepiece I spoke of when we met. This was to be imparted directly to you along with the following note stipulating specific terms that Lady MacKenzie insisted her heir follow." He handed her the timepiece along with a note.

Cate accepted both, turning the timepiece over in her hands as she received it. It was heavy and looked antique, although it was in good condition. The time piece was gold. Some shine had since worn away but it still had a warm glow to it. It looked like it had once been a man's pocket watch, but it now hung from a long gold chain, making it a pendant. The watch was unique in design with two small crosses extending from the top on either side of the knob used for opening the piece and setting the time. Cate pressed the button to open the watch. The face was off white with black roman numerals. Taking a closer look, Cate saw an inscription on the cover: Always keep an eye on your time. Cate found it curious. Holding the piece, Cate opened the note, finding it handwritten in a scrawly cursive writing and read it.

To my heir:

This timepiece was passed from generation to generation in the MacKenzie family. It came through my ancestors from father to child for centuries; eventually being passed from my grandfather to my father and from my father to me. I now pass it to you. You MUST follow the following stipulations I set forth:

Wear the timepiece on your person at all times, NEVER leave it unattended

Take care to keep the time piece in working order and always wound

Always keep an eye on your time

Good luck.

Lady Gertrude MacKenzie

Cate wrinkled her brow at seeing that line again. Strange, it was such an odd sentiment to keep coming up. Perhaps it was a family saying, she thought. Cate also found it strange that the note ended with the words "Good luck." Good luck with what, Cate wondered. The entire note was strange, in fact. Nevertheless, Cate put the timepiece around her neck as instructed and carried on with the remaining business that she had.

The paperwork took the better part of the afternoon. Afterward, Cate returned to her hotel and opted to order room service before getting some sleep. Despite not having done much for the day, the entire process had left her exhausted. The overwhelming excitement of the day's events had kept her adrenaline pumping through the day. She was still barely able to believe what was happening, but events kept pushing forward whether or not her mind had wrapped around them. She fell asleep and slept soundly for the entire night.

CHAPTER 10

*T*uesday morning brought a mountain more of paperwork to complete, but that finished most of the work, leaving the afternoon free. Given her free afternoon, Gayle asked if Cate would like to see anything while in London. Cate, still overwhelmed, didn't feel very adventurous, so she politely declined, planning on spending the time recuperating in her hotel room. Cate planned an early evening since she had an early train to catch in the morning to get to Edinburgh. She returned to the hotel, purchased some snacks from the sundries shop, ordered some room service, and curled up on the bed with Riley, renting a movie to pass the afternoon and early evening hours.

Cate turned in early, setting her alarm for 3:30 a.m. to be on time for her train, which left a few minutes after 6 a.m. Sam was prompt again in picking up Cate to take her to the train station where she met Mr. Smythe and Gayle, who were both traveling with her. Mr. Smythe planned on staying until Friday, leaving in the morning to head back while Gayle, after checking with Cate, planned to stay on through the weekend to help Cate get settled. Cate felt honored to have Gayle stay with her as her first guest. She was certain that her presence would help her feel more at home for her first few days in the castle so she accepted without hesitation when Gayle asked if she could use her help for a few extra days.

They boarded the train and got situated for the long trip. The trip, lasting about five and a half hours, would take most of the morning, putting them in Edinburgh around lunchtime. They planned to lunch there then rent a car to finish the drive north to Dunhaven. Cate had brought a book along for the trip, but the passing scenery had mesmerized her and she hadn't touched the book. She also passed some time making conversation with Gayle. Mr. Smythe joined in occasionally but mostly kept to reading his paper and some files from his briefcase. Cate had to admit she admired the man's work ethic, or perhaps the conversation lacked the same appeal of his legal paperwork. A few times during the trip Cate's hand found the timepiece that she now wore around her neck at all times as required by Lady MacKenzie's note. Her mind often drifted to the oddities of the note, however, without knowing Lady MacKenzie she concluded perhaps she was just an eccentric old lady.

As the trip progressed the conversation turned toward Cate's inheritance. "So, Cate, I understand Mr. Smythe's visit was a surprise to you," Gayle began.

"Yes, quite! Both his visit and the news he brought stunned me, especially since I had never heard of Lady Mackenzie!"

"Really? No one had ever told you about a distant relative with a castle in Scotland?" Gayle quipped.

"No, no one dropped that bombshell on me until Mr. Smythe did. To be honest, I didn't know I had any relatives anywhere. After my parents passed away, I assumed I was alone in the world."

"And all this time, you had a relative living in Scotland."

"Well, a distant relative."

"Yes, but still, it is a shame that you never got to meet Lady MacKenzie, Cate. She was an interesting woman, I'm certain you would have liked her. You remind me a lot of her! We tried to find you before she passed but were unable to locate you in time."

"Yes, that is unfortunate. I would have liked to have met her. I hope it's not too much to ask, but how did she pass away?"

"She took ill suddenly," Gayle explained. "She was diagnosed with an aggressive form of cancer which went undetected until it was too late, and she suffered a stroke soon after finding out and passed shortly after."

"Oh, that's terrible, how sad." Cate took a moment before rekindling the conversation on a brighter topic. "Speaking of my distant relative, do you have any idea from the DNA analysis how we were related?"

Mr. Smythe chimed in to answer this, setting his paperwork aside. "No, the analysis only confirms relationship, but doesn't tell us any familial relationship information beyond the general. Your relationship was in the 3rd cousin arena but we couldn't be more specific than that."

"Cate, I'm thinking your name, Kensie, is a variation of the original family name MacKenzie," Gayle added.

"Yes, I wondered that, I have to admit, for being a history professor, I have little to no idea of my family's history. I've been meaning to look into it but with everything going on, I did not yet. I plan on doing that once I get settled."

"Well, it sounds like an interesting project for a history professor!" Gayle answered. "Please let me know if I can help!"

"Thank you so much, Gayle. I agree it will be an interesting project, also!"

"What led you to become a history professor, Cate?" Gayle asked. She seemed to be a professional at small talk. Cate's introverted nature meant she wasn't a great conversationalist, but Gayle's skills made up for Cate's deficiencies.

"I developed a love of history at a young age. My parents both worked for a mid-sized natural history museum. My mother worked as an archivist there and my father was a curator. As a child, I spent a lot of time in that museum, prowling around the storerooms on scavenger hunts that my mom or her coworkers would give me. The things they had both on display and hidden away in storage fascinated me. I spent hours there making up stories about the various objects. I had a rather unique childhood."

"I'd say so, prowling around a dusty museum seems unique for a child!"

"I loved it, it was quite a happy childhood for me. I wasn't afraid of it like many kids my age would be."

"It appears you were destined to be a history buff from the start, Cate," Gayle concluded.

The rest of the trip passed with more small chitchat about Cate's previous work, her Ph.D. work and where she had lived before. Cate asked some questions about life in the U.K. and Gayle's family. She wasn't a great conversationalist but Gayle made it easy to talk. Cate sensed an instant friendship with her.

After the train trip, Cate was famished. They lunched at a restaurant in Edinburgh where Mr. Smythe ate when he traveled to Dunhaven. Cate could not recall the name but the food was excellent.

Afterwards, they picked up their rental car to begin the drive to Dunhaven which Mr. Smythe explained was a few hours northwest of Edinburgh. He had offered to drive, having driven the route several times before. Gayle sat in the passenger seat leaving Cate and Riley being able to spread out in the backseat.

Cate enjoyed seeing the countryside as they drove. She realized how remote an area Dunhaven was as they drove further and further away from what she was used to in terms of civilization. Before her trip she had read about some remote areas in Scotland but she hadn't fully understood how remote they were until seeing it for herself. This would be quite a change for her, she thought as they continued to drive.

"Almost there!" Gayle said. Cate checked the timepiece she was wearing with a surge of pride that she had remembered to wind it this morning. It showed a few minutes after 4 p.m. They should arrive in about twenty to twenty-five minutes according to Mr. Smythe's calculations. A surge of anticipation and excitement swept through Cate.

Within about fifteen minutes, Cate saw a small village appear in the distance, a ways behind it she spotted what looked like Dunhaven Castle. A few minutes later they passed through the small town of Dunhaven. If Cate had blinked, she may have missed it. Gayle informed her that there was a local grocer and a pub along with a few other local businesses and homes.

Leaving the town behind, they drove on toward the castle. Cate could see it clearly, sitting stoically in the distance. It grew larger and larger as they approached. Cate also saw the rolling lawns with their perfect landscaping surrounding the castle.

As they pulled in the drive, Cate couldn't believe this was her life. Mr. Smythe drove on toward the house as Cate gaped from the backseat. Riley, sensing Cate's excitement, was darting from window to window to peer out, wagging his tail and eyeing Cate as if to confirm that his reaction was appropriate.

As they approached the castle, Cate could see a few people standing near the front entrance. "Ah, good," Mr. Smythe said, eyeing them, "I asked the staff to meet us, they've timed it well."

"Probably got the warning call from the village," Gayle joked.

"Staff?" Cate mumbled to herself, her brow furrowing.

She said it a bit too loudly as Mr. Smythe overheard her and replied, "Yes, Charlie and Emily Fraser. Mr. Fraser oversees most of the handiwork, landscaping and the external landscaping company, Mrs. Fraser provides light cooking and house cleaning. A hired company does most of the other house cleaning. Finally, Jack Reid, the estate manager, a new addition who will also take over most of the handiwork and landscaping from Mr. Fraser soon. Lady MacKenzie hired him just before passing away."

Cate was impressed. She hadn't given much thought to the upkeep of the castle, it was good to know someone else had.

Mr. Smythe interrupted her thoughts. "Can I assume that you will keep the staff on?" he questioned.

"Ah, yes assuming they would like to stay on."

"I think they very much would, Cate," Gayle answered. "I think they may have been on edge that the new owner would do a clean sweep and bring in her own people. They will be relieved to find out that you are keeping them on."

"Oh, yes, no, I mean to say, I'd never do that to anyone!"

As the conversation came to a close, Mr. Smythe eased the car parallel to the front entrance. The youngest of the three staff, Jack, approached the car to open doors and begin unloading luggage. Cate scooped Riley into her arms and stepped out of the car. Kissing him on the top of his head, she looked up at the castle and said, "We're home, Riley, we're home."

CHAPTER 11

*C*ate stared up at the castle rising in front of her. She was on the verge of another "pinch me" moment, still having trouble believing all this was real. At the same time, she felt a strange sense of home. She wondered if she was imagining that. Perhaps she wanted so much to belong to something after her parents died that she was making things up, but she felt at peace here. It was the first time she felt that after her parents' deaths.

She took a deep breath as she stared at the gray-brown stone making up the castle's exterior. It looked expansive, at least compared to what Cate was used to. She wondered if she might end up lost, roaming through the halls. She was pulled from her daydreaming by voices conversing.

"Yes, I had Lady MacKenzie's room made up for Dr. Kensie as Mr. Smythe directed, the nearby bedroom suite made up for you, Ms. Pearson, and I had the blue room made up for you as usual, Mr. Smythe," Mrs. Fraser said.

"Perfect, thank you," Mr. Smythe answered, as he watched Jack pulling luggage from the trunk, or as they called it here, the boot of the car.

"And I had all them boxes you sent put in the library. Lady Gertrude didn't use that room much. I cannae understand what you meant by obvious but unobtrusive space so I did the best I could," she said, her Scottish dialect on full display.

"Well," Gayle said, patting the woman's arm, "let's not discuss that now, I'm sure Dr. Kensie would prefer to settle in a bit before dealing with all that."

"Oh, thank you," Cate said, stepping forward and extending her hand. "Hi, I'm Cate, and this is Riley." Cate motioned with her head toward the small dog in her arms.

Mr. Fraser was the first to take her hand, giving it a light shake. Next, Mrs. Fraser, with a rather confused and shocked look, shook it. Jack, who had finished unloading the luggage, approached and shook her hand. "Good to meet ya, Cate," he said, with a broad smile and a hard handshake that extended to her entire arm. "And a big hello to you too, Sir Riley," he said, tickling Riley under his chin. Mrs. Fraser gasped at his greeting, but Riley seemed to approve.

"Well, uh, Dr. Kensie," Mrs. Fraser began.

Cate interrupted her. "Oh, please, call me Cate."

"Well, I'll certainly not! You might not have the title…"

Mr. Smythe interrupted. "She will inherit the title along with the estate."

"Well, I shan't be referring to you by your first name, Lady Kensie, that wouldn't be proper, not proper at all!" She glanced to Mr. Smythe, then Gayle, before continuing. "Now, Lady Kensie, I'd be happy to show you to your room if you'd like to freshen up after your trip. I prepared a light meal for everyone, if you'll let me know when you'd like it served, I will have it set out for you."

"Oh, uh." Cate hesitated. She wasn't used to having a staff to do things for her and was uncomfortable ordering people around. "Yes, that would be great. I'd say maybe around five thirty to eat, if that's okay with you all?" She phrased it more like a question, shrugging her shoulders as though she wasn't at all sure.

"That would do perfectly, Cate." Gayle said warmly.

"If you would point out your bags to me, I'd be ever so happy to bring them up to you," Jack chimed in.

"Oh, the two with the luggage straps are mine. Here I can take one with me." Cate reached for one suitcase, swearing she heard Mrs. Fraser gasp again.

"Nay, lassie, I'd not have the lady of the house carrying her own bags to her room! I'd be put out on the street for it!" Jack answered her.

Cate laughed a bit. "The lady of the house," she said, emphasizing it dramatically, "can manage a bit of luggage but I won't fight you on it, it is heavy." Jack laughed. Cate felt comfortable with him almost immediately, a sense she didn't get with most people. He seemed like a friendly, down-to-earth sort and she felt an instant connection to him. She was sure they would become fast friends.

With Mrs. Fraser leading the way, they entered the castle. The foyer was as expansive and impressive as the exterior. Cate's eyes slid upwards to take in the enormous space. At the back of the large space, Cate saw a massive stairway leading upwards to a gallery-style hallway that surrounded the entire room.

"Mr. Smythe, I trust you can find your way while I take the ladies on to their rooms." Mrs. Fraser began making her way toward the staircase, Cate and Gayle followed. As they ascended it, she continued, "I had the bed you sent for the pup put into your room, Lady Kensie, I hope that was acceptable."

"Oh, yes, that's great, thank you so much, that was very thoughtful of you, Mrs. Fraser. And Riley thanks you, too!" Cate said raising Riley's paw to wave at Mrs. Fraser in a show of approval. "You hear that, buddy?" she said to Riley. "Mrs. Fraser has got you all fixed up!"

Mrs. Fraser pursed her lips together and continued down the hall, hands clasped together at her waist in front of her. Cate noticed that they had lost Mr. Smythe somewhere earlier in the journey to the bedrooms, although she didn't know where. Wherever it was, the blue room seemed far from hers.

"Ms. Pearson, here is the room I made up for you," Mrs. Fraser said, stopping outside of a doorway and motioning with her hand.

"Thank you," Gayle said, and turning to Cate said, "I'll see you in a bit for some dinner." She disappeared into the room, leaving Cate and Riley alone with Mrs. Fraser.

"The late Lady MacKenzie's room is this way," Mrs. Fraser said, turning to continue down the hall. "Mr. Smythe told me to give you that room. It was rather presumptuous of him, but I do what I'm told. If you'd like another, please let me know once you've perused the castle."

"Oh, I'm sure it's fine, Mrs. Fraser. I'm sure I'll be very happy there."

"Lady MacKenzie was, there's a fact. I suppose since it was good enough for her ladyship, Mr. Smythe reckoned it would be good enough for you, too. Here we are." She stopped in front of a set of double doors, opening them both in one smooth motion. Cate followed her into the room. She looked around, trying to take it all in. The sheer size of the bedroom suite made her apartment look tiny. There was a sitting room complete with a chaise that faced a large fireplace. To the left was a bedroom with a large canopy bed, also boasting a fireplace. Mrs. Fraser fussed with a pillow on the settee nearest the chaise lounge. Ornately carved wood and heavy draperies adorned the room. It looked like something from a movie. Cate swallowed and tried to pull herself back into reality, realizing Mrs. Fraser was waiting for the all-clear signal from her before leaving her alone.

"Thank you, Mrs. Fraser."

"Of course," she said rather sternly before making her way to the doors, shutting them behind her.

Cate, turning, took in the entire room. She hardly believed she was here. This room was as large as her apartment, and it was only one room of the castle. She no longer wondered if she would become lost wandering the halls, she was certain of it. Absentmindedly, her hand found the timepiece around her neck. "Who were you, Lady MacKenzie," she muttered, "here I am, about to live in your space, where you used to live, sleeping where you slept, eating where you ate, and I have no idea who you even were." Cate resolved to do some research into the late Lady MacKenzie.

As she was admiring the room, there was a knock on the door. "Come in," she shouted.

"Your luggage," Jack said, dragging the two bags in through the door. "Where would you like them?"

"Oh, there's fine," Cate said, pointing, "you can leave them there, thanks."

"Easy enough!" He wheeled them further into the room and left them. Turning to leave, he seemed to hesitate. He turned back toward Cate. "Say, I hope I didn't offend you earlier. I tend to come off a bit off-the-cuff. I put many people off. You seemed rather laid back, I took you at your word when you introduced yourself as Cate that I could call you that!"

"Oh, no not at all. You didn't offend me. You seem normal to me, and yes, I prefer it if everyone calls me Cate! Maybe it's an American thing."

"Ah, well that's good, before I'm out on my arse!"

Cate laughed. "I need all the help I can get, especially

from getting lost. I won't fire you because you didn't call me Dr. Kensie. I really prefer Cate."

"Mrs. Fraser will be horrified. The lady of the house having everyone call her Cate." He shivered as though it was terrifying.

"Yeah, I noticed that, I guess Lady MacKenzie was much more formal."

"Quite. She would have fired me on the spot if I called her lassie or even Gertrude."

"Good thing I'm easier going, huh?"

"Quite a good thing," Jack smiled. "Well, I'll leave you to freshen up then. M'lady." Jack said, adding an extravagant bow.

Cate laughed as he left and went back to looking around the room. She looked down at Riley who was sniffing away in her arms. "We will have fun here, Riley!" The little dog cocked his head, looking at her curiously. "Here, why don't you have a proper smell around?" Cate said, putting him down on the floor. He set to work sniffing everything. Cate watched him for a few minutes then checked the gold timepiece. It was almost 5 p.m. Mrs. Fraser would have dinner set out soon. Cate looked down at her clothes, she wore a pair of leggings and a tunic sweater for traveling. Cate imagined the expression on Mrs. Fraser's face if she turned up to her first dinner in the castle in leggings. Not wanting to send the woman to an early grave, Cate thought she had better change.

She wheeled her luggage into the bedroom area, which was separated by a large double doorway from the sitting area. The bedroom was as expansive as the sitting room. She peeked out one window before finding something to wear. Her room overlooked a side area of the well-manicured lawn. From her window she saw a winding gravel path leading to a gazebo and off in the distance, a small pond.

"Riley, you're going to love this!" she said. She hoped to explore the grounds tomorrow or Friday with him. For now, she was famished and thought Riley might be hungry, too. She opened her luggage and found his bowl and filled it with kibble. Riley heard the morsels spilling into the bowl and ran from the sitting room for his dish. Cate figured she would feed him in the bedroom today until she found a more suitable spot. Riley ate with vigor while Cate found something she deemed more suitable to wear to dinner.

Cate hoped she remembered her way back to the front door so she could take Riley for a quick walk before dinner. She would rely on luck to find her way to the dining room. On the way down, she passed Gayle's room and, as luck would have it, Gayle was just heading down to dinner.

"What luck!" Cate exclaimed. "I was afraid I would lose my way to the front door and would die of starvation trying to find the dining room!"

"No worries, Cate," Gayle said, patting her arm. "I can make sure you get there! Are you taking Riley for a short walk first?"

"Yes, for a moment to stretch his legs and do a little business. I was planning on taking him into the dining room with us after. I'm a little reluctant to leave him alone since we just got here. You don't think it will upset Mrs. Fraser if I bring Riley, do you?"

"Cate, you're a dear, but you need remember that this is YOUR home now, so you will set the rules. Mrs. Fraser will deal with Riley joining us in the dining room!"

Cate nodded, and they turned to walk down the hall toward the steps. As they walked, Gayle continued, "I think Mrs. Fraser is a little on edge because of her employment status."

"Her employment status?"

"Yes, it's a bit complex, but the long and short of it is that she was planning on finishing a few years with Mr. Fraser, then retire. It was to allow Lady MacKenzie time to find a replacement. Mr. Fraser has already begun training his replacement, Jack. I think she is on edge wondering if you'll keep her on."

"Oh, well, of course I would, yes. I don't plan on upsetting the balance of things here."

They reached the front door and headed outside. Once they were outside Gayle said in a lowered voice, "There is one other thing."

"Oh?" Cate said, raising an eyebrow while keeping an eye on Riley.

"I shouldn't discuss it but there was talk with Lady MacKenzie about changing her will. There is a cottage on the estate where Mr. and Mrs. Fraser live. She had planned to bequeath it to them as a retirement gift for their years of service. She passed away before we could draw up the final papers."

Cate took a moment, letting the information settle into her brain. She felt terrible for the older couple. No wonder Mrs. Fraser had been on edge. "That would be very upsetting. I would be happy to honor that agreement. Perhaps I should speak with Mr. Smythe about it?"

"Well, the decision is yours, Cate, but I'm certain the Frasers would appreciate it."

"Thank you, Gayle, for the heads up. I want to fit in here, I don't want to make anyone's life worse!"

"With an attitude like that, you won't!"

Riley had finished up his business so Cate scooped him up, cleaned up after him and carried him into the castle. "Lead the way to the dining room and I will try to memorize this route," she said to Gayle.

Gayle led the way to the large dining space, Mrs. Fraser had set dinner on the sideboard, as promised. Cate found the meal tasty, it would be easy keeping Mrs. Fraser on if she continued to cook meals like this! Even though they were simple, they were tasty, home-cooked meals and a far cry from Cate's usual diet of sandwiches and cereal.

As they were leaving the dining room, Mrs. Fraser appeared in the hall. "Ahem, excuse me, Lady Kensie?"

"Yes, Mrs. Fraser?"

"I have a few things to go over with you before morning if it's a good time?"

"Ah, sure."

"I wasn't sure what you preferred for breakfast and when you would like it served."

"Oh, um," Cate hesitated. Gayle had been hanging back and overheard the conversation. She glanced to Cate, encouraging her with a slight nod. "Well, if it works for everyone's schedule, I think at 7 a.m. would be appropriate for breakfast and whatever you usually make is just fine." Gayle nodded in agreement.

"I make oatmeal most mornings, I will have it ready at 7 a.m. if it's acceptable then."

"Yes, that would be perfect, thank you so much Mrs. Fraser. And thank you for dinner, it was delicious."

"You're very welcome, Lady Kensie. Sleep well."

After dinner, everyone retired to their rooms, tired from the long day and the trip. The excitement of the day had Cate wound up, so she lounged on the chaise with Riley. While relaxing, she used the time to plan what unpacking she would tackle in her first few days. After that, she promised herself that she would start exploring the grand castle and its grounds and would try to find out a little more about Lady MacKenzie and her relationship to her.

After an hour, she decided she better go to bed. She collected Riley and went into the bedroom, setting him down in his bed, which she had positioned near the head of the bed. She eyed the bed before getting into it; the bed gave new meaning to the term "climb into bed" for her. She nestled in, pulling the covers up to her shoulders. Sighing, she closed her eyes and took a deep breath. After a few moments, she popped her eyes open. She was wide awake despite the long journey. She laid quietly, trying to relax herself enough to go to sleep. After another few moments, she heard a small whine emanating from the floor. She reached over, turning on the light. "Can't sleep either, huh, buddy?" she said to Riley. Riley squinted back at her as the light washed over him then gave a big sigh. "Okay, okay, how about we share the bed tonight, that will help both of us." Cate climbed out of bed and scooped the little dog, bed and all, up and set him on top of her bed. Climbing back in she nestled closer to him, reaching out to stroke the fur on his head. He gave another big sigh and laid his head down, contented to be closer to Cate. "I wish this helped me fall right to sleep," Cate mused.

Cate continued to lay awake for another forty-five minutes, her mind too stimulated by her surroundings to relax into sleep. After almost an hour, she began to doze off. She slept restlessly all night, the ghost of Lady MacKenzie seemed to pervade her every thought. Once she woke up and swore she saw the woman standing at the foot of the bed before realizing that it was just the bedpost. She dreamt of the woman she had never met. It seemed the ghosts of Dunhaven Castle weren't willing to leave just yet.

CHAPTER 12

The following morning, Cate drowsily pulled herself out of bed. She was reluctant to sleep in since she had guests in the house and sleep was escaping her. In a half sleepwalk, she got herself dressed and took Riley out for a quick walk before heading in for breakfast.

Today, Cate was determined to navigate the castle. She was a history professor, that gave her a working knowledge of how castles and homes built in this period had operated and been changed to accommodate modernizations, so she was confident that she could make her way around. She found the dining room and set out to make her way to the kitchen. "Let's see if we can lend a hand in the kitchen, Riley!" she said, carrying the small dog with her.

Following a set of servant stairs down a flight, she came to a long hallway. She heard the faint sound of voices coming from a room at the end. She figured that must be the kitchen, Mrs. Fraser was probably preparing breakfast there, and it seemed Mr. Fraser, Jack, or both were keeping her company before beginning their day. Cate started down the hallway. Soon the sound of voices became less faint and Cate could make out the conversation. She hadn't meant to eavesdrop but she couldn't help but overhear the conversation as she moved down the hall.

"… cannae believe that they could find no closer relative to Lady MacKenzie," she overheard Mrs. Fraser saying.

"Oh, I think she's a bit of all right." Jack's voice joined in.

"Call me Cate," Mrs. Fraser mimicked. "Now we've got a typical crass American running Dunhaven Castle. I say if Lady MacKenzie knew, she'd be turning in her grave."

"Ah, come on now, Mrs. Fraser," Jack answered again. "She's not THAT bad and a bonnie lass if I ever saw one."

"Humph, she wouldn't know the first thing about being a lady. I can tell you that."

Cate bit her lower lip. What was it that her mother had always told her about eavesdropping: you never heard anything good about yourself? This would not be as easy of a transition as she thought. She decided against offering to lend a hand in the kitchen and retreated as quietly as possible back to the dining room. When she got there it was still empty, she was just about to take a seat when Mr. Smythe arrived. Gayle followed a few minutes later, only beaten into the room by Mrs. Fraser, who was carrying a coffee pot and set to pouring a cup for Mr. Smythe after offering one to Cate. She also set one out for Gayle.

Cate politely declined, she was not one for coffee. "Oh, I'm sorry, can I bring you something else?" Mrs. Fraser said when Cate declined the coffee. Cate explained that she just drank water so she wouldn't need anything else but to continue to make the coffee while Gayle and Mr. Smythe stayed on.

Next, Mrs. Fraser brought in the breakfast and set it on the sideboard. They all helped themselves to the delicious smelling oatmeal that Mrs. Fraser had made and some toppings she had laid out.

During breakfast, Mr. Smythe said that he would go into town to finish filing some remaining paperwork and that it would take the better part of the morning. He indicated that he would be back following lunch, and that Cate did not need to accompany him. As he stood to excuse himself from the table, Cate also stood, asking him if he had a moment to speak privately before he left for town.

Mr. Smythe suggested that they speak in the library and led the way down the hall to it. The library was as grand as the rest of the castle, with bookshelves extending two stories and a gallery-style hallway making its way around the top to access them. A spiral staircase led to this area. Large leather chairs were placed around the room for reading and a large wooden desk sat in front of one of the four massive windows in the room. Once they were inside with the doors closed, Cate began, "Thanks for all your work so far. I was hoping to ask you for one additional thing."

"Of course."

"It's come to my attention that Lady MacKenzie, before her death, had intended to bequeath the cottage that Mr. and Mrs. Fraser are living in to them for their retirement, but that she did not have the changes to her will completed prior to her passing away."

"Yes, that is all correct, Cate."

Cate, having always had a sense of fair play, realized the change of estate ownership affected the Fraser's entire life, from the status of their employment to the status of their home. "I'd like to follow through on her wishes and transfer the property to Mr. and Mrs. Fraser."

Mr. Smythe nodded. "Yes, that's very considerate and I can take care of the paperwork when I return to London. I'll send it on to you here for signatures and so on."

"That would be perfect, thank you so much."

"My pleasure. Is that all?"

"Oh, yes that's it, thanks."

"Then I will be on my way," Mr. Smythe said, leaving the room. About to leave the room, Cate caught sight of the boxes in the back corner. She recognized her handwriting as she approached them. "Well, now I know where to start," Cate said to herself. Despite her disinterest in the prospect of unpacking all the boxes, she didn't want to do it by herself later so she thought she'd get a start today with Gayle's help.

Cate returned to the dining room to see if Gayle had any plans before starting to unpack. Gayle was cuddling Riley as though he were her grandbaby in her arms. She was petting his belly and cooing over him. Riley was lapping it up. "I see you've discovered the way to Riley's heart: treats and belly rubs," Cate said, laughing at the scene.

"Yes, I have," Gayle said, still looking at Riley. "And telling him how cute he is." Riley cocked his head as she said the "c" word. He loved hearing he was cute.

"Oh, he loves to be fussed over," Cate answered.

After a few more moments, Gayle said, "Well, little one, it's time for your Mummy and I to begin work. Would you like to explore the castle with us?"

"He'd like to explore the castle, yard, and anywhere else he's allowed," Cate joked. "Mrs. Fraser said she put all the boxes I sent into the library, let's begin there by sorting through where they need to be in the castle?"

"That sounds like a plan, Cate. Oh, first, let's look through the place so you have a better idea of where your things might fit best."

Cate agreed; she was dying to see the castle overall and also to avoid unpacking boxes. As they were getting up to leave, Mrs. Fraser returned to collect dishes. "I beg your pardon, Lady Kensie, I was hoping to have a word with you before you set off for the day."

"Of course," Cate said. Gayle gathered Riley back into

her arms and said she would meet Cate in the library, leaving the room so that the two women could speak privately.

"Yes, ma'am," Mrs. Fraser began, stiffly, "I hope you dinnae see this as out of line, but I was always one to talk straight. I wanted to speak with you about our employment status, mine and Mr. Fraser's. I'm not sure what Mr. Smythe may have explained to you but we intended on retiring soon after finding suitable replacements. Mr. Fraser has found his in young Jack. I wasn't sure if you were keeping us on though."

"Of course, Mrs. Fraser, I don't mind at all. I would be most grateful to you both if you'd stay on as you had intended."

Mrs. Fraser nodded, tight-lipped. "Thank you, Lady Kensie." She turned to clear dishes.

Cate sensed the apprehension on Mrs. Fraser's part had not dissipated at all after finding out that her employment was not in question. She figured that it had to do with the ambiguity about what was to happen with her home and Cate made an attempt to set the woman's nerves at ease.

"Oh, Mrs. Fraser?" Cate said, before she started clearing the dishes.

"Yes?" Mrs. Fraser stopped and stood almost at attention.

"It came to my attention that Lady MacKenzie had intended to leave you the cottage on the estate that you and Mr. Fraser live in. I spoke with Mr. Smythe this morning about making sure that those wishes are still carried through."

"Oh!" The woman seemed surprised and lost for words. Cate swore she saw a smile cross the woman's face. It was fleeting, but still she swore she saw it. "I... I..." the woman continued to stammer. "Well I don't know what to say, ah, thank you, it is very much appreciated."

"You don't have to say anything. It was Lady MacKenzie's wishes and I intend to respect them."

"Well, if you say so but it's no small thing, no small thing at all and means very much to Mr. Fraser and me."

Cate gave her a nod and a warm smile.

"Well, Lady…" She paused, stumbling a bit. "Lady Cate, I suppose I should let you get on with your business. If you need any help with your boxes, let me know and I'll get Jack after it to help." With that, the woman began clearing dishes, her air of duty settling back in on her. But, it seemed to Cate, she had turned a corner with Mrs. Fraser, since she had used her first name. At least, she hoped she had. Smiling to herself, she left the dining room and headed to the library.

There she found Gayle eyeing the boxes. As she entered, Gayle turned to her then back to the boxes. "Well, it doesn't look like there are too many boxes here, we can finish this before I leave! It looks like a stack of these are clothing, we might want to enlist the help of that strapping young man, Jack, to carry these to the bedroom."

"Yes, I agree. I lugged those all myself to the post office, I don't have any desire to lug them around this place!"

"Well, why don't we take the grand tour first before we dive into that? On our way, if we come across Jack, we can ask him to move the boxes."

"Sounds like a plan, Gayle!"

"Let's start on the first floor, then move to the second?"

Cate and Gayle spent the next hour going from room to room of the castle with Riley trailing behind. The little guy started to tire as they explored the second floor so Cate carried him from room to room, setting him down occasionally so he could get a good smell of the place. Cate marveled at the castle, each room seemed more beautiful than the next. As they concluded their "tour", Cate admitted, "I feel like someone should pinch me and wake me from this dream."

"All you'd end up with is a bruise if you did that, Cate," Gayle quipped.

"I'd half expect to end up back in my apartment to be honest with you, this is quite a change for me."

"I can imagine, but I'm sure you will take it in stride. You're a MacKenzie woman, Cate! They're a tough breed!"

Cate pondered for a moment. "Wow, that is the first time I've thought about it. I guess, in some small way, I am a MacKenzie. It is nice to have a sense of belonging again. You know, it's funny but I have such a homey feeling here that I never had in Aberdeen."

Gayle smiled, then sighed, "Well, I'll bet what will REALLY give you a sense of belonging would be to have your things put in their places. As much as I hate to stop exploring your home as if it were a museum, it might be time to roll up our sleeves and do some work."

"Ugh, you may be right. Let me see if I can find Jack and have him carry the clothes to the bedroom, then we can unpack the other boxes."

"Okay, I'll meet you in the library. I can take Riley if you'd like."

"Oh, okay, thanks!" Cate handed the little pup to Gayle, and they went their separate ways.

After finding out where Jack was working from Mrs. Fraser, Cate located him working outside and enlisted his help in moving boxes. They both returned to the library. Jack began moving the stack of boxes that Cate mentioned needed to go to her bedroom while Gayle and Cate began unpacking the others.

"These are books," Cate said, "we won't have to go far to find a spot for them!"

"You have a lot of shelf space to work with so this should be an easy task!"

Cate and Gayle spent the next several hours unpacking

boxes from the library and finding places for the items. They took a brief break to eat the sandwiches that Mrs. Fraser provided them for lunch. She had delivered them on a tray complete with a side of potato chips and a pickle.

"Wow, you got on her good side, Cate," Gayle said, raising her eyebrows and diving into the sandwich, as Mrs. Fraser left the room.

"Oh, yes, I spoke with her this morning about staying on and about giving her the cottage as Lady MacKenzie wanted. I think it eased her mind."

"I'll say and it went a long way to ease my rumbling stomach thanks to her lunch delivery. I am famished!"

"Me too! I'm starving after all this work!"

They finished their lunch while chatting and taking a break from their work. Afterwards, they dove right back in after Gayle jested that if she sat much longer, she'd never go back to work. Around half past four, they finished all the boxes in the library.

"Well," Cate said, checking the timepiece that hung around her neck, "no sense in starting anything else now. Let's break for the day and start tomorrow."

Gayle agreed, and they both returned to their rooms to freshen up before dinner. Cate also used the time to take Riley out for a bit after he had enjoyed a long, luxurious nap in the library while Gayle and Cate worked.

Cate returned to her room and took a moment to sit back on the chaise. The exhaustion hit her suddenly as she leaned back into the chair. She remembered her restless night and hoped she wouldn't have another. It would be an effort to stay awake through dinner.

After a few minutes, she forced herself to get up and change for dinner. Heading to the bathroom, she caught a glimpse of herself in the mirror. "What a sight!" she exclaimed to Riley. Her disheveled ponytail was escaping from its hair tie at every angle. Her cheek had a smudge across it from unwrapping a newspaper that she had used as a protective wrapping. When she had wiped away a bead of sweat, she had also smeared a little of her makeup. The rest of her time before dinner was spent cleaning up and attempting to look presentable. She wiped away her smeared makeup and the dirty smudge from her face and tamed her hair into a low ponytail. When she felt that she was relatively presentable, she made her way to the dining room.

Mr. Smythe was already waiting, and Gayle arrived shortly after Cate. Mr. Smythe helped seat the ladies and sat down himself. "The execution of Lady MacKenzie's will has been completed," he began. "You are officially the new Countess of Dunhavenshire and new owner of Dunhaven Castle, its grounds, and its contents." Just as he finished, as if on cue, Mrs. Fraser entered the room, carrying three full champagne flutes and a bottle of what remained of the champagne. "I thought we could have a toast to celebrate the occasion," Mr. Smythe said smiling. It occurred to Cate that she had never seen the man smile.

"Oh, how lovely!" Gayle said. Mrs. Fraser made her way around the table as everyone selected a flute.

"Oh, before we toast," Cate said, "Mrs. Fraser, won't you get a glass and join us? Also, Mr. Fraser and Jack if they are close?"

Mrs. Fraser seemed surprised but answered in stride, "I would be honored, Lady Cate." The woman disappeared and returned with Mr. Fraser and Jack in tow and three additional glasses. Mrs. Fraser poured a small amount into each.

When everyone had a glass, Mr. Smythe stood, raised his and said, "To the new Countess of Dunhavenshire and mistress of Dunhaven Castle. May you enjoy many happy years here."

Cate didn't know if she was just overly tired or not, but

the toast brought tears to her eyes. Smiling and holding them back, she answered a simple, "Thank you." Everyone raised their glass to Cate before taking a sip. After everyone had taken a sip, Mr. Smythe sat down, setting his glass down and thanking Mrs. Fraser for delivering the well-timed champagne. Mrs. Fraser disappeared with her tray to retrieve the meal. Mr. Fraser finished his glass of champagne and headed after her, as did Jack, after congratulating Cate on her new ownership.

Mrs. Fraser served the dinner and afterwards a Scottish Berry Brulee that she had made for the occasion. Everyone agreed that the dinner was spectacular and thanked Mrs. Fraser for preparing such a lovely dinner. Mr. Smythe excused himself following dinner. Since he was planning on leaving early the next morning, he wanted to finish packing and retire early.

Cate and Gayle stayed up a little longer and used the time to chat in one of the drawing rooms before heading to bed. After about an hour of conversation, Cate yawned. "Sorry," she said, "it's not you, I didn't sleep well last night. Too much excitement, I think!"

"Oh no, I hope you sleep better tonight. Perhaps we should both retire, I'm getting tired myself from all that work we did," Gayle said.

"I hope so, too! Well, why don't we call it a night then. I just need to take Riley out for a pit stop, if I can wake him."

Riley lounged in Cate's lap where he had curled up after dinner, fast asleep.

Gayle laughed, "Tuckered out, buddy? You did some hard work today watching us unpack!"

Riley opened his eyes into slits and looked at Gayle, then closed them as though he was too tired to even respond. "Come on, lazy bones," Cate said, poking him gently to roust him from his sleep. It earned her nothing but a weary sigh. "I bet you'd get up for a treat," Cate said. Riley's eyes opened wide, and he bounded to his feet.

Gayle, who hadn't left yet, chuckled. "Wow, that got him up! Well, I'll leave you two to it; I'm heading up. See you in the morning, Cate. I hope you sleep well tonight."

"Thanks, Gayle. Good night!"

With that, Gayle headed toward the staircase while Cate went to the front door to walk Riley, after providing him with a treat. Then they both headed up to bed. Cate let Riley sleep in bed again; the bed was so big, she had plenty of room to share it with him. It didn't take Cate long to fall into a deep sleep that lasted most of the night.

CHAPTER 13

*C*ate awoke the next morning about a half hour before the alarm. Feeling much more rested than she had her first morning, she laid in bed basking in the good night's sleep she had gotten and the fun that lay ahead of her. She couldn't wait to continue exploring the castle along with her own heritage. Today, Gayle had suggested that they continue unpacking, then tour the grounds tomorrow. Cate had been on board with the plans, happy to have the help while she settled in.

After about fifteen minutes, Cate got up and dressed for the day. She took Riley for his morning walk, then met Gayle in the dining room for breakfast. Mr. Smythe had already departed, heading back to London and taking the rental car with him. He had left a note at Cate's seat in the dining room that he would send the papers by the end of next week regarding the cottage. The man ran entirely on efficiency.

Given Gayle's unpacking plan, Cate started to wonder if maybe his work ethic was contagious. Gayle aimed to finish all the unpacking today, so they headed to Cate's bedroom after breakfast to begin.

A few boxes in, Cate confessed to Gayle that she might have too many clothes. Gayle responded that wasn't possible for a woman and the two continued to stack shoes and hang or re-fold clothes and place them in the wardrobe.

They took a brief break when they opened a box of Riley's things and Gayle took one of his toys and began playing with him for a brief respite. At lunch time, Mrs. Fraser provided them with a repeat of yesterday's lunch, delivered straight to them. They sat down in the sitting room to eat it. With only a few boxes left to go, they took a more leisurely lunch, figuring they could finish everything up this afternoon.

As they started again following lunch, Gayle marveled that Cate had packed all this herself and had it all delivered to the post office on her own.

"Oh, believe me, I paid for it the next day!"

"I'll bet! That's a lot of work for one person! I'm glad I can be here to help you on this end at least."

"I appreciate all the help you've been."

"Oh, it's nothing, it's not every day I get to stay in a castle, so it's my pleasure," Gayle said, opening another box. She stopped for a moment, staring at its contents. Cate noticed her pausing and started toward her to see what the issue was. "Oh, Cate, is this picture of you and your parents?"

Gayle had found the box Cate kept of her parents' things. "Yes, yes, that's us, at my college graduation." Cate took the picture and reflected for a moment before placing it back in the box. It always brought a wave of sadness over her and today it was more pronounced. Here she was in Scotland, in a castle, from one of her parents' relatives and they would never have the chance to see it. Were they even aware of its existence? This was something she would never have a chance to share with them.

Gayle noticed the sadness sweep through Cate's eyes.

"Cate, I'm sorry," she said, gently. "I didn't mean to open it, I thought it was clothes."

"No," Cate said, shaking the memory loose from her mind, "no, it's fine, and it still needs dealt with. Besides, I'm used to it, I just was thinking of how crazy it is that I'm here in a castle of a family related somehow to mine but I don't know how. I was wondering if my parents knew about this place. If they did, they never mentioned it to me."

Gayle gave her a consoling smile. Cate said, "You can just put this box in the back of the closet. It's just a few of my parents' things that I kept after they died. If you want to see something more interesting related to my parents, check out that box there!" Cate pointed to the box that had been underneath the one she was carrying to the closet.

Gayle opened it, unpacked a few of the items and looked puzzled. "This is a collection of items that my dad brought back for me from his trips for the museum. Wherever he traveled, he'd bring back some unique trinket. I kept every one of them. My mom would help me put together fact cards for them after he brought them back. See this one here, it's an Egyptian cartouche. And," Cate said digging in the box, "here is my little fact card that I wrote when I was about nine years old."

Gayle studied the object and the card, written in blue ink and decorated in colored pencil and marker with Egyptian hieroglyphs. "Oh, how cute, Cate. You really had quite the unique childhood, didn't you?"

"Yes, I did. And I loved every minute of it. While most of my schoolmates were playing hopscotch, I was pretending to find artifacts in the museum's storeroom."

"So you didn't mind the long hours at the museum? Didn't long to play dolls with your friends?"

"No, I have always been an introvert, so I enjoyed the time alone with my artifacts. I learned a lot there, too. I would spend lots of time with the other museum workers learning about what they did or helping them with small jobs."

"Who knew you'd grow up practically to live in a museum, right?"

"I know! This place kind of reminds me of my childhood! I think that's why I immediately felt so at home."

"And soon we'll have you unpacked, so you can enjoy it as your new home."

Cate smiled in agreement. They finished the rest of the boxes, ending about an hour before dinner as they had the day before. Afterwards, Gayle returned to her room to freshen up before dinner while Cate stayed behind in her room. Today's refresh wasn't as taxing as yesterday's since Cate didn't look as disheveled.

Soon enough, she was off to dinner with Gayle. Despite his quiet demeanor, Cate found that she missed Mr. Smythe at dinner, though she had a good time with Gayle. She was dreading Gayle's departure at the end of the weekend. She wondered what it would be like being alone in the castle.

With all the work done, Gayle discussed their plans for the weekend. They decided on exploring the estate's grounds on Saturday and enjoying a leisurely Sunday. This allowed Gayle some down time and time to pack for the trip back.

After dinner, they moved their conversation into the sitting room, spending some time enjoying the evening together. Again, they retired early after another long day of work.

The weekend flew by too quickly for Cate. On Saturday, they explored the grounds as planned. Riley had a great time frolicking through the massive grassy areas and playing fetch with Gayle. It was like living in a park with a museum on the grounds, Cate thought. When Saturday evening came, Cate was exhausted from the day as were Riley and Gayle.

Sunday was uneventful; they both used the time to relax. Cate and Gayle spent some time playing cards and being thankful that they could spend a day lounging. It was Mrs. Fraser's day off, but since Cate had a guest in the house, she offered to make meals. Cate was grateful to have her help. She offered her a day off later in the week but Mrs. Fraser would have none of it.

Before dinner, they took one last walk together around the grounds. As each second passed, Cate dreaded Gayle's departure more and more. While she was used to living alone, she had been enjoying the company of having other people with her and she regretted the time ending. Dinner, at least for Cate, was dampened a little because it was Gayle's last dinner at the castle. Still, the dinner and conversation were overall enjoyable.

Jack had been enlisted to drive Gayle to Edinburgh to catch the train. Since it would be a long day, Gayle retired early. Cate opted to stay up a little longer, lounging on the chaise with Riley. She occupied her thoughts with all the things she wanted to begin tomorrow on her first day alone in the castle. Hoping this had settled her mind enough, she headed to bed.

Cate's tactic didn't work, and she ended up having a fitful night of sleep again. Even with the lack of rest, she arose early to see Gayle off. Gayle reminded Cate that she was just an email away if she needed anything, which helped comfort her as the car pulled down the drive. As she watched it disappear from sight, she turned again to look at the castle. "Well, Riley, it's just you and me now, kid. Let's do some exploring!"

CHAPTER 14

$\mathcal{C}$ate looked up at the castle for another moment before heading inside. She had seen a great deal during her tour with Gayle that she looked forward to exploring in more detail on her own. Cate hoped to find any old family materials that led to a clue about how she and Lady MacKenzie were related. Any materials about her ancestors who lived in the castle before her also interested her.

What she had seen of the castle had impressed her. The rooms were impressive in size and detail, making each unique. There appeared to be a wing that was added at a later date, with the styles being kept similar between the original structure and the new structure but with subtle differences that only a history buff like Cate would notice. Despite the small differences, the work in both areas was impressive.

The decorating was also impressive. Cate was disappointed that she had never gotten the chance to meet Lady MacKenzie since the woman seemed to have possessed an exceptional aptitude to maintain the estate, its contents, and keep the castle up-to-date while maintaining its centuries-old charm.

"Where shall we start?" Cate asked Riley. Setting him down, he, with his nose to the ground, headed toward the sitting room that Cate and Gayle had been using in the evenings. Cate followed him. The large area of the sitting room centered around a massive fireplace. A grouping of furniture including a burgundy velvet couch detailed with wooden carvings, coffee table, and a few matching armchairs were placed near the fireplace. Further from the fireplace, other pieces of furniture sat closer to the outskirts, including a large wooden desk set in front of one of the room's floor to ceiling windows and a bar for serving pre- or post-dinner drinks. Heavy burgundy draperies garlanded the windows. They were thick enough to block out the light when drawn and, Cate assumed, some cold weather that undoubtedly descended on the region during winter. Paintings adorned the walls, some of people, some of landscape scenes. An avid fan of this style of art; Cate imagined spending hours just enjoying the art in this room and the rest of the castle.

Riley continued to smell around the room for a few moments before settling down on the large area rug near the fireplace. "Tired already?" Cate joked. "You have a rest while I explore the rest of the room." Cate spent about an hour in this room looking at the various pieces. She had planned on looking through drawers and storage areas of the room after she had given a more cursory exploration to the entire castle in her effort to glean any details about her ancestors.

She spent another three hours exploring the rooms on the main floor including a smaller study, the large library, the dining room, a solarium, a tea room, and a portrait hall. Cate spent a good amount of time in the portrait hall studying paintings of people who had lived in the castle in the past, fascinated by the people who had preceded her and were likely her ancestors.

Cate headed downstairs to explore the servant's area, including rooms such as the pantry and kitchen along with storage for the estate's dishware and silver. She had enough time to finish this area before lunch then she planned to head upstairs and look through those rooms.

While downstairs, Cate ran into Mrs. Fraser in the kitchen. The woman seemed startled to find Cate and Riley "below decks" as she put it. "Oh, Lady Cate!" the woman exclaimed, pressing a hand to her chest. "You startled me."

"Oh, sorry, Mrs. Fraser, I didn't mean to. I was just exploring a little."

"Exploring? Down here? There's not much that's impressive down here, Lady Cate. Is there something that I can help you with?"

"No, not at all. The servant's area is just as impressive as upstairs from a historian's perspective. It's fascinating how they built these homes and how they were run."

"I dinnae see what would be of interest in the kitchen other than the food," Mrs. Fraser said. Cate wondered if she was trying to make a joke. "And speaking of food, I've nearly got lunch prepared if you'd like to head to the dining room or perhaps take it in the sitting room or library?"

"Actually, if you wouldn't mind, I had hoped to eat down here with you for lunch. I'd like to get to know you, Mrs. Fraser."

"You want to eat here? At the servant's table? In the kitchen?" Mrs. Fraser was aghast.

"Yes. Well, if you don't mind. If you'd prefer to eat alone, I would understand."

"Well…" Mrs. Fraser looked around the room, seeming stunned by the request. After recovering, she answered, "I don't mind. I doubt Mr. Fraser or Jack would mind, so please make yourself at home."

Cate took a seat at the table while Mrs. Fraser set the table. Mr. Fraser and Jack came within a few minutes.

"Joining us for lunch today, m'lady?" Jack asked.

"Yes, I'd like to get to know everyone, if no one minds, that is."

No one objected so Cate stayed for lunch, asking more about each of them. She learned that Mrs. Fraser had lived on the estate her entire life, she was the daughter of one of the maids and had stayed on. Mr. Fraser was a local from the village who had worked on the estate since he was a young man. Jack was also from Dunhaven and, after doing some traveling as a younger man, settled back in his hometown. With Jack as estate manager, Mr. Fraser was finishing out his career before retiring in the next few years.

Cate found the lunch and conversation enjoyable and she learned much about the staff that she would work with. She thanked them all for their hospitality and Mrs. Fraser for another excellent lunch.

After lunch, she headed to the upstairs to explore the bedrooms and suites. In the upstairs, she found several potential sources of information for her research and ancestor search. At the very least, her findings would provide her with several hours of entertainment. She found several trunks in a closet area containing what looked to be old papers, journals and clothes.

She spent the entire afternoon going through the upstairs, leaving herself just enough time to freshen up before dinner. At lunch, Mrs. Fraser had asked if she preferred to take her dinner in her sitting room or another room downstairs since she wasn't entertaining. Cate opted to have a tray in the library, reading a book and relaxing as she ate.

After a bit of reading, Cate headed up to bed. Even after the relaxing evening, she found herself unable to sleep, tossing and turning for yet another night. She thought she would sleep well after her restless night the night before, but her mind wouldn't settle. It was her first night alone in the castle. As she lay in bed, listening to the silence of the castle, she wondered if she had watched too many haunted castle movies. Despite the sense of belonging that she felt immediately when she arrived, she couldn't deny that being alone for the night was spooky.

She kept a firm hold of the gold timepiece, checking it occasionally, watching the night pass slowly as she lay awake. She found it calming to rub it between her fingers and thumb like a serenity stone. It was a habit she was developing.

As time crept past midnight, Cate had nodded off. The sound of loud ticking woke her. For a moment, she was confused by what may have woken her, then, she realized it was the timepiece she still held in her hand. Shaking off sleep, she opened the watch. The ticking sounded loud and seemed to have slowed almost to a stop. Opening it, she saw the time was about five minutes after one in the morning. The second hand ticked slowly. Without thinking, Cate shook it. While the ticking was no longer loud, the watch continued to be slow. Cate tried winding it but it didn't seem to help.

"Great," she said aloud, exasperated, "Not even a week with the family heirloom before I've broken it." She resolved to call around to determine if there was anyone in the nearby area who could fix it or to find a place where she could send it to be fixed in the morning. She lay back in the bed, hoping this wouldn't keep her up. Just as her head hit the pillow, Cate thought she heard another noise. Sitting up again, she listened hard. Straining, she thought she could just make out a light tinkling noise, like music. She sat for another minute, thinking she must be imagining things. She was alone, other than Riley, so no music should be playing. After a few more moments she was sure she heard music. Cate tiptoed across the room, straining to make out where it was coming from.

Glancing toward the bed, she didn't see or hear Riley stirring. The soft noise didn't seem to bother him enough to wake him. The little pup must have been nestled deep in the covers, Cate couldn't even see him. Turning back, she crept toward the sitting room. As she began approaching the door to the hall, it sounded as though the music got louder then ended as in a crescendo. She hurried to the door, pulling it open. Listening hard, she heard nothing. Still listening, she crept down the hall a bit, but there was nothing but silence. Puzzled, she stood in the hallway for a moment. She considered going further but her nerves held her back. The castle was not as welcoming during the night as it was during the day. Molly's words about it being haunted rattled around in her head.

Sighing, she gave up and headed back to bed. She chalked it up to being overtired and tried to go to sleep for what seemed like the thousandth time that night. After about half an hour, she drifted off. She slept restlessly, dreaming of the castle in older times, filled with people enjoying a house party mixed with the ghosts of the people she saw in the portrait gallery.

CHAPTER 15

*C*ate awoke the next morning hating herself for lying awake as long as she did. How silly she felt, she had been over-tired and hearing things. She probably drifted off and dreamt that she heard music. Yet, she heard it when she got out of bed, too. Had she been sleepwalking or imagining things while still half-asleep? It hadn't disturbed Riley, and she knew the little pup had to have more sensitive ears than she did.

Even more perplexing was the timepiece. Last night, it slowed almost to a stop; she thought she had broken it. This morning, it was keeping time just fine, ticking away as though nothing happened. At least she didn't need to call a repairman, so she could cross that off her list.

Cate decided that after breakfast she would start her day with a walk around the grounds with Riley. "What do you think, buddy? Would you like to explore outside today?" she asked the little dog. Riley's reaction was to give Cate a kiss on her cheek, which she took as approval of her plan. Judging by the scenery outside, Cate thought Riley needed his new tartan coat for a little added warmth. Heavy fog surrounded the castle. She planned on bundling up, too. She wasn't used to the cooler weather yet. Aberdeen was a good bit warmer at this time of the year compared to Dunhaven.

There was something romantic about the way the mist clung to the moors surrounding the castle. She enjoyed the muted scenery that surrounded her before the sun began to burn off any of the morning's fog. Riley enjoyed exploring the new area, frolicking through the grassy knolls. Cate enjoyed watching him prancing around the estate as though he were the lord of the manor. It warmed Cate's heart to see the little dog so happy in his surroundings. It seemed Riley felt a sense of belonging here, too, which counted for a lot in Cate's book.

Their walk took up most of the morning hours, with several games of fetch added in. Cate returned to the castle in time to freshen up before lunch. Given her lack of sleep last night, she planned to have a relaxing afternoon reading a book.

After lunch, she settled into one of the big leather armchairs in the library with a volume that she found there. After an hour of reading, Cate's mind began to wander to the events of last night. She swore the watch had been slow, and she was sure that she heard music coming from somewhere in the castle. Given the late hour, she started to wonder if she dreamt it all. After giving brief consideration to that idea, she ruled it out. She had been fully awake. The music lasted several minutes, enough time for her to climb out of bed and walk around searching for the source. She couldn't have imagined it and it was too real for her to have dreamt it. She was letting her imagination run wild, having read too many gothic romance novels. Or it was her subconscious reacting to Molly's teasing about haunted Scottish castles.

She checked the timepiece, again noting that it seemed to be working without issue. It was almost half-past two. Cate decided to look around the downstairs to see if she could find anything that could have produced the mysterious music last night. She needed a break from reading. Her lack of sleep threatened to make her doze off in the chair; if that happened, she would never sleep again tonight.

She rousted herself from the comfort of the oversized chair. Riley, lounging on the floor nearby, lifted his head. "Want to explore, Riley?" she asked. In response, Riley laid his head back on the carpet, too tired from his morning excursion to explore anything. "All right, all right, I'll carry you," she said, scooping the dog up, not wanting to leave him alone in the castle yet.

Apart from her bedroom suite, Cate was most familiar with the library and knew the music couldn't have come from that room. She left the library to explore the other rooms. She spent the rest of the afternoon making her rounds, meticulously checking each room for signs of some device that played music. She found none. In the tea room, she found an old gramophone, but it was only decorative. The Victrola in the small study was unplugged.

Returning to the library, she laid Riley down in his previous spot. Riley must have known this was a fool's errand. Cate had searched and searched and come up empty. She sighed as she eased back into her chair, now ready to chalk the experience up to being over-tired and over-stimulated by her surroundings. All homes had their own set of sounds and idiosyncrasies that one must get used to. She must have heard some noise, the wind or bells outside or something that sounded like music. The explanation far from satisfied her but it would have to do for now since she had no other clear explanation.

Picking up her book again, she opened it to where she had left off as Mrs. Fraser arrived with a tray of dinner. She read as she ate dinner, trying to clear her mind of the incident and let the book consume her thoughts. Mrs. Fraser collected the tray from her and said good night, leaving Cate alone in the castle after she finished cleaning up.

Cate listened again to the silence of the castle. She returned to reading her book, trying not to let an eerie pall creep over her evening. Again, her conversation with Molly sprang to mind. She pushed it as far to the back of her brain as possible, trying not to give in to any hysteria. She didn't believe in ghosts. At least, that's what she told herself.

As she read, her eyes began to get heavy. I'll just put my head back for a moment, she thought. As soon as her head hit the cushion, she started to nod off. Her head began to loll to the side, and she jerked herself awake, pulling herself back to reality. Drowsy, it took her a moment to wake up.

As she sat taking a few breaths to clear her mind, she noticed something moving out of the corner of her eye. She whipped her head around, following the movement. One of the heavy draperies appeared to be moving, swaying gently back and forth. Cate shook it off as being a draft from a window. They were old and probably leaked air like crazy. Oddly, though, Cate didn't feel any drafts in the room. She didn't need any unnerving experiences before bed; she would never sleep.

The drape continued to move, shifting directions in a larger motion. If this large of a movement was coming from a drafty window, Cate was sure she would feel the air. She would need to investigate. There had to be an explanation, at least she hoped. Cate rose from the chair, steeling her nerves, swallowing hard. Taking a deep breath, she took one step toward the moving curtain. It stopped moving as soon as she took a step. Whatever unseen force had been at work suddenly halted. Had it felt her presence? Was it now gone?

She felt her heart beating hard in her chest; her pulse quickening as she continued to stare at the curtain. As she was calming down, settling her mind that it was nothing, the curtain began to whip back and forth again. Cate's heart rose to her throat, and she instinctively backed a step away. This was no gust of wind. No drafty window could produce this. Swallowing hard again, Cate squared her shoulders and raised her chin. She was brave; she had to know what was happening. She pushed herself to take one step forward, then another, and another, and another.

As she approached the drape, she reached forward, keeping a safe distance from it, just in case. She was almost ready to pull back the curtain when the source of the movement revealed itself. Riley popped out from under the curtain, his black and white face peeking out from under the tartan drape. Cate clutched her chest in relief. "RILEY!" she exclaimed. "You scared me half to death!" In her dazed state after dozing off, she failed to notice Riley wasn't still asleep in his spot on the rug. She raced over to Riley and scooped him up, ruffling the fur on his head. He gave her an appreciative kiss on the cheek.

"I suppose we've been watching a few too many of those spooky movies, Riley. Thanks to Molly, that is! That's enough excitement for one night, buddy!" Cate said. "Let's head to bed, before I scare myself again."

CHAPTER 16

Despite the evening's unexpected excitement, Cate slept soundly that night, exhausted from her previous sleepless nights. The next several days passed without incident, with Cate trying to get plenty of outdoor time with Riley to tire herself out enough to sleep well. She also had her first experience with the cleaning company, finding it strange to see a group of people descend upon her home and clean it for her. They discussed their typical schedule with her, asking if they should make any modifications.

It also helped that she was getting used to the castle. Life here was becoming normal to her, or at least routine. That sense of belonging that she first felt when she arrived at the castle grew stronger with each day.

She received the papers from Mr. Smythe to transfer the cottage from her ownership to the Fraser's along with instructions on signing them and sending them back via courier to his office to file. Cate signed them and had Jack take them to the courier on one of his trips into town.

At week's end, she received an email from Gayle asking

how her first week in her new home went. She responded that she was getting along well, omitting her two scares, so she didn't look like a foolish girl giving in to ghost stories. Already fading from her memory, she chalked them up to being overtired. The transition to Scottish country life continued to go smoothly for Cate. Not having a mountain of work to occupy her time was unusual. She replaced it with being able to read the books she had been meaning to read for months and creating a research plan for looking into her family and the castle's history.

Cate started with the resources at the castle. During her exploration of the castle, she saw several journals and photo albums that might be of interest even if they explained nothing about her family and its history.

Left alone in the castle on Sunday, she spent the day inside. It was a chilly day with on and off rain. The darkened skies and quiet castle added to the ambience of a haunting. She used the time to look through some materials she found while exploring. Cate wanted to keep her mind busy, so she picked several photo albums and carried them to her sitting room. She loved the fact that she could hole up in her own private space within the walls of the castle. Maybe she was just used to the smaller space from apartment living but the privacy of the rooms, even when she was alone, comforted her.

Curling up on the chaise lounge with Riley and a heavy blanket to keep the chill off of them, she took one of the photo albums off of the top of the stack she made earlier on the side table next to the chaise. This album contained pictures from the early twentieth century. She spent a good hour looking through the album, studying it with interest but learning nothing from it.

Picking up the second album, she started to page through it. More recent, this album contained some pictures of Lady

Gertrude MacKenzie. Since this album contained photos of the castle's last occupant and her benefactor, Cate was very interested in it. She took her time paging through the book, even looking at pictures of Gertrude as a baby with great interest. A quarter of the way through the album, the pictures were of Gertrude as a small child. Another quarter of the way through, the album contained pictures of Gertrude as a young woman, in her late teens to early twenties.

Interested in all the pictures, Cate studied not only Gertrude but the castle and its interior in the background. The pictures were labeled, so Cate was getting a sense of the family, seeing Gertrude's mother, Mary, and father, Oliver.

When Cate turned the page again, a new face stared out at her. A child who looked about six years old stood outside the castle with Gertrude, who was a young woman. Cate didn't see any other children in the album, so she guessed this wasn't a sibling of Gertrude. Cate read the written caption at the bottom of the picture. What she read made her gasp. Riley popped his head up at Cate's expression of surprise, trying to determine the reason behind it. Below the photo, the caption read: Lady Gertrude with Cousin Logan MacKenzie. The small boy's name caught her eye, Logan MacKenzie. Logan was her father's name. His last name was Kensie, but what was the chance that Gertrude had another relative named Logan. "Logan MacKenzie?" she said aloud. "Riley, perhaps this is my dad!"

She stared for another minute at the picture. Could this boy, standing outside of the castle with Gertrude, have been her father as a child? If it was, had he forgotten this visit because of his young age? Coming to a castle didn't seem like something you would forget, even at the tender age of six, but it may have happened.

The album became very interesting to Cate now. She

examined several more pictures of the boy in various rooms of the castle. In addition, on the next page, Cate found a picture of the boy with his parents. She read their names: Charles and Sophie MacKenzie. Her grandparents' names were Charles and Sophie Kensie. Coincidence? Cate didn't believe so. Had her grandparents changed their last name or had there been some miscommunication on their paperwork when they moved to the U.S.? If it was the latter, why was the story never told? And if it was the former, what prompted them to change their name? Cate now had more questions than answers. She thought because her parents didn't talk much about their families there was nothing to tell. All she was told was that her grandparents moved to the United States when Cate's father had been a small boy. Cate's grandparents passed away before her birth so she didn't have much information about them. Her parents didn't have any photos of them so she couldn't tell if the people in the picture were younger versions of her grandparents or not.

Cate hoped to find more information, confused but intrigued by this turn of events. She looked through the rest of the album, but outside of the pictures of possibly her father at six years old, she found no other clues. There were no more pictures of Logan MacKenzie nor any other mention of her grandparents.

Cate set the album aside, intending to keep this one here in her room to study again. She went through the others she brought up with her but found no further traces of family visits from whom she thought ended up being the Kensies she knew and loved.

As interesting as she found the other pictures, Cate's mind continued to dwell on the image of the small boy that she presumed was her father. She hoped to find more information in some other journals or photo albums in the castle.

Cate considered searching for more information but

given that it was almost evening, she decided against it, concerned that it might interfere with her sleep. She promised herself to get an early start in the morning searching for more clues. She decided to spend the rest of the evening reading. However, the photo of the boy kept creeping into her mind and she found that she couldn't concentrate on the book.

Pushing it from her mind, Cate turned in early, hoping that getting into bed at an early hour would mean a decent night's sleep. Unfortunately for Cate, she was in for a sleepless night full of tossing and turning, wondering and postulating, questioning and going over every conversation that she ever had with her parents, trying to find anything that would connect her to the castle or the MacKenzie family.

When morning rolled around, Cate was determined to seek answers despite her exhaustion. She moved her daily walk around the grounds with Riley to later in the day, digging right in to search for more information on her father's connection to the family. "Sorry, buddy," she said, apologizing to Riley, "I promise we'll go later, but you know how I am when I get my mind on something. I'm like you with a bone." Cate winked at him. She started by looking through the other photo albums she found.

Cate spent hours pouring over those photo albums but found no additional information. Frustrated, Cate took a break and went for her walk with Riley to clear her head. As she walked, her mind continued to pour over the information, or lack of information, that she had so far.

When Cate returned to the castle, she looked through the album she kept out yesterday. When she got to the pictures of Logan MacKenzie, she studied the images hard. It was impossible to tell if this was her father. There seemed to be a resemblance but that could be said for many pictures of children. Cate closed the album, sighing. Staring at the same photos again gave her no new information. Her questions continued to be left unanswered. But she was convinced this must be her father. The chances of another Logan with parents named Charles and Sophie related to the MacKenzies had to be small.

"What do you think, Riley? Is this Grandpa Kensie in his younger years?" The dog gave her no definitive answer.

With no answer from Riley or anywhere else, Cate gave up at least for the evening. Over the next few days, Cate looked for any more information on her father or her grandparents within the photo albums again, but didn't find much. In the portrait gallery, she found a family bible with a family tree written inside dating several generations. It showed Gertrude and her parents, Oliver and Mary, and their parents, and so on, however a large ink stain obliterated any additional information about Oliver's generation of the family. Cate tried to glean any small details from underneath the ink by holding the book in every possible position but she was unable to see what was under the ink blot. Someone's careless handling of ink obscured any information.

Cate determined that she needed to change strategies. Perhaps if she could track down when the name change occurred she would learn more. She resolved to pursue this avenue.

CHAPTER 17

Over the next two days, Cate searched all the major ancestry sites for any information on her grandparents and when they may have changed their last name from MacKenzie to Kensie. She found a few immigration forms from when her grandparents moved the family from England to the United States, but they listed the last name as Kensie. So they had been the Kensies since their immigration to the States at least. Cate tried to search for birth records of her father and grandparents but couldn't find much listed online in the U.K. databases. She hated admitting defeat, but this path wasn't leading her anywhere at the moment.

As she headed into the library for lunch, an idea struck her. There must have been a way for Mr. Smythe's law firm to find her. Perhaps they were aware of how much the families knew of each other. Cate sent a quick email to Gayle just as Mrs. Fraser came in with a tray for her.

"Well, have you found anything out about yourself?" Mrs. Fraser asked as Cate shut her laptop.

"Afraid not," Cate answered, deflated. "I hope to have better news soon."

"I almost forgot to tell you, Lady Cate, I packed all Lady MacKenzie's personal belongings away and put them in the tower room. That was the best place so they wouldn't be in your way but you could access them. Well, what wasn't donated according to her wishes. I dinnae think you've been through those boxes yet. I dinnae know if anything there would help you but I thought I'd mention it. Even if it doesn't help, most of her personal items were there. I just packed everything up for you to go over whenever you have the chance."

"Oh, thank you, Mrs. Fraser. I'll take a look this afternoon."

Cate ate her lunch quickly, determined to spend her afternoon with the new stash of potential clues. After she finished lunch, she checked her email. Gayle, efficient as ever, had already responded to her inquiry.

Dear Cate,

Lady MacKenzie had given us information about a branch of the family in the United States. She knew your father's name and had an old address of his we used to track down his current status and, eventually, to find you. I'm sorry we don't have more information than that. Good luck with your search and please let me know if I can be of any further assistance.

On another note, it sounds like you are settling in well! Castle life suits you!

Best, Gayle

So, Lady MacKenzie knew she had family in the United States. She even had an address for Cate's father. The main question in Cate's mind now was if her father knew of his family in Scotland. Sighing, she realized she might never answer those questions.

But, she had a new treasure trove to look through in the tower. Turning to Riley, she said, "Let's explore something new!" She gathered Riley into her arms and headed to the tower. Mrs. Fraser had brought Riley a bone which he had enjoyed chewing on over lunch. Cate took it with her and settled Riley into a corner to continue enjoying his bone.

Cate eyed the stack of boxes. Lady MacKenzie accumulated many things during her life at Dunhaven. She had her work cut out for her. With this number of boxes, it may take her more than the afternoon to finish. "No time like the present," she mumbled to herself. She picked a stack and dove into the first box.

Cate sifted through box after box finding nothing helpful to her heritage mystery. What she did find was many interesting items that told her a bit about who Gertrude MacKenzie was including a few decorative items that had adorned her dressing space, some perfumes and lotions and other personal things.

There was one more box in the stack Cate started. Cate planned to call it quits after looking through that box. Opening the box, she found a large wooden jewelry box inside. She opened it and discovered that it was a music box, playing Fur Elise when wound and opened. It contained several notes and letters. These must have been special to Lady Gertrude if she kept them close in her jewelry box. Cate opened a few and read them with interest. They were the typical things you would keep close as keepsakes: a note from her mother on her twentieth birthday, a card she received from her mother prior to her death. Cate carefully set them aside and reached into the box for the next item. As she opened the folded note, several pictures fell out. They were snapshots of various things in the United States. It seemed Lady Gertrude took a trip to the States in 1975 according to the dates on the pictures and kept some pictures close at hand for her to reminisce over. Cate looked through the pictures. There was one of the Statue of Liberty, one of Times Square, and another of the White House, all marked with captions underneath. Cate flipped through the pictures, then stopped dead as she got to the fourth photo. This time there was no mistaking her father, now appearing close to being in his thirties. He stood in the middle of the picture between two women, smiling. Cate's mother stood on one side of him and on the other side was none other than Lady Gertrude MacKenzie. The caption read Visiting Cousin Logan and his new wife.

Cate sat in stunned silence for several minutes. Lady Gertrude MacKenzie visited her father as an adult. And her father certainly met and mingled with Lady MacKenzie. But he never mentioned her. Cate could not figure out why. From the time she was a child, her parents told her she had no living relatives. Both her parents had been only children so there was no close family nor any other relatives spoken of. Her father never mentioned a visit from a Scottish relative who lived in a castle nor that she was still alive and was Cate's closest living relative.

As Cate contemplated all this, she absentmindedly rubbed the gold timepiece between her thumb and finger. Suddenly, Cate heard the ticking of the timepiece. She thought it was just the quietness of the room and her pensive mood, but the ticking seemed to grow louder and louder, and again, the second hand started to slow down. Cate opened the timepiece; it was ticking slowly, barely at all.

What was wrong with this thing? This time she wasn't

half-asleep and wasn't imagining it. She would need to have the watch looked at; it wasn't working properly. Maybe Gayle could assist in finding someone to help with it. Since she would no longer be in the office today, Cate decided to deal with it tomorrow.

Cate's thoughts returned to the picture she found. The discovery that her father knew Lady MacKenzie, met her as an adult and was very much aware of their relationship surprised her. Why would her father keep something like this from her? Was there some family feud? It would explain the inkblot in the family bible. Perhaps it wasn't just carelessness that caused it, but maybe a deliberate blotting out of a branch of the family that was no longer welcome at the castle. But then why bequeath the castle to her? Lady MacKenzie was aware that Cate's side of the family was her closest relatives. If there had been a rift in the family, why not will it to someone else?

As she thought, Cate made her way to the large towering window in the room. A steady rain fell from the sky. Strange, Cate thought, there was no rain in the forecast today; it had been bright and sunny earlier. Turning away from the window, Cate continued to think through all of her questions. As her mind churned, Cate began to absentmindedly rub the timepiece. Her thoughts turned to it and its defect. She had broken the watch, the item that seemed such an important part of the inheritance. Or at least, it had broken on her watch, no pun intended. Cate felt heartsick about this on top of the idea that it was possible that no one in the family wanted her to inherit the castle.

Looking down, she opened the watch. Much to her surprise, it was ticking away as if nothing happened to it, like it never slowed. Cate frowned at the timepiece in her hand, wondering what was going on with it. It was working again, but she still planned on having it checked before the thing really went kaput on her. She already had enough unanswered questions, questions that would probably remain unanswered; the last thing she needed was another mystery.

Without being able to accomplish much more today, Cate decided that she would take a tray of dinner in her room tonight, so she headed to the kitchen to tell Mrs. Fraser. Cate gathered Riley and his bone, long since discarded in favor of a nap, and left the tower room. As she walked, she looked outside one of the hallway windows. Bright sunshine glared back at her. The storm, it seemed, had passed rather quickly.

CHAPTER 18

*A*s planned, Cate emailed Gayle the next morning, opting to do it before breakfast as it was consuming her mind. She informed her that she believed the gold timepiece, that had been so important to Lady MacKenzie, seemed not to be working properly. She asked if Lady MacKenzie had a repairman or if there was one that Gayle could recommend to fix it.

After sending the email, Cate made her way to the kitchen before breakfast. Mrs. Fraser was busy preparing the meal. Cate pitched in to help despite being sure that it made Mrs. Fraser uncomfortable.

"Good morning, Mrs. Fraser."

"Good morning, Lady Cate. Did you find anything you could use in the boxes?"

"Yes! I found a picture of my father with Lady MacKenzie! She had visited him shortly after he married my mother. I had never known!"

"Really? Well, I'm glad you found something to help you."

"Mrs. Fraser, you grew up here, right?"

"Been here since my birth, yes."

Cate took a stab in the dark. "Do you remember anything being discussed about my family? Or my grandparents visiting?"

Mrs. Fraser thought a moment. "Nay, I cannae say I've heard anything about your family. When Lady MacKenzie was ill, Mr. Fraser, and I wondered what would become of the place since there didn't seem to be a relative in sight to take it over. We didn't even know if there was a relative out there."

"I see. I thought you may have heard something being here all your life."

"Nay, I've not heard a whisper of anything about your side. Never met your grandparents or your parents and never heard of you, Lady Cate, until Mr. Smythe told us he'd located the new owner."

"Well, it was worth a shot. I may have questions I will never have answers to."

"You mean your father, he never told you about any of this?"

"Not a word. I never knew I had a relative, even if she was distant. I wish I did, I would have liked to have met her. She seemed like a very interesting person, someone I would have liked."

"Aye, Lady Cate, she was and very kind, too; the picture of grace. You're not much different from her to be honest. Well, that's your breakfast ready. Anything else I can do for you?"

"No, no, that's all. I'll carry it up myself, thanks, Mrs. Fraser. Come on, Riley!" Cate called the little dog to follow her.

Cate decided over breakfast that she would move on to her other project, finding more about the castle's history and its inhabitants. It seemed like she was at a dead end on her family's connection to the MacKenzies and why it was kept a secret. She wasn't giving up but for the moment she would move on.

Cate planned to write a book about the castle, its history and its owners if she could gather enough interesting information. It seemed like an appropriate project for a former history professor and she had always wanted to write a book.

Since there was no rush to begin, she spent the morning enjoying the grounds with Riley, and gathering her thoughts for the book. While they were walking, she ran into Jack, pruning back a large birch tree.

"Well, if it isn't Lady Cate and Sir Riley. Good morning to you!" he yelled from the ladder as he climbed down.

"Good morning, Jack! How are you today?"

"Ah, I cannae complain, lassie. I'm alive and breathing this beautiful Scottish air!" he said, giving Riley a scratch under his chin. "And how are you and the good Sir Riley this morning?"

"Good, thanks. Although, this beautiful Scottish air is just a bit on the chilly side for me!"

"Chilly? Ahhhh, lassie, this is nice, warm weather! If you think this is chilly, you've not seen anything yet!"

"Ha! Well I'm not freezing but Aberdeen was a lot warmer than this at this time of the year!"

"Not considering moving back for all that warmth, are you?"

"Never! I'm made of tougher stuff than that, you know!"

"There's the spirit, lassie, there's the spirit. Well, I better get on with it before Mr. Fraser catches me idling my time away talking about the weather but if there's anything I can help you with, you let me know."

"Thanks," Cate said, beginning to turn away. She turned back. "Actually, I could use your help with something."

Jack stepped back off the ladder. "Name it, Cate."

"Well, I'd like to go into town, I was wondering if you had

a morning this week to spare to drive me in. I'm not sure that I trust myself to drive on the right side of the road yet."

"Ah, well, good thing you're asking me, because we drive on the left side of the road, Cate," Jack said with a wink.

"Very funny. I meant I don't know if I'll drive on the correct side of the road."

"Well, I can definitely help you with that, lassie. I'd be happy to take you into town any morning that you want, just name it."

"Ok, how is tomorrow morning, then?" Cate asked. The cleaning service was scheduled to come in, so Cate figured it would be an appropriate day to be out of the castle.

"Tomorrow morning is fine with me. Shall we leave around nine? I dare say you'll not find much open before then."

"9 a.m. sounds great! I'll see you then!"

Instead of beginning book research, Cate spent the rest of the day sorting through Lady MacKenzie's personal belongings. She hadn't decided what she would do with anything, but she wanted to make more progress with the boxes. While she didn't acquire much information for either of her research projects, she learned more about Lady MacKenzie as a person, or at least she felt as though she did. It was a strange feeling to feel close to someone that you had never met, but Cate did feel closer to her.

$\mathcal{C}$ate and Riley enjoyed a quick walk after breakfast the next morning. Then Cate left Riley with his favorite ball, tucked away in her bedroom suite and met Jack at the front of the castle to head into town. "I hope we have enough time to tour the entire town. We might need a second day," Jack joked.

"I'll bet. I heard there's a grocery store and everything."

"Well, you heard right, lassie. There's a small grocer and a pub!"

"Ah, sadly, though, my real interest is in the town's library."

"The library? Ack, you're kidding me? All this fuss for the library?"

"The library, yep."

"You've got a whole library here in the castle. But you want to go to Dunhaven's library?"

"I was hoping they might have some information on the castle that we don't."

"New research project, eh? Well, right-o, then, let's get

you to the library. If you want to get wild and crazy, we can visit the bookstore and even a church."

They got into the car. "Very, very funny. Maybe we could check out the pub afterwards, too?"

"Now, you're talking, lassie, now you're talking. At least we've got something to look forward to!"

Jack fired the engine and pulled the car down the drive. Within a few minutes, they were in town. The town was much smaller than Aberdeen, but Jack had exaggerated its tiny size. While the town was small, it had much more to offer than just a library, a pub, and a few churches. Cate found the town to be the perfect size.

Jack dropped Cate off in front of the library, telling her he planned to park and make a quick stop at the local hardware store to pick up a few things from a list that Mr. Fraser had given him. He told Cate that he would meet her at the library afterwards.

Cate headed into the library; it was small compared to the libraries at Aberdeen and Aberdeen College. A young woman behind the circulation desk greeted her. Cate smiled and whispered a hello to the girl as she approached the desk.

"Hello, ma'am, something I can help you with?" the girl asked politely.

"Yes, hello, I'm Dr. Cate Kensie. I'm the new owner of Dunhaven Castle. I was wondering if you had any information on it, perhaps old building plans or anything they might have filed with the municipality? Maybe any articles or texts written about it by locals?"

"Oh, hello, Dr. Kensie. Let me see if the librarian can help you. I'm not sure what we have."

"Oh, great, thank you!"

The young woman disappeared into a small office behind the circulation desk. After a moment, an older woman appeared through the doorway.

"Hello, Dr. Kensie. A pleasure to meet you," she began, in a deep Scottish brogue. "I'm Mrs. Campbell, the librarian. Within our private archives we have some things that may interest you. I also know that we have the book *The Mysteries of Scotland* in which the castle is mentioned if you'd like to see that?"

"That sounds great, thank you so much!"

The woman took Cate to a back room, which looked like a storage room. Cate was familiar with these types of rooms, where they kept private materials and a small space was provided for perusal of these materials. Cate set her tote bag down on the floor near a small desk in the room while the librarian pulled several materials from the shelves. Setting them on the desk, she left Cate to look over them while she went to retrieve the other text that she had mentioned.

Cate looked over the materials provided by the librarian. They included plans for the castle when it had been modernized and plans for the added wing along with a few other historical documents involving the castle's building and operation. One of the documents noted the castle served as a recovery space for officers after the first World War.

As she perused the documents, the librarian placed a book down before leaving her alone again. Cate picked up the book the librarian left as she was looking over the documents. The book appeared to contain ghost stories from various areas, homes, and castles across Scotland. Cate checked the index for a reference to Dunhaven Castle then thumbed to the indicated page. There was a short entry detailing why the author included Dunhaven Castle in the book.

Dunhaven Castle, located just outside of the town of Dunhaven in northwestern Scotland, has long been the site of mysterious occurrences. During its construction, one worker died on the site in a freak accident with falling bricks, while another disappeared without a trace. Following the construction, those working at the castle insisted that the ghosts of those who met their demise on the property or who had never been seen or heard from again haunted its halls. Many of those working in the castle often left, some of them in the middle of the night, unable to continue working in the home after experiencing random sights and sounds at various times of the day or night. The castle's owners, the MacKenzie family, were often left without servants at short notice.

Stories of these phantom occurrences were not confined to only those who worked at the castle after its construction. Visitors to the home and other workers have continued to tell tales of occurrences, all bearing a resemblance to the original tales from early servants: phantom sights and sounds presenting at all hours of the day and night. Visitors and workers at the castle tell tales of being woken from their sleep to hear music coming from nowhere or to hear conversations

from people that were never to be
found. They tell stories of seeing
people roaming the halls that
disappear when followed. All those
that experienced some form of
manifestation at the castle, when
asked, have indicated that they
believe it to be haunted by the ghosts
of those that gave their lives in her
construction.

Throughout the history of the castle,
the MacKenzie family has refused to
comment on the stories about the
castle. The current occupant was
contacted for comment during the
writing of this book; no response was
received.

Cate read the text with great interest. Others had heard
phantom music in the castle. When Cate had explored the
place in the middle of the night, it was because she had heard
music. Had she experienced the same thing as she had read
from the book? Maybe Molly was right and her new home
was haunted.

A moment of panic washed over her. Cate shook her
head, refusing to give in to it. The castle was NOT haunted,
what a ridiculous idea. Molly was only joking when she had
said that. Ghosts were not real, there was a reasonable explanation for everything that had happened. Cate was an
educated woman, she would not give in to ghost stories. The
book was sensationalizing a few strange occurrences, prob-

ably to drive tourism, Cate mused. And it was easy to sell the tale of a haunted castle; there was no shortage of stories about the topic.

Cate set the book aside, planning to focus on the other materials that the librarian had provided her. This was what she had come for. Since she was meeting Jack shortly, Cate didn't have time to take notes on any of these documents. She wanted to study them in depth at home. She decided to ask the librarian if she could take them.

Gathering everything, Cate made her way back to the circulation desk. She spotted Jack coming through the door as she approached the desk. Perfect timing, she thought.

The girl behind the desk smiled at Cate. "Did you find everything you were looking for?"

"Yes, the librarian helped me to find everything that I needed. I'd like to take a more thorough look at these materials. Is it possible for me to take them home?"

"Ah, those are in the private collection, I'm not sure..." the assistant began.

"Oh, I'm a historian, so I'm well versed in document preservation and so on, I'll be very careful with them."

"Um, well, I'm just not sure, I don't think we're supposed to allow those to leave, and the librarian has stepped out, so I'm not sure I can help."

Jack made his way to the desk and chimed into the conversation. "Why, don't you know who you're talking to, lassie? This is the world renowned Dr. Cate Kensie. Are you going to be the reason she can't complete her research? Why, she might make our little hamlet famous one day. Of course, if we're not famous we can all blame you, I suppose."

The assistant seemed flustered, but she was blushing at Jack. Cate didn't blame her; he was a rather good-looking man, he reminded her of a younger version of a certain Scottish actor whose name was escaping her at the moment.

"Well," she stammered, smiling at Jack then turning to Cate, "I suppose if you're a historian, it won't hurt. Let me just mark down what you're taking and you can be on your way."

"Thank you, it's much appreciated. And like I said, I'll be careful and have them back before anyone misses them!"

The assistant made a short list of what Cate was taking, smiled at her and wished her a good day. Cate gathered the materials and headed out the door with Jack. After storing her treasures in the car, they made their way to the pub that Jack recommended for some lunch.

After ordering, Jack began by asking, "So, it's a bit warmer where you came from, eh?"

"Yes," Cate answered, taking a sip of her ale, "it was already non-coat weather where I came from!"

"So, were you prepared for our weather? Have you been here before?"

"No, I've never been to Scotland. But, I searched it on a weather app before coming, so I guess I was as prepared as I could be!"

"Never been, eh? Well, at least you've done things right for your first trip."

"I have?"

"Sure. The right way to do things is to come to Scotland for the first time after you've inherited a castle."

"Oh, right, that's what I thought everyone did, so I just followed suit!" Cate joked back.

"What do you think of your new home? Do you like it here?"

"Well, I've only been here two weeks, so it's early to judge, but on the whole, I do like it! I already feel much more at home here than I ever did in Aberdeen. And I went from living in an apartment with three rooms to living in a castle, I can't complain! I assume you like it here since you came back?"

"Sure, I mean, it's home. I traveled a bit, worked on a fishing boat for a while, but when my father passed away, I came back and continued the Reid tradition, taking over his job on the estate. He died of a heart attack and I decided it was time to come home and fulfill my duties here. You know, keep an eye on my grandfather and so on."

"Oh, I'm sorry to hear that, Jack. Your dad worked at Dunhaven, too?"

"Aye, that he did lassie, that he did. There's always been a Reid as the estate manager for as long as any of us can remember. My grandfather before my father, and his father before him and on and on back through the line."

"Oh, wow, I hadn't realized that. I'm sure you know more about that place than I do."

"I don't know about that, oh Cate the historian, but I spent a lot of time there while growing up. I remember that watch you've got on always being around Lady MacKenzie's neck. Funny how you remember things like that, eh?"

"Oh," Cate said, grabbing the watch, "yes, apparently, it was important to her. She left me a hand-written note as part of the inheritance telling me I needed to wear it at all times. I thought it was odd, but I guess it was just really important to her."

"Must have been!"

"Which makes me feel even worse," Cate said, sighing.

"You lost me, Lady Cate, feel worse about what?"

"Oh, I think I may have broken the watch."

"Oh, broken it? You Americans, riding roughshod over everything. How did you do that, drop it from the turret?"

"No idea. But it keeps slowing down, sometimes it seems almost to stop. Then it starts up again as if nothing was wrong. I need to have it looked at."

"My grandfather could take a look if you'd like. He's not a genuine watchmaker, but he's good with those kinds of things. He might have some experience with it from when he worked there."

"Oh, that would be great! I asked Gayle about someone, but I haven't checked to see if she recommended anyone or not."

"I'm sure he could peek at it after lunch if you don't mind an extra stop?"

"Not at all, I'd like to make sure it works properly, I'd feel terrible if anything happened to it on my watch, no pun intended. It has been in the family for so long."

As they finished their conversation about the watch, their food was served. Cate and Jack spent their meal discussing some places they had each traveled. Cate told Jack that she had traveled somewhat during her graduate work, but nothing outside of the States. She had traveled far less after her parents passed away and she adopted Riley.

After lunch, Jack took Cate to his grandfather's house, a charming cottage on the outskirts of town. After thanking the man for agreeing to look at the watch, Cate handed it over.

"I can remember this watch from when I was a young man on the estate," the elderly man said, taking the watch from Cate.

"Oh, yes, Jack mentioned that you worked there. And his father, too."

"Aye, lassie, there's always been a Reid on that estate, it's tradition! Wouldn't seem right without us!"

"Well, I'm glad to have Jack there!"

"Now let me see the watch. Think you may have broken it, do you, lassie? Let me take a look." The man held it under a large magnifying glass. He had all the tools of the trade despite not being a watchmaker. He carefully opened it with jeweler's pliers. Holding the piece with reverence, he eyed the inside. "Now, come on over here, Jackie, take a look at the inside and I'll show you some important parts."

"Yes," Cate said, as the man worked with the timepiece, pointing out various elements of the mechanism to Jack, "I was telling Jack, it seems to slow suddenly, almost to a stop and it ticks very loudly when it does that. Then, it will just start back up again as if nothing was wrong with it."

"You hit the nail on the head with that last one, lassie!"

"I'm sorry, I don't understand, what did I do?"

"You're right, nothing is wrong with it."

"Are you sure? It seems to slow almost to a stop, it's done it a few times now, that can't be normal."

"I assure you, it's right as rain, this watch."

Cate wasn't so sure. "I trust your experience, Mr. Reid, but, would it still be prudent to have a watchmaker look at it, just to make sure it's in tip-top shape?" Cate hoped she didn't offend him but she was certain the watch's behavior was abnormal.

"Nay, I'd not recommend that, lassie. Not at all."

"Really?" His recommendation surprised Cate. "May I ask why?" Whether he felt it was needed, what would be the problem with having a second pair of eyes look at it?

"It's quite an expensive piece, an antique, in fact. I'd not let it out of my sight. Lady MacKenzie was never without it, I'm sure that's why."

"Did she ever have it serviced, I mean, that you know of?"

"Nay, she never did. If anything needed fixing, I took care of it, she would have trusted no one else outside of the estate to care for the watch."

"Hmm. That's interesting. Well, thanks so much for looking, I'm glad to know I haven't broken it at least!"

"You're welcome, lassie, I'm happy to help."

"Well, we'll be on our way," Cate said. Jack said his goodbyes to his grandfather, giving the elderly man a clap on the back and half a hug. Cate found it charming that he treated his grandfather with such respect. Cate thanked him again before leaving and making her way to the car with Jack.

"Well," Jack said as they climbed into the car, "at least you've got the official word that you haven't broken it."

"Yeah, that's a relief. I've not ruined my inheritance only a few weeks in." Cate laughed.

The rest of the ride was quiet. It still surprised Cate that the watch was working as it should. She hated to feel this way, but she wondered if the older Mr. Reid was certain of his diagnosis. Her thoughts turned to how adamant he was about not having the watch serviced. It seemed strange. Did he not want his lack of experience to show if there was something wrong with the watch? Or was he worried about the piece being stolen or damaged? Either way, it seemed odd. Surely there were professional jewelers who could be trusted. Perhaps Gayle would have an answer. It couldn't hurt to have someone else check it.

When they arrived back on the estate, Cate thanked Jack for taking her into town. He helped her carry her bounty from the town's library into the castle's library.

Cate would look at the files later. She wanted to stretch her legs with Riley on a walk around the estate before dinner. Before heading out, she checked her email to see if there was a response from Gayle and found one waiting for her. Gayle never took long to respond.

Dear Cate,

To our knowledge, Lady MacKenzie never had the watch serviced at any outside locations. I don't believe either of us (meaning myself and Mr. Smythe) ever knew of any issues that she had with the timepiece. Mr. Smythe did indicate that she usually trusted Mr.

Stanley Reid (Jack Reid's grandfather) with mechanical work and suggested that you check with him if you believe the timepiece may be malfunctioning.

I hope you continue to adapt to your new surroundings with ease and find Scottish country life charming! If you need anything else, please do not hesitate to reach out.

Best,
    Gayle

Cate frowned at her computer. So, Lady MacKenzie had never had trouble with the watch. And she trusted Jack's grandfather to maintain it. It was another vote of confidence in Jack's grandfather as a watch repairman; and no suggestions to take it to an experienced jeweler. It seemed rather odd, but Cate guessed they had much more experience than she in these matters. Perhaps the watch was that valuable that even they did not trust it to leave Cate's care. Vowing to be extra careful with the watch from now on, Cate went to find Riley for his pre-dinner walk of the estate with her.

Cate and Riley enjoyed a quiet and uneventful evening after their walk and dinner. Cate curled up with some old photo albums she had found, not looking for much of anything, just enjoying the photos of the castle's past and her ancestors, however they were related. Soon she dozed off on the chaise and thought it might be best to head to bed, hoping she could sleep after the day's events. Molly's joke about the castle rattled through her head again. The passage from the book came to mind. What Molly intended as a joke may turn out to be a warning.

CHAPTER 20

s she crawled into bed, she tried to bring her research to the forefront of her mind and push the entry about the castle from the library book to the far reaches of her mind. Cate was not one to give in to silly legend and lure. She had heard enough of these tales. As a historian, there were always tales abounding about hauntings and ghosts, unexplainable events, legends that drove history. They were rarely unexplainable, rarely true, and usually embellished beyond belief to make them more interesting for fireside chatting and evening dinner conversation.

Still, Cate had experienced some things described in the blurb. She almost wrote it off as her overly tired imagination, but reading someone else's experiences, experiences that matched with hers, seemed to confirm that this was not a figment of her imagination.

As she lay awake in bed, she wondered if her new home was haunted? "Cate," she said aloud, "you're being ridiculous. There are no such things as ghosts." She thought perhaps saying it aloud would make it more real. Still, she lay awake replaying the events she experienced, sitting up a few times, swearing she saw something move in the corner of the room or heard something.

As she tossed and turned, she became more paranoid, as one did when they dwelt on things of this nature. Climbing out of bed, Cate paced the room. Nothing in the corners, she noted. Expanding her pacing area, she made her way around the sitting room. Nothing there either, as she well knew, despite her paranoia. Still unable to sleep, she made her way around the castle. Perhaps the walk would tire her out enough to sleep.

Cate wandered through the massive hallways. Moonlight drenched everything, giving many areas an eerie glow. It did little to ease her fear. Cate forced her mind to appreciate the beauty in what she saw. She wandered in and out of rooms, trying to take in details, forcing her mind to focus on mundane things rather than allowing it to go at lightning speed to ghost stories.

In one bedroom closet, Cate found a box of personal belongings from someone who must have lived at the castle. Cate sifted through the box. Among the personal effects, there appeared to be several journals. These piqued Cate's curiosity, triggering her inner historian. Ghost stories were pushed to the far corners of her mind as excitement over personal journals from an occupant of the castle rose to the forefront.

Paging through, Cate's heart leapt at seeing the hand-written pages. Most people would have yawned and tossed them back in the box, but history coursed through Cate's veins. Finding a direct link to the past like this, a primary source, was every historian's dream. Cate flipped through each journal. She considered reading the journals now, but she was getting tired. Wanting to savor the moment and enjoy them, she collected all journals from the box and made her way back to her room. She set the journals on the side table next to the chaise, excited to look at them tomorrow.

Returning to the bedroom, she climbed back into bed. Riley lifted his head to acknowledge her return, then settled back in with a big sigh. With something new on her mind, sleep came more easily to Cate despite her excitement over her find.

Cate awoke the next morning still excited about her discovery, feeling like a kid at Christmas. After jumping out of bed, she quickly dressed for the day, glancing at the journals and admiring her discovery before heading down to breakfast.

During breakfast, Cate determined that she would begin her day with her research items from the library after a leisurely morning walk with Riley. She would save the journals for an evening treat. After the walk, she spent the morning taking detailed notes on the materials borrowed from the town's library, making it through about half of the items. After lunch, Cate further investigated the closet where she found the journals. With Riley in tow, Cate spent the better part of the afternoon inspecting its contents. She found several interesting items of clothing from previous decades and some framed photographs leading her to conclude that the belongings in the room where the property of Mary MacKenzie, Gertrude's mother. This made Cate even more excited to read the journals, she hoped they may give her some information into her family's connection to the castle.

Much to her chagrin, just prior to dinner, she received a call from the town's librarian. Word had gotten out that the assistant allowed Cate to borrow materials from the private collection. The librarian explained that there was a "mistake" made when the assistant allowed her to remove those items from the library and asked that Cate return them as soon as possible. Cate assured Mrs. Campbell that she would bring them back first thing in the morning. Unfortunately for Cate, that meant she would have to finish her notes this evening before returning the materials in the morning. Not that she minded, but she was anxious to look at the journals before the library materials. She buckled down after dinner and finished her remaining notes on the items she had borrowed.

The following morning, Cate decided to be adventurous and use the estate's car to drive herself into town to return the documents. After informing Mrs. Fraser that she wouldn't be there for lunch, she loaded Riley into the car with her and headed into town. She made it to the library without driving on the incorrect side of the road. Feeling proud of herself, she parked the car near the same spot that Jack chose when he brought her to town.

She returned the documents to the library and thanked the librarian, telling her that despite it being a mistake, she appreciated access to the documents to study and take notes on. She informed her she was well-trained in document preservation and assured her that the items were in the same shape as when they left the library. While the librarian agreed, she remarked that document preservation was best left to librarians. Cate found the remark humorous, it was quite a stretch to infer only librarians knew how to handle documents properly.

Afterwards, Cate explored the town with Riley. She was excited to see what the town offered and wanted to admire its unique charm. The new smells entertained Riley, and he enjoyed the attention he received from the local townspeople. Cate found many charming shops that she was sure she would enjoy exploring over and over. A few shop owners were dog-friendly, so she took her time exploring those shops with Riley. Many of the shop owners and staff were curious to meet her since she was the new owner of the largest property in town. Most of them were also curious since she was an American. Cate had many interesting conversations with the locals and most of them made her feel very welcome.

She spent the better part of the day exploring the town, electing to lunch at the local pub again. She made it home just before dinner. In her former life, she would have made herself a bowl of cereal for dinner but here Mrs. Fraser had prepared her a nice light meal after her day out. She had to admit, she was getting used to being taken care of.

Despite being eager to read the journals she found, Cate found herself exhausted after her day of exploring and opted for some light reading before bed. She turned in early in the hopes of getting an early start to her day tomorrow.

After her sleepless night the night before, Cate slept soundly and arose early the next morning. She took a short walk with Riley after breakfast before a storm blew in, bringing thunder, lightning, and soaking rains to the area. It was the perfect opportunity to stay inside for the day with her prized find. She hoped the distraction would keep her mind from wandering to the haunting rumors. In weather like this, every castle seemed haunted.

Before settling down with the journals, Cate retrieved the family bible containing the family tree in case she needed it to help identify names brought up in the journals. Sitting down with a cup of hot chocolate and a plate of cookies courtesy of Mrs. Fraser, Cate curled up on her chaise with what she considered a good book. Riley lounged on the rug near the foot of her chaise, enjoying the fire that Mr. Fraser built to take the chill off the rainy day.

Cate picked up the first journal on the top of the stack. She glanced through it, trying to find any dates or markings that showed the year the journal was written or the order of these journals. She wanted to read the journals in order, if possible. There were no markings, but she noticed something odd. Several pages appeared to be missing from each journal, torn from the books. It was such a shame, Cate mused. Perhaps though, the main ideas were intact.

Cate observed the handwriting in some books was messier than in others. She thought perhaps it showed that the person was getting older. Or, it could have meant that they were writing hurriedly. She tried to use this to piece together an order but wasn't able to.

Giving up on trying to determine the order, Cate closed them all except the first one she picked up and set them aside. She began to read the first page.

... heard the soft music as if it were floating on the air up the stairs. It was nice to hear the sounds of life in the castle again no matter how strange. I stood at the top of the stairs with my eyes closed enjoying the sounds of the music. I imagined all the people below in elegant gowns of their time period, dancing impeccably, laughing, drinking, enjoying. I thought of sneaking down to have a peek but I still have not brought myself to explore during these events.

Cate set the book down, taking a sip of her hot chocolate and a bite of a cookie. The entry seemed to describe a party being held at the castle. It seemed strange to her that the lady of the house was not attending the party. How odd, Cate thought. Perhaps these journals were not Mary MacKenzie's or maybe she wrote them at a young age and wasn't talking about Dunhaven at all but rather her family home. She didn't know much about any of her predecessors so it was possible that Mary MacKenzie also came from a wealthy family who would have hosted such parties. As a young child, she wouldn't have been in attendance. Cate imagined Mary as a small child longing to go to her parents' ball, standing at the top of a grand staircase listening to the music play, watching for a glimpse of the ladies in their elegant gowns as they passed by.

Cate's thoughts turned toward the journal. Perhaps these were older than she realized, coming from a childhood version of Mary. She studied the first entry; it didn't look like a child's handwriting, although Cate couldn't be sure. Penmanship was a different matter in the era when Mary was a child, so it was comprehensible that this could have been the writing of someone around the age of ten. If these were her childhood journals, not only would it be interesting to see things from a child's perspective in a different era, but that may also explain the torn out pages. Perhaps they were failed attempts at making an entry, or those that showed poor penmanship, ink blots or something else careless a child may have done and torn out to dispose of. Maybe an older Mary re-read her journals and tore out things she didn't want to remember or keep recorded, childish thoughts that she perhaps regretted later.

Cate was still fascinated by the journals. There were so many possibilities; it was such an intimate way of knowing someone, reading their inner thoughts. Even if they didn't provide her with information about her own family, they would be fascinating to read from a historical perspective.

Before reading further, Cate determine some research on Mary MacKenzie may help not only to learn more about her background but also to have a better visualization for the words written in her journal. Cate set the journal aside, intending to grab her laptop, a pen and notepad. The appeal of another sip of hot chocolate and a second cookie were too strong for her, though, and she lay back on the chaise for an extra moment enjoying the snack. The fire gave the room a warm coziness despite its size. Cate glanced outside, watching the rain fall steadily down from the gray sky. She took a moment to remember her panic and uncertainty about moving here. It seemed silly to her now. She had been here for a few weeks and was already settling in and finding herself happy and very much at home. Even the cooler weather and rainy day didn't dampen her growing fondness of her new home. She took another bite of her cookie. And she couldn't beat the food, she thought to herself.

Cate spent another few moments enjoying the snack and the dreary day while she let her thoughts slip away to imagining the great ball Mary spoke of in her journal. She pictured people in fancy gowns swirling around the room, laughing, enjoying each other's company. What a different life they must have led, Cate thought, both because of the time period and their upper-class lifestyle. Things changed quite a bit in the almost one hundred odd years since Mary was a child.

Cate tried to imagine a world without computers, lacking instant access to information and other people, where the written word was the most common form of communication and of recording thoughts. How different life must have been, perhaps simpler in some ways despite the absence of modern conveniences.

Cate finished her cookie and the rest of her hot chocolate then forced herself off the chaise to get her materials. She began by noting the dates of birth years and death years for Mary from the family bible and her maiden name, Campbell, to give some context to when she may have been writing the journals. Setting up her laptop, Cate navigated to one of the online ancestry records sites and began searching for any information she could find on Mary MacKenzie née Campbell. There wasn't much information but from what she pieced together, Mary had two sisters and one brother. The third child of four, she had been born into an affluent family but one that did not have any titles associated with their family legacy. She was twenty-four years old when she married Oliver, who was ten years her senior.

Cate didn't spend too much time digging into Mary's lineage since it wouldn't have coincided with hers, but she got enough information to have a basic understanding of Mary's young life while reading the journals.

Before closing her laptop, Cate did the customary check of her email account. Nothing but ads, it amazed Cate how quiet her life had become without the constant barrage of student requests or departmental demands from Jeff. She closed her laptop and set it aside just as Mrs. Fraser brought a tray of lunch in. Cate hadn't realized the time. She was thankful to see Mrs. Fraser had prepared a light salad for lunch. Cate felt stuffed with cookies so she was happy for the lighter lunch. Mrs. Fraser cleared away the now empty cookie plate and hot chocolate mug, asking Cate how her reading was going.

"I hope you don't mind, I took it upon meself to bring your lunch up to you. Figured you were all nice and cozy here, why move yourself just for lunch."

"Thanks, Mrs. Fraser, I appreciate that. I am cozy. Although, I think you may spoil me."

"Well, isn't a lady in the world that doesn't deserve some spoiling now and again."

Cate smiled at her as she finished clearing the dishes and headed out of the room. After lunch, Cate thought she would stretch her legs a bit, take Riley for a brief trip outside and revisit the room where she found the journals to see if any of the torn out pages were lurking in the box.

The rain was still coming down at a good clip. Cate was glad she invested in a small raincoat for Riley, otherwise the soaking rains that poured from the sky would have drenched the poor pup. Despite remaining mostly dry, Riley was unhappy as the thunder rumbled above them, giving suspicious glances at the sky and offering the occasional bark in retort to the loud sounds. Even with the bad weather though, Cate admired the beauty of the Scottish countryside. Mists clung to the hillsides, shrouding them as if with a fluffy blanket. It was no wonder stories of hauntings at the castle were bandied about. The setting couldn't be more perfect for a haunting, Cate thought, as she listened to the thunder grumble overhead and the fog surround the neighboring countryside and even shroud part of the castle.

After Riley finished his duties outside, Cate entered through the servant's entrance of the castle, hanging their soaked coats in the entryway to dry. She made her way back to the bedroom closet where she found the journals. Looking through the box, she found no additional pages. She was disappointed but still hopeful that she would learn a great deal from the few pages she had to work with.

Cate went back to her sitting room and again settled on her chaise. She noticed that Mr. Fraser had taken the opportunity while she was out to refresh the fire. It burned steadily in the fireplace, keeping the chilly day at bay. Even with the warmth of the fire, Cate draped a blanket over her legs and curled up under it. Seeing the blanket unfurled on Cate's lap, Riley leapt onto the chaise and curled himself into the crook of her legs for a nice nap. Cate gave him a pat on his head as he let his head rest against her calf.

She picked up the journal again, giving the first entry a quick re-read. Something about it seemed odd to her, but she couldn't put her finger on what it was. She thought for a few moments, trying to see if she could identify the source of that impression but she wasn't able to. She chalked it up to a barrier in language between generations and turned the page to read more.

The next entry seemed to detail a similar experience. Mary wrote about the buzz of having guests in the house. Again, Mary noted that she tried to "stay out of sight" and "take everything in." Not uncommon for a child in a large estate during the era of "children should be seen and not heard." Still, it appeared Mary was on the verge of adulthood or a very mature child. She wrote as though she were much older than a youngster who would have been unwelcome at parties and other household events.

Cate began to think perhaps this was why the writing seemed so odd to her. She read the next entry to see if it gave her impression more credence.

... strange to think I could meet my husband as a young man or child or at least see him once again. The very thought gives me goose pimples and the feeling as though someone has walked over my grave. As inviting as it seems, it is terribly dangerous. I can see why my husband

The page ended. Cate turned to the next page, but the entry did not continue. It appeared several pages were torn out and then another entry appeared which seemed to be unrelated to this one. Cate set the book down, confused by what she just read. Mary MacKenzie referenced her husband. "Well, that's odd, Riley," Cate said aloud to the dog. "Looks like this entry was made by Mary as an adult, after her marriage. Why is she not attending events in her own home?" The pup didn't offer any answers.

Granted there were entries missing but there weren't

even close to enough pages gone to have grown from a child-hood Mary to an adult one, so the entire journal had to be from Mary as an adult, Cate surmised. Cate sat dumb-founded, pondering the entries she read. She couldn't under-stand why if Mary was an adult, married or otherwise, she wasn't attending parties within either her parents' home or her husband's. If the parties had been in her husband's home, Mary would have played an integral role in hosting the event, even if the couple were not living at the castle yet. If it were the former, her parents would have paraded Mary among the guests with her primary goal having been to secure a suitable suitor and a successful match for marriage. Why would Mary have been hiding upstairs, not able to bring herself to even sneak a glance at the event?

Cate thought perhaps Mary was ill, however, if she was physically ill, most likely the party would have been post-poned. If it hadn't been, she would have attended it, ill or not. Women of that era were informed that they should not take ill often as it may displease their husband.

If she was mentally ill, that was quite a different story, but there didn't seem to be any signs of mental instability in the writings. Perhaps that was why several pages were missing though, Cate thought. Perhaps Mary was unstable and had ripped pages from the diary or someone else had and only left the ones that sounded sane.

Perhaps she would know more when she read all the journals. Perhaps there would be a clue in one of them to point her toward what may have happened to either the journals or Mary. Cate checked her watch, about an hour and a half remained before dinner. She read a few more brief entries before stretching her legs and taking Riley for a walk.

Cate spent the next hour reading the rest of the first jour-nal. As interesting as it was, it gave her no more clues about what was happening. It covered more of the same experiences, or rather snippets of experiences. Mary discussed a few parties she attended, and a little about raising her daughter after her husband's death. It gave Cate a little more context knowing that Mary was writing after her husband's death, but the mystery of why she avoided social events in the castle deepened.

Standing up and stretching, Cate noticed the rain had slowed up a bit. She gathered Riley to take him for a walk before dinner. She didn't come to any conclusions after pondering what was going on in the journals while they were outside. She hoped that the remaining journals would shed more light on the matter and planned to read another during her dinner.

Heading back inside, she found both Mr. and Mrs. Fraser in her sitting room when she arrived. Mr. Fraser was tending to the fire again while Mrs. Fraser arranged the blanket on the chaise, her tray of food placed on the edge.

"How are you enjoying this beautiful Scottish weather we're having?" Mr. Fraser said, adding some logs to the fire.

"It's a nice day to stay in!" Cate answered.

"That it is," Mrs. Fraser agreed. "Is there anything else you'll be needing?"

"No, that's all, thanks. Why don't you two go home early and get settled in, this weather is terrible, I don't want anyone out in it on my account."

Mr. and Mrs. Fraser exchanged glances. "Well," Mrs. Fraser hedged. "I'd like to finish the dishes from dinner and I'm sure Mr. Fraser would like to add some logs to the fire before we leave for the night."

"Oh, don't worry about that, Mrs. Fraser. I'm capable of washing a dish or two and I can add some logs if we get cold enough. Please go home and get out of this dreary weather."

"Well, I guess if you insist, Lady Cate. Then we'll see you tomorrow morning."

"I do insist," Cate said. "See you tomorrow!"

With that they both left, leaving Cate to her dinner. She settled in with the second journal from the stack, hoping to find some answers. After reading about half, Cate was no closer to learning the truth about anything. Again, the entries were vague and brief. Several pages were missing, causing the entries to be nothing more than snippets or pieces of a full entry. It made it very hard to read or glean anything from.

Cate glanced through the other three journals again. All had pages removed. She sighed; they likely contained more of the same. She considered diving into the third journal but remembered her promise to Mrs. Fraser. Glancing at her empty dish sitting on the tray, she figured she better take care of the dishes before she did anything else. Picking up the tray, she headed downstairs to the kitchen. She expected to find a few dishes from the dinner preparation waiting in the sink to be washed. Instead, the sink was empty, all dishes cleaned, dried and put away. Cate shook her head, Mrs. Fraser had been kind enough to clean everything, leaving Cate with only her own dishes and utensils to wash.

It was quick work since Cate had so little to do. She washed, dried and returned everything to its appropriate place. She tidied up the kitchen a bit, so it looked as though she had never been there, hoping Mrs. Fraser would appreciate that, then headed back to her sitting room.

The fire was dying out and, since Cate planned on staying up longer, she threw a few small logs on top and poked them around with the poker, before plopping back onto the chaise and cuddling under a blanket with Riley. She picked up the third journal and began to read. About halfway through the journal, Cate was frustrated and tired. She decided it was a good stopping point for the day and set the book down on the table. Collecting Riley, she took him for a short trip outside before heading to bed.

Despite being tired, Cate laid awake for a long while before falling asleep. She couldn't stop her mind from going over the questions she had about the journals. Realizing she may never have the answers to any of these questions, she dozed off.

CHAPTER 21

The next day brought bright sunshine and warmer weather, a complete contrast to the previous day. Cate enjoyed most of the day outside, giving Riley a break from being cooped up in the castle. She also wanted a break from her research and the journals, both of which were proving fruitless. Sometimes the best thing to break through a brick wall was to take a break.

Cate spent most of the day enjoying the grounds of Dunhaven Castle. She loved watching Riley enjoy them too. He bounded happily around the yard with a silly grin on his face, stopping to sniff the grass or the air every so often. Seeing Riley so happy with his surroundings added to Cate's feeling that she made the right decision in moving. Aberdeen was fast becoming a distant memory in Cate's mind.

After lunch and an afternoon walk, Cate spent more time looking through trunks and boxes in the castle. Not wanting to re-examine Mary's belongings, she picked a different room. Finding a closet full of trunks and boxes in one of the other bedrooms, Cate glanced through them, trying to make a mental inventory of what was there so she could explore it in depth later. It looked like some trunks held clothes from a long gone-by era, from another century. She also found some hand-written letters that looked promising to explore. She sat down on the floor, taking one out to read.

As she read, she absentmindedly began to rub her thumb on the watch that hung around her neck, a subconscious tic that was becoming a habit. As she did, she heard the familiar loud ticking and slowing down of the watch. She sighed, annoyed that the watch was misbehaving again, particularly after she had been assured nothing was wrong with it.

She looked at the watch face; sure enough, the second hand ticked slower and slower. Grabbing her phone, she decided that she would record a video of what the watch was doing to share with Jack and his grandfather. Something was not right, perhaps the video would help them diagnose the problem. Swiping to unlock the phone, Cate noticed the large letters on the lock screen: NO SERVICE.

Cate crinkled her brow, not understanding why she lost her cell signal. Even with the spotty signals she had been getting in the Scottish countryside, she had not experienced much of an issue anywhere in the castle or on the property.

Cate selected the camera app on her phone and switched it to video mode. She aimed the camera at the watch and began to narrate the video. "As you can see," she said, "the seconds are ticking by on the video but not on the watch, it's definitely slower than it should be. And no matter what I do," Cate balanced the phone and began to shimmy the watch a bit, then wind it again, "it doesn't help. See", she said, aiming the camera back on the watch after bobbling the phone to wind it, "still slow. Then, sooner or later, it's back to normal like nothing was wrong." She swiped the watch face to clear it of any fingerprints and continued to film when abruptly, the watch started to tick faster and faster until it began to keep perfect time again. "See what I mean," Cate narrated, "now it's back to normal, I don't get it!" Cate let the video run a few more seconds so they could see that the watch was now keeping perfect time then shut it off.

She planned on sending the video to Jack via text message but remembered her lack of signal. She opened her text app, ready to climb to her feet to find a spot with a signal, only to discover the signal returned. It was odd, Cate had never moved yet the signal, not there moments ago, was now extremely strong. The crinkle on her brow deepened. Were the two incidents related? Was there some kind of electro-magnetic disturbance that affected both the watch and her cell phone? Or maybe the signal was just intermittent within the closet. Either way, Cate would send the video off to Jack with a note describing it and asking him to show it to his grandfather whenever he got a chance. Perhaps he would have some answers that would explain this.

Cate turned her phone display off. Her stomach growled, and she noticed that it was almost dinnertime. She would continue exploring these items another day. Collecting Riley, she carried him back to her room, setting him in his bed while she freshened up before dinner.

After she finished her dinner, Cate spent more time reading Mary's journals, hoping that she would find at least a shred of information. Polishing off another journal before bed lead her no closer to the truth and gained her no further information beyond a few pieces of stories. The disjointed nature from the missing pages was becoming aggravating. It was like trying to build a jigsaw puzzle with half the pieces removed.

That night, Cate laid awake, tossing and turning in bed struggling to piece together the puzzle without all the pieces. A habit that she often indulged in with her research projects, it never led to any solutions. Nevertheless, she couldn't stop herself from obsessing nor stop her mind from spinning. As the time passed, Cate's theories ranged from a mental illness to the idea that these were stories Mary penned. Cate considered the latter. Perhaps to pass the time, Mary wrote stories in a journal rather than accounts of her life. Perhaps the torn out pages were her form of editing. As her mind parsed through theories, Cate stared at the timepiece clasped in her hand. She wondered if Mary ever wore this around her neck. Staring at the pendant, she willed it to provide her with some information from Mary.

Unfortunately, the timepiece wasn't talking. Cate frowned at it, letting it rest back on her chest. She listened to its rhythmic ticking, thinking about all the generations before her that had worn this watch and listened to the same sounds. Her mind turned toward the video she sent to Jack. She wondered if he had shown it to his grandfather. He hadn't texted back other than to confirm receipt and indicate that he would show it to him. She hoped they could identify what the issue might be. Her mind again focused on the ticking noise; the watch was working, for the moment. She felt herself relaxing as she listened to the steady rhythm of the timepiece, dozing off to its calming sounds. Cate dreamt of house parties and balls of days gone by held at the castle.

CHAPTER 22

*T*he next morning brought more rain to the area; a foggy mist enveloped the castle. Looking out the windows was like looking through a veil of fabric that had been stretched from the sky to the horizon. The cool and damp weather kept Cate inside for most of the day, only venturing out to take Riley for brief walks. Cate went back to the closet she explored the day before, continuing her investigation. Having dreamt of fancy parties and balls all night, she, like a kid in a candy store, wanted to look at the clothes and maybe even try some on. They looked like they had been from the 1800s, perhaps near the 1850s. She'd never worn legitimate period clothing before; she was curious to know what it would feel like to wear a frilly hooped skirt characteristic of this period.

Cate returned to the room's closet after breakfast and began opening the trunks filled with the clothing. She took dress after dress out, holding them up to imagine what it might look like on her before folding them with care and placing them back into the trunk.

"What do you think, Riley?" she asked the small dog,

holding up a pink and white dress against her body. Riley cocked his head to the side as she spun around the room with it against her. "Do I look pretty?" Riley's dark almond eyes sparkled at her. "Should I try it on so you can really tell?"

Cate giggled a bit while she slipped her clothes off and the dress on, feeling like a child trying on her mother's clothes. She did her best to fasten the dress in the back, appreciating why most women needed a lady's maid to assist them with dressing. Cate felt the weightiness of the dress on her body; it was heavy like a good drapery. She tried to swirl in it, finding it more awkward than she expected. As luck would have it, there was a full-length mirror hidden behind a sheet tucked in the back of the closet. Pulling the sheet down, Cate viewed herself, pulling her hair up to complete the centuries old look. She gazed at herself for another minute, wondering what her life would have been like in this era. Seeing the watch dangling, she picked it up and began to rub it, wondering who from this era wore it.

Finally, her mind snapped back to reality. "Well, Riley," she said swinging around in the dress, "what do you think of the full effect?" She turned to face the small dog, but his spot was empty. The smile disappeared from her face, now where did he get off to, she wondered.

"Riley! Riley!" Cate called out a few times but saw no sign of the small pup. She checked around the trunks and other items in the closet. She looked around the room, there was no sign of him. "RILEY!" she called louder. "RILEY, COME!" Still nothing. It was unusual for Riley not to listen when she called him, Cate started to worry that he may have wandered off.

Widening her search, she looked around the bedroom. Again, she saw no sign of Riley. She called out a few more times as she looked around the room, but he didn't respond and she didn't see him. Cate was becoming concerned about the dog. She feared he might have gotten himself lost or trapped. Living in a place this size, it could take them days to find him, if not longer. Cate felt panic set in. He was her entire life, she would be heartbroken if something happened to him.

She tried to calm herself and think logically. He had to be somewhere close. She double-checked the closet again, then the bedroom. Heading to the hall, she looked up and down, trying to decide which way to go first. The heaviness of the dress made it difficult for her to move around but her worry over Riley stopped her from changing first.

Cate called down the hall, facing in both directions. She saw nothing. Most of the doors were closed so he couldn't have gotten in those rooms. Cate wondered if he made his way back to their bedroom. She tried to run, finding it awkward in the piles of fabric that surrounded her. Picking up her skirts to the best of her abilities, she hurried herself down the hall, making her way to her suite. She glanced inside, finding it empty. Racing through the sitting room, she looked in the bedroom area. It was empty, also, and even stranger, Riley's bed seemed to be missing. She hadn't moved it, but it was not there. Cate wondered what was going on. Perhaps Mrs. Fraser moved it while cleaning.

Cate retraced her steps to where she had been. This time, she continued down the other way, making her way to the main staircase. She would look there and then perhaps enlist help.

Arriving at the top of the stairs, she saw Mrs. Fraser walking on the lower level across the giant entryway.

"Oh, Mrs. Fraser! Mrs. Fraser!" Cate called, out of breath.

The woman turned to look at her and Cate realized she was not Mrs. Fraser. Instead, another, younger woman returned Cate's gaze.

"Oh, I'm sorry, I thought you were Mrs. Fraser," Cate apologized. Cate bypassed any pleasantries, in a panic to find Riley. "I'm looking for my dog, Riley, have you seen him?" Receiving no response, she continued, "Could you find Mrs. Fraser and ask her to help me look?"

At the bottom of the stairs, the girl's eyes were wide, and she was white as a sheet. Cate wondered what was wrong with her; she looked as though she had seen a ghost. Abruptly, the girl turned and fled the room. Cate wrinkled her forehead, was she running to tell Mrs. Fraser? She had made it sound urgent, but it wasn't an emergency. Cate then realized she still was still wearing the centuries old dress; no wonder the girl reacted that way, the poor girl assumed she had seen a ghost.

It was of no consequence now. Cate turned to make her way back down the hall, intent on finding Riley. As she walked, she wondered who the woman was and why she was in the castle. Perhaps Mrs. Fraser found her replacement and was training her, but she mentioned nothing to Cate, which seemed odd.

Cate pushed the thought aside; she'd deal with that mystery later. Right now she must find Riley. She checked the timepiece to determine how long he had been missing. "Seriously?" she exclaimed, exasperated. The timepiece was almost stopped again. "Useless! I don't know how long he's been gone!" she said out loud and she shook the watch in frustration. Feeling guilty, she patted it, rubbing it gently almost as an apology; a silly gesture since the watch wasn't a living thing, but it made her feel better. As if on cue, the watch started to tick faster and faster until it returned to normal.

"At least one thing is sorted." She sighed. "Ok, Cate, think, he's a little dog, just calm down, he couldn't have gotten far."

Cate spoke to herself out loud to calm herself and think rationally. "Let's retrace our steps."

Cate entered the bedroom and opened the door to the closet. As she stepped inside, shock and relief washed over her. Riley was sitting on the floor. "RILEY!" Cate cried, rushing over to scoop up the small dog. "I thought I had lost you! Where have you been?" Cate hugged him close, kissing the top of his little head. A few tears of relief escaped from her eyes and rolled down her cheeks. Riley gave her an appreciative lap on her face for all the attention, not seeming to understand why Cate was so exasperated.

Cate breathed a sigh of relief; she had been so worried about the little pup. She took an extra moment to hold him close, still wondering where he could have gone. It appeared he had been in the closet the entire time. After a moment, Cate figured it didn't matter, at least her precious Riley was back and she took that as a win. "We better go tell Mrs. Fraser that we found you, Riley!" Cate stood up, feeling the weight of the dress. "I better change my clothes first though!"

As she changed, she caught sight of herself in the mirror. Her makeup was smudged from shedding a few tears of relief. She thought she better clean up before going to see Mrs. Fraser so, after she changed, she gathered Riley up and hurried to her bedroom.

As she went to the bathroom, she noticed Riley's bed back in its normal spot. It was not here when she looked before. Then again, she had been certain Riley had been missing when he had been in the closet the entire time.

She fixed her smeared makeup and headed downstairs, Riley in tow, to speak with Mrs. Fraser. Arriving in the kitchen, she found Mrs. Fraser preparing her lunch. The other woman was nowhere in sight. "You can call off the emergency, Mrs. Fraser, I found Riley."

"Emergency?" Mrs. Fraser looked up from her work, not understanding what Cate was talking about.

"Yes, didn't the other girl tell you? I thought I lost Riley, but I found him, thankfully."

"Other girl?" Mrs. Fraser asked, perplexed.

"The other girl. I saw her in the entry hall. I told her to come and get you to help find Riley. She ran down the hall, did she not tell you?"

"I'm the only one in the place, Lady Cate. No cleaning service here today and both men are outside."

Cate was dumbfounded. She struggled to get the word "what" out to Mrs. Fraser. Clearing her throat she followed up with, "I thought…" she stammered, "I thought maybe you hired your replacement and were training her?"

"Nay, I haven't hired a replacement to train, Lady Cate. As far as I know, we are the only ones here."

"Mrs. Fraser, I saw a woman standing right at the bottom of the stairs. She was wearing a long black dress and a white apron."

"Long black dress and white apron?" Mrs. Fraser said, puzzled.

"Yes, I SAW her, no mistaking it. She stood right there in front of me, I spoke to her!"

"Did she speak to you?"

"Well, no." Cate said after some thought. "But I didn't imagine her."

Mrs. Fraser went back to her work without a word. Cate pursed her lips. "I can't believe I'm actually going to say this but… do you think she could have been a… a ghost?"

Mrs. Fraser laughed. "A ghost? Lady Cate, you don't believe that nonsense, do you?"

"Well, no, I mean, I didn't but I read in a book from the library that many people have claimed this castle is haunted. I never believed in that stuff either but, how else can I explain the woman who was standing there, dressed oddly, now that I think about it. But she was there plain as day."

Mrs. Fraser continued to chuckle. "She didn't disappear in a puff of smoke or float down the hall, did she?"

"No, no she didn't do any of that, I don't mean a story-book ghost. What if she was a spirit trapped in this castle? How else do you explain what I saw?"

"I'm sorry to poke fun, Lady Cate, but I dare say it was your imagination running wild after having those silly tales planted in your head."

Cate considered the woman's words. "So, Lady MacKenzie never mentioned anything strange happening? No 'hauntings' when she lived here?"

"Nay, Lady Cate, no hauntings and Lady MacKenzie would have driven you right out of the castle with that talk. She hated those nasty rumors that the castle was haunted by people who died building it or whatever. I remember they contacted her before they wrote that bloody book. She wouldn't even return that man's call she was so furious about that rumor."

Cate pondered that information. Why would Lady MacKenzie be so adamant against any rumors of hauntings? Perhaps it was just one of those things that stuck in her craw. Either way, Cate couldn't deny what she saw. Then again, perhaps it was her overactive imagination. She was half panicked from having lost Riley, who ended up not being lost after all. Maybe her mind was playing tricks on her. She wasn't sure of anything anymore. Riley was there the entire time, but she had been sure he was gone. Was she sure the maid was there? Maybe she was letting her imagination run wild.

"Time for your lunch, Lady Cate! Did you want it in the dining room or the library?" Mrs. Fraser's announcement brought Cate's mind back to reality.

"Um, I think I'll take it in the library, thank you! Here, I can carry it up there." Cate set Riley down on the floor to take the tray.

"If you'd like. Thanks." Cate turned to leave the kitchen, calling Riley to follow behind her. "Oh, ah, Lady Cate?"

"Yes?" Cate said, turning to face Mrs. Fraser.

"I'm sure it was just your imagination earlier. I'll bet you were just tired and worried about Riley if you thought you lost him. I'm sure there's nothing to it." Mrs. Fraser smiled reassuringly to her.

"You're probably right, Mrs. Fraser. Thanks!"

Cate turned and left, making her way to the library with her lunch. She planned to read a book during lunch and then go over some notes she had collected about the castle and its history and create a plan for moving forward with her research.

Despite her best intentions, she couldn't keep her mind focused on research after what just occurred. The encounter with her "ghost" kept running through her mind over and over. As she did with most things, she picked the encounter apart, detail-by-detail.

The girl never spoke, to her memory, she did act like she saw Cate though. Her dress seemed strange, old-fashioned, as if from another era. Cate wondered if she imagined it, but she couldn't believe her mind could create something so lifelike.

After lunch, Cate saved Mrs. Fraser a trip and returned her tray to the kitchen. Afterwards, she explored the area where she saw the girl while on her search for Riley.

Standing in the entryway, Cate glanced around for any sign of the maid. She didn't know what she expected to find, but she looked for anything to lend credibility to what she saw. She stood where the girl had been, peering all around.

Nothing gave her any sign that anyone had been there earlier.

Cate climbed the main staircase and stood where she had been before, looking down to where she had seen the figure. She tried to imagine all the details in her head. She was certain it couldn't have been in her imagination, the details had been so real to her. So what was it she had experienced? She didn't believe in hauntings, but she had no other explanation for it.

As she pondered this, her phone chirped. She checked it to find a new text message from Jack. He had shown the video to his grandfather while running some errands in town. His grandfather said the watch, despite the behavior in the video, was functioning as it should and everything on the inside appeared to be ship-shape. He didn't think it was anything to worry about and suggested keeping it wound daily but nothing beyond that. He called the anomaly a tic of the mechanism, pun intended.

It was a frustrating response; Cate couldn't believe the watch was working, yet she had no reason to distrust Jack's grandfather's opinion. Perhaps it was, as he called it, a tic that the watch had developed. It never seemed to last long. Cate would continue to monitor it or see if she could reproduce it, but decided not to have it looked at further as suggested by both Gayle and Mr. Reid.

Cate texted a thanks to Jack and went back to staring at nothing trying to determine if she was going crazy or if she had seen a ghost. If the castle was haunted, Cate wondered why Mary never mentioned it in the journals. Perhaps she had, and those were the missing pages; that could explain the missing text. It sounded as though Lady MacKenzie didn't care for that talk, perhaps the entire family was sensitive to it and thus never mentioned it. Or perhaps Lady MacKenzie tried to remove all references her mother made to it by tearing out the journal pages that cited it.

After a few more minutes of pondering, Cate decided she, again, would not solve anything. She returned to the library to continue her work. Before resuming studying her notes, she took out her laptop and hunted down anything she could find on the web that discussed hauntings at the castle. Other than some conjecture on discussion boards and a few random posts on the author of *The Mysteries of Scotland*'s page, there was nothing.

She toyed with the idea of emailing Molly and telling her she may have been right about the castle being haunted but decided against it, afraid Molly might think she was becoming a mad eccentric after only a few weeks in the castle.

Cate returned to her work and made a copy of the family tree so she could study and annotate it. She also noted that she discovered Mary's journals. She had a few letters from another era too, but she didn't know to whom they belonged. Cate had planned to look at the letters after she finished toying with the dresses but losing Riley had distracted her. She made a note to explore them further.

Cate decided that she would continue to explore the letters tomorrow. She wondered if she could also reproduce the issue with the watch and her cell phone's loss of service. Her mind wandered further, pondering if she could reproduce the ghost. Maybe she should hold a séance. She watched enough of the campy 1960s soap opera, Dark Shadows, to know the basic tenets. She laughed out loud at the thought of her, Mr. and Mrs. Fraser and Jack sitting around a table, hands touching in a circle calling out to the ghosts of the past to hear and answer them. It all seemed silly when she considered it, but, it didn't take away the idea that she had seen a girl dressed in clothes that appeared to be from another era standing at the foot of the main staircase staring at her as though she was the one out of place.

After a few hours of note-making and perusing the library's books for anything relevant about the castle, Cate called it a day for her work. She concluded that if the castle was haunted, she would be presented with more evidence.

Despite her convictions, Cate had a restless night of sleep. Waking at the least sound, expecting to see ghostly maids popping out of the corners. She swore at one point she awoke and could make out the figure of a woman floating around in a gently moving curtain sheer. She spent the night on pins and needles alone in the castle, waiting for the sun to rise and banish all ghosts from the halls.

CHAPTER 23

*F*inding herself exhausted again the next morning Cate decided she could use a break from her research. She surmised this may be the cause of her restlessness. While she realized that she hadn't been making good progress, she told herself there was no rush; she had a lifetime to continue. She also felt she needed a break from the castle. She headed into town for a little shopping and Scottish culture.

Cate again took Riley with her to explore the town. She left him in the car for a short period while it was still cool and cloudy in the morning so she could look in the few stores that didn't allow pets. Cate enjoyed her shopping trip and made a few purchases along the way, including a little porcelain figurine of a small dog that reminded her of Riley. She planned to send it to Gayle as a thank you for helping her unpack. She also purchased two postcards from a local shop owner that had a picture of Dunhaven Castle on the front.

After returning to the car, she dug a pen out of her purse and wrote three notes. One to Gayle to be sent with the porcelain dog expressing her thanks for the help; the second two she wrote on the postcards: one for Molly, her department secretary from Aberdeen College and one for her old neighbor, Mrs. Kline. Both cards were almost the same. Cate passed along her best wishes hoping both were doing well, said that her move had gone well and that the picture on the front showed her new home, Dunhaven Castle. On Mrs. Kline's card, she wrote a P.S. message stating that she was not joking, just in case there was any question.

Cate, with Riley in tow, headed to the post office to have the postcards mailed, and the figurine packaged and sent to Gayle. After taking care of this task, Cate did a little more shopping before having lunch in town. While there, she also bought a lovely flowering plant for Mr. and Mrs. Fraser as a housewarming gift, since the cottage would soon be under their ownership. While she didn't know the name of the plant, she thought the flowers were lovely and hoped the Frasers would enjoy it.

After lunch, Cate returned to Dunhaven Castle and spent the afternoon walking the grounds with Riley. She presented a very surprised Mrs. Fraser with the housewarming gift at dinner, telling her that the paperwork should soon be complete and the cottage would be all theirs. Mrs. Fraser seemed touched that Cate had given them a gift upon their acquiring the cottage. At the end of the day, Cate thought the break had done her good, and she was ready to return to her research tomorrow. She turned in early and got a sound night's sleep.

CHAPTER 24

$\mathcal{C}$ate awoke refreshed and determined to make some progress on at least one of her many mysteries. After having a hearty breakfast courtesy of Mrs. Fraser and taking Riley for a short walk around the property, Cate settled in the library, ready for work.

To begin, Cate needed to get re-organized. Her mind was a mess from the recent events, so she took out a blank sheet of paper and started to make some notes. She titled columns across the top, listing each thread that she was exploring: MacKenzie Family History/Dunhaven Castle History; My connection to MacKenzies; Temperamental Watch; Possible Haunting?.

In each column, Cate planned to make a list of questions, what she already learned from her research, and any materials she had come across with information about each.

In the first column about the MacKenzie's and castle history, Cate jotted a note that this was her primary research project and it was comprised of building a history of the castle and those who influenced its development. Cate already had a good deal of information on this including building plans for the castle and the family tree. She noted this and determined that additional work included finding more details about each individual and their impact on the castle through histories, letters, journals, and other similar sources. Cate noted that she found the journals of Mary MacKenzie, mother of Gertrude and some letters from the 1800s, but she did not have much information on these.

In her second column, Cate listed that her primary question was to determine what her relationship was to the MacKenzies, specifically Gertrude. She noted that she knew the relationship was on her father's side, as evidenced by the pictures she found. She also surmised that the relationship extended to her paternal grandfather, but beyond this she wasn't sure. She made a notation to find the birth record for her grandfather, Charles Kensie or possibly Charles MacKenzie. Also, she noted that perhaps Gayle would know the best way to track down this information.

In her next column, Cate jotted down that she witnessed the watch slowing down on three occasions. She recorded that on the last occurrence she noticed that her cell phone also had no service at the same time. She jotted a memo asking if this was connected or not. Also, she remarked that Mr. Reid said the watch was in perfect working order. Then, she listed that she would continue to monitor these two incidents.

After she finished cataloging this information, Cate took the watch from around her neck, opened it and laid it on the desk next to her. She intended to keep tabs on it to see if it slowed at all.

In the last column, Cate wrote about the book entry stating that the castle was believed to be haunted. She then detailed the two incidents that she experienced, the first one with the phantom music and the second with the phantom maid. Was she crazy making this column, she wondered? But there were several unexplained incidents that she needed to get to the bottom of. She hoped fleshing out the details in an organized way would help her.

After finishing her notes, Cate felt much more organized and ready to conquer her projects and solve her mysteries. She planned to continue to update her note sheet every few days to keep on top of all the information that she had and what she still needed to learn. Before diving into some books she pulled from the castle's library, Cate sent a quick email to Gayle.

Hi Gayle—I hope you are doing well. I dropped something in the post for you yesterday; I hope you receive it soon and like it!

I had another question for you. As I try to trace my ancestry back to the MacKenzies, I found that I need more information about my great-grandparents. Do you know the best way to find birth records? Specifically, I'm looking for the birth records of my grandfather so I can identify his parents. I'm not sure of where my grandfather was born, but his name was Charles Kensie or perhaps Charles MacKenzie. I'm not sure but I'm working off the premise that our last name was changed from MacKenzie to Kensie somewhere along the way.

Any help that you can provide would be much appreciated!

Thank you, Cate

Cate closed her laptop and looked at the stack of books she pulled from the shelves. "No time like the present," she said, diving into the first book.

In the course of a few morning hours, Cate felt she

learned a good deal about Scottish culture throughout some major periods of history. She was just finishing with one book describing the culture that surrounded the building of Scottish castles when Mrs. Fraser arrived with a tray of lunch.

"Thank you so much, Mrs. Fraser! Perfect timing!"

"Learning a lot, Lady Cate?"

"I think so! It's a new area of study for me, my focus was American History in graduate school, there's a lot I have to learn."

"With all these books, it almost looks like you're back in school!"

"Yes, it does!"

"Well, I'll leave you to your work."

"Thanks again, Mrs. Fraser."

Mrs. Fraser left Cate alone. Looking at the mountain of notes she made during the morning, Cate spent lunch re-reading them and organizing them.

After lunch, Cate thought she spent enough time hitting the books. She took Riley for another walk, then left him napping in the library and closed the door firmly behind her so she knew Riley couldn't get out and become lost. She made her way to the bedroom closet to have another look at the letters she found.

Once in the closet, Cate got comfy on the floor; pulling the letters out of the trunk. She scanned a few of them, trying to get a sense of who they were from or any defining information that would give her a more exact sense of when they were written.

As she read, spreading the letters out on the floor, Cate heard the familiar sound of slow ticking. Clutching the watch tighter, she lifted it and opened it, seeing that it was slowing down, just as it had in the past. Cate grabbed her cell phone, still holding the watch in her left hand. It read NO SERVICE in large white letters on the lock screen.

"Ah ha!" Cate exclaimed. "No signal and a slow watch. Now, if I move around, can I get my signal back?" Cate headed back to her bedroom. She knew she had a regular signal there. She hoped to make it before the watch returned to normal.

Standing up, holding the watch in her left hand and her cell phone in her right, she left the closet and the bedroom, turning toward her bedroom. She walked at a moderate pace, determined to get to the bedroom before the watch returned to normal timekeeping but also wanting to keep an eye on her cell service. For the duration of her walk, the phone read NO SERVICE.

As she entered the bedroom, the phone still read NO SERVICE. She walked around a bit, focusing on the phone and watch, but still never recovered service. The watch still ticked slowly. Cate sat on the chaise, trying to figure it out. She opened her phone and thumbed through a few apps, nothing would connect. Turning her attention to the watch, Cate stared at its slowly ticking hands. She was no closer to the truth despite having made a connection between these two events. She made her way back to the other bedroom's closet. At no time did she recover service.

Sighing, she let the phone fall to her side and gave the timepiece a rub across the face as she pondered the mystery. As she did, she noticed the ticking accelerate. The second hand was picking up, returning to its normal speed. She grabbed her phone. Holding it next to the watch, she watched the lock screen until the watch was ticking away normally. Within seconds of this, the phone's signal returned.

Cate was convinced these two incidents were connected, but she had no clue how or why. She was determined to find out. Perhaps she would ask Jack. In the meantime, she thought she should add this event to her note sheet to keep good track of everything.

Cate headed to the library to jot down the event. Riley lifted his head to acknowledge her return. "Another weird watch event, buddy!" she told him. After adding it to her note sheet, she texted Jack, telling him that the watch had slowed down again and she noticed it happened at the same time as her cell phone lost service. She asked if he had any thoughts about it, questioning if there could be some interference affecting both the watch and her phone.

Checking her email, Cate saw a new message from Gayle.

Dear Cate—I look so forward to receiving your package. I am positive that I will like whatever you have sent and thank you so much for thinking of me (although you didn't need to send anything, I was happy to help!).

Regarding the information about your grandfather's birth, let me see what I can track down for you and get back to you. Please give me about a week and I'll give you an update.

Best,
   Gayle

Cate shook her head in amazement at Gayle's response. She was so helpful and always willing to jump in and provide her services. Just as she finished reading the email, her cell phone chirped. Checking it, she saw an incoming message from Jack: *Some kind of EMP? I can run it past my grandfather. Let's talk tmw?*

Cate considered the idea that it could be an electromagnetic pulse, or EMP, causing the watch to malfunction. She texted back: *No idea, maybe something like that, although nothing else seems to be affected. Talk tmw*

After sending the text, Cate did a quick Internet search on things that affect cell phone services. She ruled out a few obvious things like a jamming device but many discussions of what affected service were over her head. Giving up, she closed her laptop. She would have to wait to discuss it further with Jack. Maybe once the two of them put their heads together, they could figure it out.

As she closed the laptop, Cate glanced down, feeling a pair of small feet on her right leg. Riley's dark almond eyes stared up at her. "Okay, buddy, you've been cooped up for most of the day, let's go for a long walk before dinner, okay?"

Riley responded by wagging his tail at her in approval. Cate gathered the little guy up into her arms and headed toward the door to get his harness and leash. They both enjoyed a long walk before dinner and a relaxing evening. Cate pushed the thoughts of her mysteries as far from her mind as she could, opting to stream some of her favorite shows on her laptop.

CHAPTER 25

*A*fter breakfast, Cate took Riley for a long walk before settling in to do some research for the day. Along her walk, she hoped to run into Jack to see if he and his grandfather had any clues concerning what might be going on with the watch and her cell service.

About halfway through the walk, Cate found Jack trimming some shrubbery near the edge of the property.

"Well, good morning to you, Cate, and to you, good Sir Riley!" Jack called.

"Good morning! How are you doing today?"

"Can't complain! I see we're coatless today, adjusting to our weather, are we?"

"Haha, it's a bright sunny day, so I left the coat inside! So, did you talk to your grandfather about the watch?"

"Yes, we couldn't come up with anything. The watch is old; he didn't think there would be any parts in common with a cell phone."

"I tried to look around on the Internet yesterday, but I saw nothing that made sense."

"Maybe it was a coincidence?"

"Possibly, but that's the second time it's happened and when I walked around I had no cell service even where I usually have it. That's the strange thing, and as soon as the watch started keeping normal time again, my service came back almost immediately."

"That is strange, but still, possibly a coincidence? I can't figure out anything that would affect both." Jack shrugged. "Sorry I don't have a better answer."

"No, it's okay, I don't either, nothing makes sense, so maybe it is just a coincidence. Maybe I'm reading more into it than there is." Cate shrugged back. "Well, I'll let you know if it happens again or if there's anything else that I notice that can shed more light on what's going on. I know your grandfather said everything was functioning properly but there's something strange going on or that watch has a strange tic, no pun intended."

"Yeah, let me know. My grandfather took care of a lot on the estate, so if he says nothing is wrong, I'd believe him. But I agree it is a strange tic, pun intended." He laughed heartily.

"Okay, will do!"

"Oh, before you go, let me toss a branch here for Riley, I've barely spoken to the lad, I think he's insulted."

Riley looked up, eyes gleaming as Jack brandished a stick. "Yes, you'd better, he'll be highly insulted."

"Can't insult the master of the house, I might lose my job!"

Cate laughed as Jack tossed the branch away and Riley chased after it. "Okay, see you later."

"Good day, Cate."

Cate followed Riley as he retrieved the stick and brought it to Cate. It looked like they had a new play toy for the rest of their walk.

After finishing the walk, Cate returned to the library to continue her research on the castle's previous residents. She was making good progress with mapping out some previous residents and their contributions to the castle's development and history. With the research she had done so far, Cate hoped soon to have enough for at least an introductory chapter of a new book.

She finished her notes after lunch and spent the rest of the afternoon in her sitting room reading the journals from Mary. She hadn't read the journals for several days because reading them was frustrating, given all the missing information. Even so, Cate felt they were somewhat insightful. And she hoped to find some mention of her father in them since Mary met him as a child or at least to find something that explained his relationship to the family.

She settled on the chaise and began reading the fourth journal where she had left off. It didn't take her long to finish what she hadn't yet read in the journal; she learned little more than she already knew. The journals spoke of parties or events within the castle; Mary must have entertained often.

Sighing, Cate considered giving up and trying to find something else to occupy her interest before dinner but she had only one journal left to go. Eyeing it, she figured she might as well finish it before moving on to other sources of information. She hated leaving things unfinished.

The journal, like all the others, was missing pages and only contained pieces of entries. Cate settled in to read more of Mary's stories of balls and house parties. At least Cate learned about life at the castle decades ago.

Cate had about half a journal left when she found something interesting. As she went to turn the page, Cate noticed something odd. Having read about four and a half of these, she had gotten used to the feel of the pages. This one seemed too thick. Looking carefully, it appeared as though two pages were stuck together. When Cate looked closely, she could just make out the thin line of two separate pages. It appeared as though the pages may have been wet and dried stuck together.

Cate rubbed the corners, trying to see if the pages would loosen but they did not. She tried to get the edge of her fingernail between them but she made little progress. Concerned that she would tear the sheets and ruin the pages, she decided against pushing harder than this.

Cate leaned back, pondering. She had studied document preservation and restoration and had even done some as a child with one of her mother's coworkers. Most times these situations were lost causes but there were some tricks that one could try if the document was not too important to risk damage.

Cate recalled a similar situation happening at the museum. An industrious worker told her that steam could sometimes do the trick then demonstrated on a few stuck onion paper pages. Grabbing the book, Cate headed to the kitchen. If she was lucky, a little steam might do the trick and loosen the pages without destroying their contents.

When Cate got to the kitchen, Mrs. Fraser was already preparing a few things for dinner.

"Lady Cate?! Did you need something?" a startled Mrs. Fraser said.

"I do, but not what you might think! Could you point me toward a pot to boil some water?"

"Aye, but might I ask what you plan on boiling? So I can give you the right size."

"I'm not going to boil anything, I just need some steam. I've got this journal," Cate waved the journal in her hand, "and there are a few stuck pages. I'd like to see if I can get them unstuck with a little steam."

Mrs. Fraser pulled a pot from a cupboard and began filling it with water then put it on the stove to heat. "Do you suppose it will work?"

"I don't know, but I hope so. I've never tried this before, but I have seen it work in the past. I'm hoping it works on this since the pages are not glossy or thick."

Mrs. Fraser watched as the water began to boil, creating plumes of steam floating up. Cate carefully held the journal to allow the steam to hit the pages but not close enough to be splashed by the boiling water. Cate moved the book around in an almost circular motion trying to coat the pages with the steam allowing no part to become too damp.

After a bit of work, Cate removed the book from the steam and tried the pages.

"Any luck?" Mrs. Fraser, who had been looking on with curiosity, asked.

Grimacing, Cate answered, "Nope, not yet, still stuck. I've got to be careful not to tear it, too. I'll try more steam."

Cate moved the book over the steam again, testing the pages every so often to make sure they weren't getting too damp. After a short while, Cate tried again. Mrs. Fraser watched with interest.

"HA!" Cate shouted.

"Did it work?"

"Yes, I think so, I've just got the edge but if I'm careful, I think I can get it," Cate said between clenched teeth as though admitting any success may jinx her efforts.

Mrs. Fraser craned her neck to watch Cate work. Carefully, inch-by-inch, Cate slowly peeled the pages back. Finally, she got them apart. "There." She breathed a sigh of relief. "Got it."

"Hey! Good work, Lady Cate! I have to admit, I cannae believe that worked," Mrs. Fraser exclaimed.

"Thanks! I'm glad it worked! It's always a gamble. Now I just need to let these pages dry and I should be able to read them."

"Will you be having your dinner in your sitting room to continue reading?"

"Yes, I will, thank you! I'll try to dry this off now with my hair dryer."

"Okay, Lady Cate, I'll bring your tray to you when it's ready."

"Thanks, oh, here, let me empty the pot and dry it before I go."

"No need, don't fuss with that, Lady Cate. I've got it." Mrs. Fraser was already removing the pot from the stove and emptying it while waving Cate out of the kitchen.

Cate was so excited that her trick worked! She hurried back to her room to dry the pages. A few minutes on low heat with the blow dryer and the pages were soon dry enough to read. Cate was careful not to over-dry them so they didn't become brittle. She was just returning to her sitting room when Mrs. Fraser brought her tray in with her dinner.

"Did you get it dry?"

"I did, I was just about to read it, perfect timing with dinner!"

"Happy reading, Lady Cate!" Mrs. Fraser said as she left the room, pulling the double doors slightly closed.

Cate sat down, taking a few bites of dinner before diving into the exposed entry. Excited as she was, she was also famished. After a few bites, she turned her attention back to the journal. Finally, an entry that was longer than a page, she thought. Refreshing herself on the previous page's entry she read:

As I continue these excursions, I can not help but feel the...

The unveiled page continued the sentence:

... tremendous responsibility to pass along to Gertrude. I can scarcely wrap my head around it sometimes, yet I cannot deny the proof right in front of my eyes. Since my husband has passed the timepiece to me, a mere caretaker of the awesome object, I have struggled to comprehend the enormity of the responsibility that has been given to me and that I will pass to Gertrude.

I have documented what I have learned so far and plan to keep a complete record, which Gertrude will surely need to destroy after gleaning any information that she can from my writings. It is the only way I can pass a complete record to her. While this task was thrust upon me because of the direst of circumstances, I vow to do all I can to make it easier...

The page ended. The remaining pages were torn away, leaving another incomplete record. What little remained on those pages still left Cate stunned. Mary seemed to have created the journals to establish a record for Gertrude. What it was a record of, Cate did not know. All that she read seemed to have been meaningless descriptions of parties, get-togethers, and other castle happenings. It didn't seem to be earth-shattering information. Yet Mary seemed to think it was significant enough to be documented. Phrases and words like "tremendous responsibility", "enormity", "awesome object", and "direst of circumstances" seemed to lend gravity and importance to the writing. Yet what Cate had read did not seem important in the least.

Cate scanned the entry again. Mary also specifically mentioned the timepiece that now hung around Cate's neck. This object seemed to be of immense importance to Gertrude and also to Mary. The words about Gertrude destroying the journals echoed in Cate's head, too. Could this explain the missing pages? Perhaps Gertrude destroyed the journals or the relevant parts that tied the entries together in any meaningful way. Had these pages been left because they were stuck together?

Turning to Riley, Cate said, "What in the world is THIS about, buddy? Rather mysterious way to refer to this old timepiece, huh?" While the entry didn't say much, it said more than any other entry, at least to Cate. It further confirmed the importance of the timepiece that Cate inherited and perhaps some of the reason Lady Gertrude took such great care to pass along hand-written instructions about it.

Cate wondered what in the world was so special about it and what enormous truth Gertrude was protecting by destroying the journal pages? Cate eyed the timepiece, willing it to share its secrets. Sighing, she realized she could learn nothing from it. Taking another few bites of food, she pondered what it meant. Was it somehow connected to the slowing of the timepiece? Was there some meaning behind that? Or was Mary just mentally unstable and took to writing fanciful stories in her journals? If that was the case, why did Gertrude destroy so much of the books?

Cate finished her meal, reading the rest of the journal. She gleaned no more relevant or useful information.

Cate found it hard to sleep later that night. She repeatedly went over the words from the journal. Mary considered whatever she was referring to in the journal to be a huge responsibility. And someone, perhaps Gertrude, as suggested in the hidden entry, thought it important enough to conceal. Cate stared at the timepiece she held in her hands, apparently this was a vital piece of the puzzle, but how did it fit? What was its importance? This was the only mention of that object from all the journals she found. Were there other mentions in the pages that had been torn away?

Sighing, she let her hand with the timepiece in it fall to her chest, rubbing it as thoughts raced through her mind. It wasn't long after she let it rest against her she heard the now familiar loud ticking and slowing of the watch. She bolted upright in bed, opening the timepiece and watching it as the second hand slowed to a crawl. Cate watched it for several more minutes before a thought struck her. She rubbed the watch again. She watched with amazement as the second hand started to move faster and faster until it was keeping perfect time.

Cate's brow furrowed. Was it possible she was causing the watch to malfunction? Could friction from the rubbing cause it to slow? That didn't explain the loss of cell phone signal but it could explain the malfunctioning timepiece. Perhaps no one else in the family had trouble with it because no one else in the family had developed the habit of rubbing the watch that Cate had.

Cate thought for a moment. She wanted to try again to see if her theory was correct, but she was afraid she might damage the watch. Perhaps it was best left untried until she ran her theory past Jack and his grandfather. She would text him in the morning. Cate relaxed back into her bed, determined to go to sleep. After a bit of a struggle, she drifted off to sleep, dreaming again about the past occupants of the castle.

CHAPTER 26

The next morning, after breakfast and a walk with Riley, Cate settled in the library to go over some of her research notes. Before sitting down with them, she texted Jack: *I may have a theory about the watch, meet for lunch to talk?*

After sending it, she set her notes out to go over the information that she had already acquired. After reviewing it for an hour, Cate supposed the next logical step might be to do some interviews in town, especially with the town's librarian to ascertain what information she could gain or where other resources may be.

While she still had several sources to look through at the castle, she wanted a multi-pronged approach to gather as much information as possible before putting words on a page.

With her notes sprawled, Cate opened her laptop and searched for the number for the library. After noting its hours, she checked her watch and found that the library was open for the day. She called the number listed and explained who she was and asked to speak with the librarian.

As luck would have it, the librarian was in and was eager to meet with Cate to discuss her project and provide any information she could. She told Cate her schedule was open if Cate would like to meet with her today. Cate accepted the invitation and told her she would meet her in about 30 minutes. With the appointment set, Cate hung up.

She gathered her notes, making sure she had a pen and plenty of space in her notebook. Satisfied, Cate gathered up Riley for a quick pit stop before heading into town as her phone chirped. Checking the phone, she saw a message from Jack: *In town on errands, won't be back for lunch, later?*

Cate texted back: *Heading to town for a meeting, meet at pub for lunch?*

Before she had even made it outside with Riley, her phone chimed again. Checking her phone, she saw Jack's response: *Deal! Noon?*

She responded an affirmative and headed out the door with Riley, after telling Mrs. Fraser that she wouldn't need lunch today.

Since it was a cloudy, cool day, Cate took Riley into town with her, leaving him in the car with a few windows cracked while she went to the library. As Cate walked into the library, she spotted the same assistant behind the desk, the one she had gotten into hot water. The girl eyed her warily. Cate approached the desk and informed her she had an appointment with the librarian. Before the assistant answered, the librarian emerged from her office.

"Dr. Kensie, a pleasure to see you again! Please, come into my office."

"Hello, Mrs. Campbell, nice to see you again, too. Thank you for meeting with me so quickly." Cate followed her behind the desk to her office. The office was small and dimly lit, filled with boxes of books and other library paraphernalia. It appeared to be part storage room, part office, as was the norm for many small town libraries. The librarian motioned to a chair opposite the desk which Cate took, opening her notebook and uncapping her pen.

Mrs. Campbell sat down behind the desk, folding her hands on the top and leaning forward. "Well, Dr. Kensie, I hope I can be of help to you, I understand from your call that you're doing research into the castle's history?"

"Yes, that's right, oh and please call me Cate. Do you mind if I record our conversation?" Cate waved the recorder she brought in the air.

"Oh, no, not at all."

"Thanks." Cate clicked the button to record. "I have been doing some research into Dunhaven Castle. It's of great interest to me as a historian and the new owner. I'd like to get a better sense of its history from anyone who may have lived in the area and who knows of any information or sources of information. I believed you would be a great starting point since, as the town's librarian, I suspect you may also double as the historian for the town as well?"

"Oh," Mrs. Campbell began, acting a bit coy, "well, I'm not sure I'd call myself a historian per se but, yes I'm the person who is charged with keeping the town's history. I am president of the historical society here in town as well."

Cate's suspicion was correct, Mrs. Campbell had a double role in town. "Oh good! I'm glad I assumed correctly! You'll be a great starting place. So," Cate said, turning to her notes, "I've got the basics of who, what, where, when and why with the castle. I was hoping you would share some less objective details about the castle. For example, local stories that have been passed along about why particular things were done or anything else that might be connected?"

"Oh, you mean the, ah, legends?" Mrs. Campbell raised an eyebrow.

"Yes, if there are legends, I'd love to hear them, they are exactly what would be a perfect addition to my book."

"Well," Mrs. Campbell began, settling into her chair looking like the cat who caught the canary, "you have heard about the hauntings, haven't you?"

"I read a short blurb about it in the book you provided on my last visit, yes."

"Of course, I didn't say anything when we first met, I didn't want to ruin your experience in your new home. I don't believe in such things, but." She paused. "There have been, eh, stories."

She paused again, eyeing Cate. The woman was enjoying the suspense. Cate fed into her excitement. "Stories? Please go on."

"Yes, stories, tales, legends. Of spirits, ghosts, terrors in the night, phantom sounds, shrieks and screams of the dead but not gone." She went on dramatically, she loved a good tale. "Some say they were ghosts of the builders; someone was murdered during construction, you know. Others say various spirits of staff who died on the estate come back to haunt their employers long after they were put in their graves."

"Any description of those spirits? What they looked like, where they appeared?" Cate glanced up from her note taking.

Mrs. Campbell raised her eyebrow at Cate again. "Any form in particular you'd like more information about? You haven't had a run-in with any of the dearly departed, have you, Cate?" She grinned.

"No," Cate said flatly. Cate wasn't sure what "run-in" she'd had when she encountered the maid in the entryway, but she wasn't going to admit it to Mrs. Campbell, at least, not yet.

"Well," Mrs. Campbell was already continuing, having lost her bid for another juicy haunting story from the new owner of Dunhaven Castle, "there is the tale of the young man who disappeared during the construction. He is rumored to roam the halls, with various sightings across the estate from the gardens to the castle's interior. He's described as a tall, dark-haired figure in tattered clothes with a menacing expression."

She continued, "Then, there are tales of phantom maids, appearing all over the place, endlessly bustling around, continuing their household chores long after their deaths."

"And of course, there're the tales of those who have lived there. Those who have been sent screaming into the night when they are awoken by ghastly howls, screams, and shrieks that seem to come from all directions at once."

"Interesting," Cate commented as she took notes. It fit with most stories of hauntings, wildly embellished by each passing narrator to make the tale more luridly interesting around a campfire. "Do you think there's any truth in these tales?"

"Oh, not me." She shrugged. "I don't believe in such rubbish, but that doesn't stop the tales from circulating, of course."

"Or from being printed in books," Cate quipped. "Speaking of, I noticed in that book that Lady MacKenzie chose not to comment when contacted by the author. Do you know the reason for that?"

"Lady MacKenzie despised the talk of the ghosts and goblins haunting the castle. My guess is primarily because it was her family home. She took a lot of pride in the place, as she should have, and it bothered her to hear people talk negatively about her family home."

"Was that common for all the MacKenzies or just Lady Gertrude?"

"I'm not sure, but, I think Lady Gertrude was more of a recluse, particularly toward the end of her life, than her father was, for example. Those who knew him described Lord MacKenzie as a very personable and outgoing sort."

"Did she take after her mother?"

"Again, without personal knowledge, only from what I've been told, no. The previous Lady MacKenzie was known as gracious and friendly."

"Hmm, very interesting. Any interesting tales about any of the residents?"

"Well, there is a tale about Lord Randolph MacKenzie, I think he was the third proprietor of the castle."

"Yes?"

"Well, he traveled extensively. The rumor was, he brought back a girl from one of his travels. He kept her locked in the tower room and used her to fulfill some of his more base desires." Another eyebrow raise.

Cate summarized the story in her notes. "Another interesting tidbit!"

"So," she said leaning forward onto the desk again, "will you be able to use anything I've said in your book?"

"Oh, yes, you've been very helpful."

"Oh excellent, I'm so glad I've been of help. And how exciting that some small part of what I've said may end up in a book one day! Is there anything else I can help with?"

"Not right now. If I think of anything, though, I'll contact you to follow up as I begin writing."

"Oh, please, feel free, I'm happy to provide you with anything else that might help fill in gaps."

"Well, thank you so much for your time, Mrs. Campbell, I'm sure we'll be in touch," Cate said, capping her pen and closing her notebook.

"Of course, of course. I'm happy to help and please don't hesitate to contact me if you need more."

Both women stood, Cate extended her hand to shake Mrs. Campbell's and told her that she would find her own way out. Exiting the office, Cate skirted around the circulation desk, with the library assistant still giving her the evil eye, and headed for the door. Checking her watch, she had about thirty minutes before she planned to meet Jack for lunch so she collected Riley from the car for a short walk around town. He enjoyed visiting some of his favorite shop owners and appreciated getting treats from them even more. Before heading to the pub for lunch, Cate settled him back in the car for an early afternoon nap. "You wait for me here, buddy. I'm going to meet our pal, Jack, for lunch." Riley acknowledged the mention of Jack's name with a wag of his tail. "I'll tell him you said hello!" Cate said to Riley before heading to the pub.

She found Jack already waiting in a booth; he waved her over.

"Thanks for meeting me," she said as she sat down. "Riley says hi."

"No problem, I'm dying to hear your theory about the watch. Oh and tell the little lad that I say hello, too and I look forward to another game of fetch very soon."

Before they could discuss anything further, the waitress arrived at the table to take their order. After ordering, Jack joked, "Fish and chips again? Really?"

"It's good and I'm not very adventurous, I guess."

This generated a hearty laugh from Jack. "Oh, right, this coming from the lassie who moved to a new country and castle sight unseen."

"Not true! Mr. Smythe showed me pictures," Cate joked back, "so I saw it." She made a "so-there" face at him.

"Ah, you're right, not very adventurous moving to a new country when you saw pictures." He laughed again. "Okay, down to business, what's your theory on the watch?"

"One word: friction." Cate grinned.

"Friction? Care to elaborate?"

"Yes, friction. I've developed this kind of habit of rubbing the watch in my hand. I think the friction from my fingers may affect it. It happened again last night just after I was rubbing the watch. When I thought back, I believe every time it's happened it has been when I've been handling the watch like that. Here, let me show you."

Cate grabbed the watch and began rubbing it. Nothing happened. Cate frowned. She tried again. Again, nothing. She sighed, disgusted, "This is what I was doing last night and when I rubbed it again, the watch sped up and went back to perfect time."

"Are you sure it wasn't just a coincidence?"

"I thought of that but, from what I remember, it's typically happened when I've been rubbing the watch."

"Except now."

"Except now, yes," she said, deflated, trying to watch again, "except now."

"I'll run it past my grandfather and see what he says. Assuming, though, that you've got something here, like maybe it worked last night because it built up all day with friction, how does that explain the cell phone signal loss?"

"That's the only piece that doesn't fit into this scenario, I don't know. But maybe I'm on to something even if this isn't exactly it. You could be right; maybe it's a build up. Although, it's happened earlier in the day, too, so that wouldn't fit well there," Cate said, turning pensive.

"Well," Jack said as the waitress returned with their food, "perhaps we're moving in the right direction. Keep tabs on it. For now though, let's enjoy our meal."

After lunch, Cate returned to the castle with Riley, planning on taking him for a long walk after he had been cooped up in the car for most of the morning. While she walked, she pondered the situation with the watch. She thought she had been on to something with the friction idea and had been disappointed when she wasn't able to reproduce the phenomenon at lunch. She frowned down at the watch. She wasn't doing very well on any of her mysteries since moving to the castle.

At least she had gotten some good information for her book. She focused her thoughts on her conversation with Mrs. Campbell, the librarian. Much of what she told her would add a good deal to the book. It was interesting to interweave historical fact with accounts from people who had grown up with legends and lore. These often made the most interesting pieces of a book.

Cate started piecing together how she would pepper in the quotes from Mrs. Campbell with the topics in her book. She could gather quotes from a few other people too, like Mrs. Fraser and Jack's grandfather. Both had a lifetime of experience with the estate and would be excellent sources to interview. She was sure there would be others from the town who would be interested in giving her some quotes, perhaps members of the historical society.

She resolved to ask Jack if his grandfather would mind doing an interview for the book. As she walked, another idea formed, and she decided to email the author of *The Mysteries of Scotland* to see what details he could provide about Dunhaven Castle.

As the path turned her back toward the castle, Cate contemplated some other sources that she planned to use in her text. It reminded her she still needed to finish reading through the letters she had found in one of the bedroom closets and continue to look through the castle for additional personal sources that could augment the facts she had gathered already.

Checking her watch, Cate decided to do that tomorrow,

planning to spend the following morning with the letters she had already found and tomorrow afternoon scouring the hidden depths of the castle for additional resources.

Upon returning to the castle, Cate headed for the library, planning on organizing her notes from the meeting with Mrs. Campbell and finishing up a few odds and ends before dinner. After about an hour and a half of reviewing her recording and written notes, adding and editing the information, Cate was satisfied and gathered everything, storing them back in her research folder.

She opened her laptop and searched for information on how to contact the author of the book that mentioned Dunhaven Castle. It didn't take long to find the author's webpage and information on contacting him. Cate opened a blank email and typed a brief message, introducing herself and requesting from him any information about sources he used in putting together the entry on Dunhaven Castle in his book. She stated that she was requesting the information since she was researching the estate. She was careful not to mention that she was the new owner. She did not want to be asked to provide a quote for his next book or blog.

After sending the email, Cate scanned the list of new emails that appeared in her inbox. Most of them were junk, but there was an email from Gayle with the subject: THANK YOU!

She opened it and read.

Dear Cate, THANK YOU so much for the thoughtful gift. I love the little porcelain dog figure! I have him (I assume it's a him) set on my desk. He reminded me of Riley so I named him Wiley after the funny story you told me about your neighbor's insistence on calling him by the incorrect name! Each day, I will look at him and think of you and Riley. I hope you are doing well and enjoying castle life!

By the way, I hope to have some information for you soon about the birth records for your grandfather.

Best,

Gayle

Cate smiled at the email, she was glad that Gayle enjoyed receiving the small figurine and found it amusing that she had named it Wiley. Cate's mind wandered to her old neighbor, Mrs. Kline. She wondered if she had received the postcard she had sent her, deciding that she probably had not since she expected that it would take some time to reach the States. Cate pondered how the older woman was doing, thinking she may be lonely with Cate's departure. Cate was one of the few people who talked with her; most others avoided her or told her they were too busy. She reassured herself that someone had already moved into her old apartment and Mrs. Kline was now enjoying having a new person to spy on. Cate chuckled to herself, imagining the woman hovering at her peephole, eyeing everything the newcomer was bringing into the apartment and their various comings and goings, planning her perfect moment to spring out and introduce herself.

Her thoughts turned to her old department. She imagined Molly sitting behind the desk, Jeff in his office. She pictured her old office, small and windowless, packed with her things. What a huge change she had undergone in the past few months. She could still sometimes scarcely believe it was true, yet, as she looked around, she couldn't deny that she was sitting in a castle, HER castle. She had worried so before arriving that she wouldn't settle in or that she was making a mistake. This couldn't have been further from the truth. She had felt at home from the moment she had set foot on the grounds, feeling kinship with the souls of those who had lived here before.

She glanced back at the screen, seeing the email from Gayle. In the few minutes that she had before dinner, she typed a quick answer back telling Gayle that she was glad she liked the figurine and that she loved the name. She also wrote that, while she was looking forward to getting the birth record information, there was no rush.

Cate just finished the email when Mrs. Fraser appeared with a tray of dinner. "Thank you so much, Mrs. Fraser." Cate smiled. "Oh, before you go, I hoped to ask a favor of you."

"Ask away, Lady Cate."

"I was wondering if you'd let me interview you sometime for my book on Dunhaven Castle. Since you've been here all your life, I suspect you have some great insight on the castle and how it's changed over the years. I'd love to have some personal accounts from someone with as much knowledge as you and a few quotes for the book I'm working on."

"Me? Well, I don't know how much use I'll end up being for you, but I would be happy to help if I can.

"Oh, great! Thank you! Would you have some time tomorrow morning after breakfast?"

"Well, I can make the time whenever you'd like to do it."

"I don't want to inconvenience you if that's not the best time."

"Nay, that's a fine time."

"Okay, great. We'll plan to do it then, Mrs. Fraser. Thanks again!"

Cate ate her dinner, spending the rest of her evening streaming her favorite TV show. She took Riley for a short walk just before sunset, both of them enjoying the exquisite views of the sun setting over the moors. She turned in early, planning a full day of research starting first thing in the morning.

CHAPTER 27

*C*ate admired the sunrise from her bedroom window. She was eager to start the day and her interview with Mrs. Fraser. When she finished breakfast, she carried her own dishes downstairs and offered to help Mrs. Fraser tidy up the kitchen before beginning the interview, so she wasn't left with the work after the interview. The woman would hear none of it, insisting that she would take care of everything after the interview.

Cate brandished her recorder asking if she could record the conversation and after receiving an affirmative from Mrs. Fraser, she clicked the recorder on and opened her notebook to begin. "So, Mrs. Fraser, you've been on the estate your whole life, correct?"

"Yes, I was born here, daughter of a maid and groundskeeper. Lived my whole life on this estate."

"You must have a great deal of knowledge of the place and its inhabitants, I assume?"

"I know the castle inside and out. Know every hallway and back stair, every nook and cranny. Now the people I didn't have much contact with, being a child. But when I got older and took on a position here, I got to know their habits and preferences. I started here when Lady Mary was still overseeing the household and of course was here for Lady Gertrude's entire time as mistress of Dunhaven Castle."

Cate asked some specific questions about each, asking Mrs. Fraser to provide some details on their habits and preferences, how the two women differed and how the estate changed in the years that Mrs. Fraser had been there.

Emily Fraser provided a wealth of knowledge on the inner workings of the castle and how it changed over the years. Cate's interview took almost two hours, with Cate getting several pages of excellent information to add to her book. At the close of the interview, Cate thanked her again; telling her she provided much information. Cate was sure she had enough for a whole chapter of her book. Mrs. Fraser seemed stunned that anything she said would be used in a book. She told Cate that she was surprised but happy to provide help for her research. She acknowledged that she never dreamed she would be quoted in a book someday.

As Cate gathered her things, Mrs. Fraser asked her if she planned to work on her book for the rest of the day. Cate explained that she planned to do a little more exploring, looking for more sources within the castle for her book, so in a way, she would be working on it. She also told her she'd love to interview Mr. Fraser, but it being the warmer season, she knew he would be busy with grounds keeping. Mrs. Fraser suggested a rainy day and Cate agreed this might be a great time to speak with him. They planned for the next rainy day and Cate left the kitchen, on her way to the "1850s bedroom" as she coined it, where she found the old gowns and letters.

Along the way, she checked on Riley, finding him contentedly napping on the chaise lounge. Leaving him undisturbed, she headed for the bedroom closet containing her next target. She again settled in amongst the boxes and trunks, grabbing a handful of letters to read.

Cate found the letters very interesting. Among the correspondence were love letters from one of the castle's eventual owners to his future wife. Cate was fascinated by the difference in the discourse between men and women during courtship in the distant past as compared to today. Apparently, the young suitor had been quite taken by the young woman's beauty and wrote her several poems about it, sending them along with his official wishes to court her. It was like reading a real-life romance novel and Cate couldn't put the letters down.

About a third of the way through her reading, Cate heard the familiar loud tick of the timepiece as it, again, began to slow. Looking down, she tried to remember if she had been rubbing it and concluded that she likely had been.

This time she hoped to show Jack exactly what the watch was doing and they could both test her theory that friction was responsible for slowing down and speeding up the watch. Cate picked up her phone as she left the closet, intent on texting Jack to find his location. She hoped that she could locate him quickly. She pressed the button to toggle the display on only to be greeted with white lettering that read NO SERVICE. Cate groaned, not only was it impossible to text Jack, but if the cell signal was in any way related to the slowing of the watch, her friction idea just went up in smoke. Giving up on piecing it together for the moment, she concentrated on finding Jack. She hurried from the room and down the hallway, peering out the windows in search of the groundskeeper.

Window after window passed, but Cate caught no glimpse of Jack. Sighing in frustration, Cate hurried around the corner into another hallway, peering through more windows that overlooked the back garden. There she glimpsed movement from a tall figure and assumed it was Jack. Success, she thought! Moving to the next window, she knocked at it rapidly to attract his attention. Focusing her attention on the figure outside, he turned to face her fully, attracted by the noise. Instinctively, she stumbled back a step, surprised. It wasn't Jack, but a stranger whom she had never seen before. Collecting herself, she approached the window again. The man was just turning back to his work, having scanned the area and not seen anything of interest. Cate stared at him, not sure what to make of the situation. He was dressed curiously and the equipment that he was using to work looked like a peculiar choice given the tools she had seen Mr. Fraser and Jack using on the estate. Cate was further puzzled since she was sure if Mr. Fraser had extra help, Mrs. Fraser would have mentioned it.

Cate focused her mind back on the task at hand. Checking the watch again, it was still running slow, and she still had no cell service. She reminded herself that her main goal had been to find Jack so he could see the watch in its slowed state. Then she could follow up asking him about the man she had seen working in the back garden.

Continuing down the hall, she didn't spot Jack outside anywhere. Perhaps he was farther out on the estate than she could spot from the windows. Retracing her steps, she looked again through a few windows but spotted nothing. Without being able to contact Jack to determine a location she could wander the property for hours without finding him and it was getting close to lunch. Not that Cate was starving, but she didn't want Mrs. Fraser's efforts in preparing lunch to be pointless if she couldn't be located.

Sighing, she thought she might try her rubbing trick to see if she could get the watch back to its normal speed and just tell Jack about it later. Taking a deep breath, she rubbed the face of the watch between her thumb and fingers like a serenity stone. To her amazement, it seemed to work. The watch started to move faster and faster until it was ticking along at normal speed. This couldn't be a coincidence, Cate thought. She had to be on to something. It was too bad she couldn't have found Jack to show him.

She checked her cell phone before heading back to her room to gather Riley for a quick walk before lunch. She had a signal. The two events had to be related but then her theory made little sense. The more she thought she was on to something, the less things made sense.

Frustrated, she hoped to find some answers soon and headed back to her bedroom. As she passed through the hall, she glanced out the window toward the back garden. The mystery man had vanished. Rounding the corner, she could view another angle of the garden. She stopped dead. There stood Jack, working at trimming a row of rose bushes. He had tools and clippings spread everywhere; it looked as though he had been there quite a while.

Cate wondered if she could have missed him when she hurried past the windows. She couldn't see how she had; the tools and cuttings spread about were large enough not to have been missed.

Cate knocked at the window and opened it. Jack turned toward the castle, spotting Cate at the open window.

"M'lady!" he shouted, bowing extravagantly toward her, "Why doth though beckon from the window?" He laughed.

Cate laughed and shook her head, always a jokester. "Very funny. I beckon from the window because I've been looking for you."

"That sounds ominous."

"Did you just get here? I went past here earlier and didn't see you. That thing happened with the watch again, I wanted to show you."

"I've been here for over two hours. And I can tell you it's

true: every rose really does have its thorn. Maybe even two or three of them!"

Cate's brow furrowed in confusion. She couldn't have missed him, she thought. But where had he been when she walked past moments ago?

"Everything okay, Cate?" he hollered up when she didn't respond for a moment.

"Ah, yes, I think so, it's just that, well, I just came past and I could have sworn you were not here."

Jack looked equally confused. "I promise I've been here for about two hours, haven't left."

"No, I believe you, but I'm surprised I could have missed you. Hey, speaking of working, did Mr. Fraser hire some extra help for the garden trimming?"

"Extra help?" He looked confused.

"Yes, I saw a man a few yards down working outside the garden, I was wondering who he was."

"Ah." He glanced around as though not sure what to say. "There's no one else working with us today that I know of. If he hired someone, he didn't mention it to me and I haven't seen anyone all day."

The information left Cate with chills. Surely she didn't see yet another nonexistent person roaming the estate. Not wanting to make a bigger issue with Jack than she should, she shouted, "Hmmm, well, anyway, we can chat later about it. I'll let you get back to your roses!"

"I believe, they're YOUR roses, Lady Cate." He gave a sort of salute to her as he turned back to continue working on the trimming. Cate shut the window, hovering a moment more staring out of it. She switched angles to view it from the other side, as though she were heading back down the hallway in the direction she had been when she was searching for Jack. There was no way she wouldn't have seen him. But she knew he wasn't there when she walked past moments before.

She lingered another moment before turning to head back to her room. She gave up trying to figure out what was going on, maybe she was losing her mind or maybe she had been in such a rush that she hadn't been paying careful enough attention. Not solving it by the time she got back to her room, she pushed it from her mind as Riley greeted her, bounding off the chaise and happily prancing over, tail wagging.

No matter what was playing on her mind, Riley could always improve her mood and distract her mind. "Did you have a nice nap, Riley? Ready for a little walk before lunch?"

Riley's tail wagged furiously, and he lapped Cate's face appreciatively when she mentioned a walk. Gathering him up in her arms, she headed for the front entryway. The pair enjoyed a nice walk down the main driveway and back before lunch. The walk was enough to stir his appetite for a lunchtime bone.

After lunch, Cate spent some time online shopping for a small scanner. She wanted to scan the letters and journals that she read so far so she had a digital copy. She hoped to include information and quotes from both sources in her book and thought it might be useful to include images of the originals.

Cate ended up spending most of the afternoon shopping for things far beyond merely the scanner. She ended up with a scanner, a few texts on Scottish castles to help with her research, a new chew toy for Riley, and a new notebook for her research. Looking at the time when she finished, she decided that she wouldn't start anything else today, opting instead for a nice long afternoon walk with Riley.

After dinner, Cate tried to focus her energy on reading a novel she found in the library. After her strange encounter earlier, she could feel the tension building in her with night-fall approaching and the promise of being alone in the castle. If she kept running into these "ghosts," she wasn't sure what she would do but she was feeling more and more unsettled.

Cate read, or rather tried to read, late into the night. Loathe to go to bed, she suspiciously eyed every dark corner, expecting a ghost to come popping out at any second. She felt ridiculous, like a child afraid of monsters under her bed, but still, she couldn't shake the eerie feeling. Finally, exhausted as it approached one o'clock in the morning, Cate crawled into bed, sleeping restlessly, but undisturbed by the phantoms she imagined haunted her new abode.

CHAPTER 28

*D*rowsily, Cate opened her eyes to the first peeks of the morning sun over the horizon. Yawning, she stretched before sitting up in bed. She considered lying down to sleep in but decided against it; afraid it would inhibit her sleep that night. She forced herself out of bed, figuring a brisk walk with Riley was what she needed to get going for the day.

After the walk, she planned to take another trip to town. She was trying to get used to life in Scotland and she wanted another break from the castle, before she surrendered too far into her unscientific fears about ghosts again. Or worse, ran into another.

After breakfast and a nice long walk, Cate loaded Riley into the car and headed for town. It was a warm, sunny day, so she took Riley with her as she made her way around town. Riley enjoyed town walks, especially because shop owners often gave him a treat as he walked past.

Cate was becoming accustomed to the town; it no longer felt as foreign as the first time she had visited. Walking down the main street, Cate stopped in the shop where she had purchased the postcards, greeting the store owner as she entered.

"Good morning, Harry!"

"Well good morning, Lady Cate! And little Riley, too!" Riley stared expectantly, waiting for a treat that Harry quickly produced from under the counter. "I'm glad to see you. How are you today?"

"I'm good, thanks! How are you?"

"Cannae complain! I've got my wife helping me today, just a minute." He held up a finger. "I want you to meet her. Helen! HELEN!" he called into a back storage room.

"Yeah? What is it?" a voice answered.

"Come out here and meet Lady Cate!" he called back.

Helen appeared in the doorway, dusting her hands off from whatever she was working on. "Cate?" she asked, then spotted Cate standing near the counter.

"Aye, Lady Cate, the newest MacKenzie, our new castle owner!"

"Oh, Lady Cate," Helen said, making her way over.

"Hi Helen, I'm Cate, and this is Riley."

"Hello, nice to meet you, I've heard about you from Harry and Isla. I'm a member of the historical club, too."

"Oh, great. I was hoping to stop by one of your meetings to discuss the castle with the group. I'm writing a book on its history and it would be great to get some stories from the folks here about it."

"I'm sure you'd be welcome at a meeting, you should speak with Isla about when the best time might be. There are definitely stories about that place, that's for certain."

"Yes, Mrs. Campbell was telling me about some stories. Hauntings and so on."

"Those tales have been told around this town long as I can remember. After listening to some of them, I'd venture to say you're quite a brave girl, Lady Cate."

"Brave?"

"You'd not catch me in that castle all alone at night, there's a fact."

"So, you think there's something to the stories?" Cate asked.

"Well, I cannae say if they're true or not, but I can say I dinnae think they just came from nothing. Something happened up there at that castle to cause such a stir of tales in the village."

"Oh, well, I'd guess much of the stories are embellished upon."

"Even still, you'd not get me alone up there," Helen shook her head emphatically.

"Now, Helen," Harry began, "stop filling that poor girl's head with tales."

"Nothing she hasn't heard before, sounds like," Helen retorted.

"Well no sense in stirring her up more, the poor child doesn't want to hear about how she's sharing her new home with ghosts! She'll barely be able to walk around without checking every shadow after you're done."

Helen waved her hand at him as though she didn't agree, but didn't continue with the discussion, instead changing the subject. "How are you settling in to your new home?"

"Very well, thank you. It was quite a change for both of us," she said, motioning to Riley.

"You're from the States, right?"

"Yep, born and raised! I'd never even traveled outside of the country before I moved here, so it was quite a change. I'm still getting used to it."

"Well, welcome to you, I hope you're finding Scotland as charming as we do."

"Thank you, I am finding it very charming. Everyone has been extremely welcoming to me, I'm very grateful. Well, I'll let you get back to your day, I just wanted to stop in and say hello."

"Thanks for stopping by, Lady Cate," Harry said, offering Riley another treat before he left.

"Nice seeing you again, Harry and it was nice meeting you, Helen. I hope to see you soon at a historical club meeting."

"Nice meeting you too, Lady Cate."

Cate left the shop, wondering if she would ever get used to being called Lady Cate, and continued down the sidewalk, stopping to visit several other shops and returning to the castle just before lunch. After lunch, she spent the day outside, enjoying the warm sunshine, walking and playing with Riley or lounging on the lawn by the loch, reading a book while Riley napped in the sunshine.

On her way back to the castle in the late afternoon, Cate caught site of Jack frowning at one of the rose bushes. Making her way over, she said hello.

"Hello, Cate," Jack answered. "And hello to you, too, Sir Riley," he said, patting the dog on the head as he stood with his front legs planted on Jack's leg.

"You don't look happy," Cate said.

"I'm not. This little lad doesn't seem to be doing so well." Jack showed her the shriveled leaves on the plant. "I was trying to determine what might be wrong with it. I might have to call in reinforcements, my grandfather might have a better idea than I."

"Oh, speaking of," Cate answered, "I was hoping to interview him for my book. Since he's lived here and worked on the estate, I think he would have a great wealth of knowledge about it. If he's coming to look at the rose bush, would you mind asking him for me?"

"Ah, I'm sure he'd be happy to talk for as long as you'd like about the castle. Maybe even longer than you'd like," he said laughing, "He's probably got loads of information to share. He's out of town, so I'll ask as soon as he's back."

"I'll bet, that's why he's a perfect source for my book."

"Say, speaking of people at the castle, did you track down that extra helper you saw yesterday?"

"Uh, no," Cate frowned.

"Now you don't look happy, Cate."

Cate hesitated, unsure if she wanted to discuss her experience. It was the second time she had seen a person on the estate that no one else had seen. Jack noticed her hesitation, following up with, "Cate, is everything okay?"

"I think so."

"You think so? You don't sound so sure."

Cate watched Jack absentmindedly petting Riley as they spoke. The little dog seemed attached to him. Riley trusted him, so Cate decided she would, too. "It's just that this is the second person I've seen on this estate that no one else has seen and when no one else outside of the Frasers, you and I have been on the estate."

"The second time?"

"Yes, I saw a woman in the entry hall. I spoke to her, but Mrs. Fraser said there was no one else in the castle when I asked her about it."

"Hmm," Jack said.

"I'm not crazy. And I didn't think I believed in ghosts, but I'm wondering about those tales floating around town about this place."

"I don't think you're crazy, Cate. And I certainly don't believe those tales from town. Those people like to talk, that's all. It's Scotland, everyone's got a haunted something or other in their back pocket around here. It's just idle chatter, don't let it get into your head."

"But then how do you explain what I saw? If it's not ghosts, am I going crazy? What other explanation is there?"

"Cate," he said, putting his hands on her shoulders, "you've just moved from another country into a giant castle. I'm sure your nerves are on edge and your imagination is just playing tricks on you. You're primed to see something."

Cate wasn't so sure, but she would accept it for now. "You're right, it's probably an overactive imagination combined with the unfamiliar setting. Plus it can be kind of spooky here at night."

"Yeah, I'll bet, but I wouldn't know for sure, I'm too afraid to be here at night," Jack joked to lighten the mood.

"Funny. You should be afraid during the day, that's when I see all my ghosts." Cate laughed back. "Well, time to get Riley his dinner. I'll leave you to your sick rose, I hope it's okay!"

"Okay, Cate. Enjoy your dinner, Sir Riley!"

Cate waved and headed back to the castle. As she walked, she pondered Jack's statements. He was right; it was her overactive imagination, coupled with some sleepless nights. It had to be; she probably just thought she saw someone. At least that was what she would keep telling herself.

CHAPTER 29

$\mathcal{C}$ate awoke early the next morning after a good night's sleep, convinced that Jack was right. She reminded herself, as she did most of the evening, that no scientific evidence of ghosts existed and that her mind was playing tricks on her.

Lying in bed, she watched the first rays of morning light paint the night sky with bright streaks of orange. As she admired the sunrise, she planned her day. She would explore the castle for more material for her book. Since she had never finished the romantic letters that she found, she planned to start with them.

She checked the time on the timepiece, thinking it was another mystery she hadn't finished. Impulsively, she rubbed it to see if it would slow. She didn't know why she was surprised when, in fact, it did begin to slow down. This couldn't be a coincidence. She watched the second hand of the timepiece tick ever so slowly, taking what seemed to be an eternity to snap from second to second. She sighed and whispered aloud, "What is your secret?"

Cate heard something in the hallway; it sounded like a

236

woman's voice. She sat upright, looking at the watch. It was only 5:30 a.m., Mrs. Fraser never arrived before six. Cate decided she better check to see if anything was wrong. She swung her legs over the side of the bed then remembered she had left the watch in its slowed state. She rubbed it and, as expected, it began to pick up speed, returning to normal.

Slipping into her slippers and pulling her robe on, she went to the hallway. She saw no one in the hall. She stepped out peering from door to door, seeing no one.

"Mrs. Fraser?" she called. She received no response. "MRS. FRASER?" she yelled again, straining her ears. She heard nothing.

She returned to her room and dressed for the day, gathering Riley for his morning walk before leaving the room.

After his walk, Cate met Mrs. Fraser in the kitchen before breakfast to ask her if everything was okay this morning. "Good morning, Mrs. Fraser, how are you?" Cate asked.

"Oh, good morning, Lady Cate, you startled me. I'm doing well, how are you?"

"I'm good. Sorry, I didn't mean to startle you. Is everything okay?"

"Okay? What would be amiss?"

"I don't know, but you were here so early this morning I thought something might be wrong."

"Early? I was here just after six, my usual time."

"You weren't here around five thirty this morning?"

"Nay, I wasn't here that early."

Cate paused, lost in thought. "Is everything okay, Lady Cate?" Mrs. Fraser asked when Cate became quiet.

"Yes, must have been hearing things!"

"Oh, I don't doubt that. I'll bet the castle has a whole host of noises you'll discover. Well, I'll have your breakfast ready soon."

"Thanks, Mrs. Fraser." Cate left the kitchen. She wasn't

convinced that the sound she heard was the random groaning of the castle; it had sounded clearly like a woman's voice. Still, she couldn't say for sure and Mrs. Fraser's explanation was far more logical.

After breakfast, Cate took Riley for a longer morning walk around the grounds. As they toured the gardens, Riley suddenly bolted around a set of bushes, disappearing from sight. Cate rushed to keep up with him, rounding the row of bushes to find the reason for Riley's sudden excitement.

As she rounded the corner, she found Riley, his tail wagging furiously, enjoying a game of tug of war with a stick and Jack. With his keen sense of smell, he must have smelled Jack and raced over to say hello. "Ah, good morning, Cate! I thought Sir Riley had let himself out for a walk."

"No, but he's faster at dodging bushes than I am."

"I'll bet he is, and he's not too shabby at tug of war either, he's got quite the grip, this little one has."

Cate watched them play for a moment, Riley pulled and tugged to get the stick away from Jack. Finally, he gave a big tug and pulled it right from his grip. He pranced to Cate, carrying the stick. Jack climbed to his feet. "You win, big guy, you win. And how are you today?" He turned to Cate.

"I'm fine."

"Haven't seen any ghosts today, have you?" he teased.

"No, I haven't seen any ghosts today, thank you. BUT, I made the watch slow down again AND speed up. It has to have something to do with friction."

"Rubbing it? But, that didn't work the last time."

"No, but it did this morning. It can't be a coincidence."

"Try it again."

"Okay." Cate rubbed the watch as she had this morning. It did nothing. Cate frowned at it. "Come on you!" she said to it.

"Talking to watches? NOW, I think you're crazy, Cate." He grinned.

"It just worked." She tried and tried, but to no avail. "It wasn't more than two hours ago! This is so frustrating!"

"Maybe it doesn't like me, maybe it's shy. Did you lose your cell signal again when it happened?"

"I don't know. I didn't check, I thought I heard Mrs. Fraser talking in the hall so I got the watch back up to speed and went to check."

"What did she want?"

"Nothing, she wasn't there. When I asked her about it this morning, she said she wasn't in the castle."

Jack looked concerned. "I'm NOT crazy," Cate answered to his look.

"I didn't say you were, I'm a little concerned that someone might have been in the castle."

"Who would have been there and why?"

"That's the million dollar question. Whoever it may have been, I can't imagine they were up to anything good at 5:30 a.m. in someone else's home."

Cate's blood went cold. In all her preoccupation with haunted castles and ghosts, she had failed to consider that she may be seeing and hearing real, live people wandering the estate. The castle was large enough that someone else could be there without her ever knowing. "Okay, that's creepy on a different level but that would make sense with some things I've been experiencing. But again, why?"

"I can come up with a million reasons: a free place to live, hiding out from someone, trying to scare the new owner, who knows, but I'm getting concerned that maybe it's not your overactive imagination and your big move."

"Do you think I should call the police?"

Jack shook his head. "We don't have proof of anything. Do you mind if I look around?"

"Not at all. I'd feel better if you did, in fact. And I'd like to help! I want to see with my own eyes that no one is here."

"Okay, let's check it out, top to bottom, if your ghost is in there and alive, we'll find them."

They headed for the castle with Riley in tow. As they made their way inside, Jack suggested starting at the bottom floor, the servant's area, and working their way up.

On the bottom floor, they found no evidence of anyone having been in the castle. Moving to the main level, Jack asked where Cate had seen the woman. Cate showed him and explained the direction she had seen her walk and where she had run to when Cate had talked to her. "Okay, let's look." Jack said after she had explained everything to him. They made their way through each room, looking for anything disturbed or evidence of anyone living in the castle but found none.

"One more floor to go," Cate said as they finished looking in the last room. "Not sure if I feel better or worse that we haven't found anything yet."

"Hopefully we'll find something definitive by the time we're done searching so you can rest easier."

As they climbed the stairs, Cate said, "I'm sure we can rule out my bedroom, unless they are living under my bed and I don't know it."

"I certainly hope they aren't!" Jack laughed.

They searched every corner and closet upstairs to be sure there were no signs of anyone. They only had one room left, the room where Cate had found the love letters. As they approached the room Cate said, "I doubt anyone is in there, I've been in and out of that room a number of times, I think I would have seen them."

"Let's check it out just to be sure."

Cate shrugged. "Okay, sure."

They entered the room and searched around. "I'll check

the closet," Cate said, pulling the door open and entering it. She looked around; everything was as she had left it, no signs of anyone. "I don't see anything," she called, "but this is one place this watch loves to do its trick, maybe it'll work here and you can finally see it!" She rubbed the watch and this time, it worked as she expected, slowing down to a crawl. "HA!" she exclaimed, "I was right! Come and see!" She grinned at the watch, then looked up, waiting for Jack. He didn't come in. "Jack!" she called. There was no answer. "JACK!" she yelled louder, but received no response.

She headed for the door, leaving the closet, "Jack?" she said as she scanned the room. He was nowhere. Where could he have gone? Wherever he was, Riley must have followed him. Cate frowned. Where could they have gone?

She went back into the closet to check for him in case he had slipped in without her noticing. She didn't see him, so she figured she had better start searching. Before she left, she turned the watch back to its normal speed not wanting to forget to do it later. She was beginning to think Jack would never see it in person.

Heading back out of the closet, she collided right into Jack. He caught her just as she stumbled backwards, almost falling onto her backside.

"Cate, where have you been?"

"Where have I been? Where have YOU been?"

His face scrunched up in puzzlement. "I've been right here the whole time. I called and called you but you didn't answer. I looked in the closet and you weren't here."

It was Cate's turn to be surprised. "I heard nothing. I called and called to YOU and you didn't answer. I looked in the room and back in here and neither you nor Riley were here."

The two stood for a moment in silence, trying to make sense of what had just happened. Suddenly, an idea struck

Cate. "Do me a favor, I'd like to test something. Go out and close the door, wait about ten seconds, then open it and see if I'm here, then close the door and wait another few seconds and open it again."

Jack looked beyond confused. "Cate, what are you talking about?"

"Just trust me, try it."

"You're the boss." He shrugged.

Closing the door, he left Cate alone in the closet. She began counting in her head to ten seconds as she rubbed the watch, it slowed down to a crawl. She waited for the door to open as she got to the ten second mark. Nothing happened. Before she could begin her second count, she heard voices. She raced to the door to open it, figuring that it was Jack talking to Riley. Astounded, she found no one there, but the bedroom door was open. She was sure it had been closed. Jack must have left; why would he do that?

She headed for the open door, peering into the hallway. She saw no one. "Jack?" she called down the hall, but received no answer. She listened for any sounds; she was sure she heard voices. Maybe Jack had taken Riley for a quick pit stop outside, she surmised. She walked down the hall to see if she saw them in the garden, but she saw no one from the window. She made her way to the closest servant stairs and called down them, "Jack?" Again, no answer.

She was confused, but suddenly realized she had been wandering around for well over the ten second time frame she had given to Jack. She headed back to the closet, checking the room again for signs of Jack and Riley and finding none. She opened the closet door and found it empty. Closing the door behind her, she rubbed the watch and it return to normal speed. Knowing she was well over the time frame she had given to Jack, she expected the door to be open, but it wasn't. Just as she made her way over to it, the door opened and Jack appeared.

Cate was surprised, but thought maybe they had gotten their wires crossed. Going out on a limb she said, "Please tell me this is the first time you've opened that door."

"This is the second time I've opened the door, the first time you weren't here. Cate, where did you go? Is there a secret passage in here?"

Cate swallowed hard, considering what she was about to say. It made no sense even as the words started out of her mouth, "I don't know where I went, but I think it has something to do with this watch."

"You don't know where you went? What could it possibly have to do with the watch?" Jack was full of questions.

"I was standing here in the closet but the door never opened. I heard voices, I assumed it was you and opened the door myself but there was no one. I walked all over looking for you and Riley but couldn't find you."

"What?" Jack laughed. "Cate, are you playing a prank on me? Come on, where is the secret passage or secret panel?" He peered around the room.

"I'm not joking, I wish there was a secret passage or whatever, but there isn't, or if there is, I don't know about it. You two were not here."

"Cate, I can't believe that."

"I'm not sure I want to believe it either, but it's the truth, I didn't see you and the only thing that changed was this watch's speed."

Jack paused. "I don't know what to say, I can't think of a relevant question to even ask, I don't understand any of this."

"Me either, but I can think of one question to ask."

Jack looked at her hard. "What's that?"

"If you didn't see me here, where was I?"

CHAPTER 30

"None of this makes any sense to me, Cate," Jack admitted. "If you never left, where were you? You were not here."

Cate sunk down to sit on a trunk as a wave of nausea passed over her. "None of it makes any sense, you're right. Are you sure you didn't miss me?"

"Cate, there's no missing you, you're standing here plain as day in front of me. I didn't miss you."

Cate considered the situation, but a satisfactory explanation escaped her. "Is it possible," she said, thinking out loud, "there is some mechanism that moves this closet? Perhaps there is a secret passage or panel that we aren't aware of that interacts with the watch."

"Okay, but the closet looked the same just minus you. So, an identical space must be replacing it. And if we're moving, what mechanism is that quiet that no one would hear it? And how could the watch control it?"

"I don't know, but something strange is going on."

"That's the only thing we know for sure, something strange is going on. Damn! A fine time for my grandfather to be traveling, he'd be the perfect person to ask." Jack looked down at Cate. "Cate, are you okay? You're white as a sheet."

"Yeah, well I mean other than me disappearing with no explanation, I'm okay. I just don't know what to think anymore."

"Well, until we know what to think, it might be best that you're not fiddling with this watch, we don't want you disappearing for good."

A wave of panic swept over Cate. "Maybe you're right. We do not understand what it's doing or where I'm going, maybe I shouldn't mess with it."

"I'm not even sure you should keep coming to this closet, it may be something similar to what you suggested earlier being triggered by something we don't know of."

"Good point." Cate stood up to leave but sunk right back down onto the trunk.

"Whoa, you okay, Cate?"

"Yes, just a little woozy. I think I'm letting my fear of the unknown get to me a little too much. I'm sure there's a reasonable explanation for this."

"Maybe you should lie down."

Cate was about to decline and insist she was fine, but she wasn't sure she was. She was disconcerted by her disappearing and reappearing. She forced her mind to think logically, but it could come up with no logical explanation at present. She told herself that there was a reasonable explanation, as was often the case with strange events like this, but she still couldn't shake the eerie feeling that something was amiss. It made her head swim and threatened to bring her breakfast rising into her throat. "Maybe you're right," she agreed. She felt childish and silly, like a heroine in a gothic novel with a case of the vapors, but she needed some time to think and relax.

"Here, let me help you to your room."

She struggled to her feet, unsteady at first, then, feeling stronger, and with Jack's aid, made her way to her room. Riley followed behind, not sure what to make of everything but sensing Cate's anxiety.

As Cate climbed into bed, Riley attempted to jump onto the bed. Jack placed him on the bed and the little dog curled up by her side and stared at her as if trying to determine the source of her nervousness. "I'll tell Mrs. Fraser that you're not feeling well and to bring your lunch here," Jack said, as she settled into bed.

"Thanks." Cate answered.

As he left the room, he turned and said, "Don't worry, Cate, I'm sure there is a reasonable explanation, we'll figure it out."

Cate nodded in answer. As he disappeared from sight, she laid her head back, her hand stroking the fur down Riley's back to relax both of them. She took a few deep breaths, trying to clear her mind, but she found it impossible to push the thoughts of what happened from her mind. Jack's words echoed in her head: "You weren't there, Cate, you weren't there," and she again wondered where she was. It was a terrifying idea to think she had disappeared and not even known it. It was even more terrifying wondering where she had gone. Wherever she was, she couldn't see or hear anyone who was in the same room as her. Was she in some spirit realm? None of it made sense.

Riley stared up at her, still unsettled by her strange behavior. "It's okay, Riley. I'm fine. At least, I think I'm fine. I don't know which way is up anymore." She thought of her "disappearance," of little Riley left behind, searching and not being able to find her. It made her feel woozy all over again.

As Cate fretted over the morning's events, she heard footsteps in the sitting room. She sat upright, startled by the noise until she heard Mrs. Fraser call out, "Just me coming in, Lady Cate. I've got your lunch."

Cate scolded herself for being so silly; of course it was Mrs. Fraser. She had to stop letting her new environment lead her into jumping at every noise. "Come in, Mrs. Fraser," she called back.

Mrs. Fraser pushed the door to the bedroom open, carrying a tray. "Well, what's this about being sick?"

"Oh, it's nothing serious. I just felt a bit woozy, probably too little sleep or something," Cate said.

"Well, lucky for you, I was making some of my famous chicken soup. It's just what you need for whatever ails you." Mrs. Fraser set the tray down next to Cate. "And I brought a bone up for Riley, too, to keep him occupied while you rest. Now here, lean forward and let me straighten your pillows."

"Oh, that's unnecessary, Mrs. Fraser. Thank you so much for the soup and the bone for Riley."

"Now come on, don't make me ask twice." Cate leaned forward, not wanting her to ask again and allowed her to fluff and straighten the pillows. "Leave it to a man to just dump you off in bed and not bother to get you settled. There we are, that should do. Now you just sit back and enjoy your soup, I'll be back to check on you later." Before leaving, Mrs. Fraser set the bone down on the floor and settled Riley with it.

Cate obeyed Mrs. Fraser and ate her soup. It was obvious why they referred to it as famous; it was delicious. She watched Riley chewing his bone on the floor; he also seemed to enjoy Mrs. Fraser's lunch.

The lunch seemed to fortify her a bit. She felt much better than she had earlier. Eating also seemed to clear her mind. She was being ridiculous, there was a plausible explanation. People didn't just disappear and reappear. She firmed her resolve with each passing moment. She would unravel this and she would not panic over it while doing so.

Mrs. Fraser returned just as Cate was climbing out of bed. "What's this? Up already?"

"Yes, I feel much better. Your chicken soup does work for whatever ails you! I was going bring the tray down on my way to the library."

"Nay, I won't have it, back to bed with you."

"Oh, but I feel fine!" Cate felt like a child bargaining with a parent to play outside after being ill.

"You need rest. Young Jack says you were white as a sheet, could barely keep to your feet when he brought you in here. I'd say you still look a mite too pale for my taste. Now back to bed."

"I always look too pale for my taste," Cate joked, referencing her light complexion. "Besides, I can't just sit here, I need something to do, at least. I'll get my laptop and my notes and then I'll get back into bed, I promise."

"I'll have none of that. You're not running around the place ill on my watch. I'll send young Jack with it or fetch it myself."

Cate sighed; she would not win this battle. Giving up, she climbed back into bed. Mrs. Fraser pulled the covers up over her, turning them back to rest on her lap. "There we are, now I'll send up a plate of cookies for you. Got to keep your strength up." Cate had to admit, this wasn't too bad. She hadn't had someone worry about her strength in quite a while, although she now felt silly over the entire incident.

"Thanks, Mrs. Fraser."

Cate waited in bed for her laptop and other research materials. She didn't have long to wait, it couldn't have been over fifteen minutes before she heard movement in the sitting room and saw Jack appear at the doorway. His hands were full. "Let's see, I've got cookies," he said, placing the plate on the bedside table, "a laptop and a folder marked Castle research. Did I get everything?"

"Yep, you got everything. Sorry, Mrs. Fraser wouldn't permit me to get out of bed to get it myself."

"I heard, the old toughie has forbidden you to leave your bed. Sorry, that's my fault; I'll admit I was worried, and I told her you were awfully pale. You look better now though."

"I feel better, I think I just panicked. There must be a reasonable explanation."

"Well, we don't have to solve it today. I'm with Mrs. Fraser on this one, take the day to rest."

"With everyone fussing over me, I'll be back to normal in no time."

"There's the spirit. Is there anything else you need?"

"No, I think this is everything, thank you!"

"You're welcome, Cate," Jack said, leaving the room.

Left alone, Cate opened her laptop first to check her email. She found three emails waiting for her amidst the junk mail: one from Gayle, one from Molly and one from the author of *The Mysteries of Scotland.* She opened Molly's first.

Cate—OMG!!! I just got your postcard. I'm glad to hear that you're doing so well. Is the joint haunted or not? I posted your postcard in the department office for everyone to see. Don't be surprised if you get a few emails from people asking to visit. I'll be the first, can I visit yet? LOL

Enjoy your new adventure!!
   Molly

Cate smiled at the email, Molly could always make her laugh. She pressed the Reply button and emailed back describing how at home she felt and told her she was welcome to visit any time she wished. She side-stepped the haunting question, now not sure if she could send an honest and dismissive answer.

Cate moved on to the email from Preston Scott, the author of *The Mysteries of Scotland*.

Good day Cate! Lovely to hear from one of my esteemed readers and thank you for your inquiry. I gathered the information for my stories from visiting the local towns themselves and speaking with residents. Many castles have tales to tell and many of those living near them love to tell those tales! I find this a most effective way to gather information (and fun, too!).

Good luck with your research project. I wish you all the best with your book. If you need a critique, I would be happy to provide one for you!

My highest regards,
   P. Scott

The email left Cate with no more information than she already had. But, at least the author had answered. Cate moved on to the email from Gayle, hoping for a better result.

Hello Cate, I hope you are doing well. I have the information that you requested about your grandfather. We searched the records to find the birth certificate for both your grandfather, Charles, and your father, Logan. I had digital scans sent, and I attached them to this email.

As you can see, your grandfather was born in Scotland as Charles MacKenzie to Lucas and Amelia MacKenzie (additional

information including dates are in the attachment). Your father
was born in Dublin, Ireland to Charles and Sophie MacKenzie.

Your grandparents' name changed (deliberately or not) from
MacKenzie to Kensie when they emigrated to the States.

I hope this information helps you in your search and if I can be of
any further assistance, again, please reach out.

Best,
  Gayle

Cate was thrilled. The information answered her question. She now knew when the name change had occurred, although she did not know why. She also had her great-grandparents names, which she hoped she could use to identify the link between herself and Gertrude.

She opened her notes, took out her pen and pulled out the family tree she had copied from the family bible. She scanned the tree for the names listed in Gayle's email. She found them at the same level as Gertrude's parents. It looked like her great-grandparents were Gertrude's grandparents, making her grandfather and Gertrude's father cousins. This made Cate and Gertrude second cousins-once removed.

Cate filled in the remaining piece of the family tree where the inkblot had been in the family bible. The blot had covered her grandparents and anyone in their line. Cate was pleased; one mystery solved. She had established her relationship to Gertrude, and she confirmed that she belonged in the castle. It was exciting to have found the answer to one part of her research.

She took out her summary sheet with her overall notes and documented what she had found. The only questions left in this column was why she never knew of her distant relatives and why her family's surname had been changed. Even with the unanswered questions, Cate took satisfaction in crossing this research question off the list. She struck a line through it on the paper as a final form of closure.

Turning back to her laptop, she sent a reply to Gayle.

Dear Gayle—Thank you so much for providing the information. It helped immensely with my research. Using the information that you sent, I filled in the family tree that I have been working on and determined my relationship to Gertrude (second cousins-once removed).

I now have a sense of how we fit into the family puzzle, although I don't know why the surname was changed and this side of the family was never mentioned.

Again, thank you for your help. I hope you are doing well. Please send my regards to Mr. Smythe. I hope you can find some time to visit in the summer so I can thank you in person. Riley and I would love to have you back with us at the castle!

Cate

P.S. Riley and I are doing great! He has made a new friend in Jack, he loves to play fetch with him.

Cate sent the email, leaning back on her pillows, she took a moment to savor the end of a research thread. She glanced at her summary sheet, smiling at the struck-out question. She turned her attention to the other items on the sheet, including the timepiece. Her mind snapped back to the mystery unraveling around the object and the events of this morning. She frowned; she had distracted herself for a bit with other work but now the mysterious events of the morning were front and center in her mind again, unnerving her as they had earlier.

Cate distracted herself by turning her attention to the cookies Mrs. Fraser sent. She nibbled on one, still unable to distract her mind even with the rich, buttery flavor. Cate forced herself to study the other items on her summary sheet, hoping the distraction helped her like it did before.

She spread her research notes out across the bed, taking stock of what she had. She organized them in what she envisioned the chapters of her book would be. With the chapters arranged, she opened a blank document on her laptop and typed in a proposed table of contents. Under each chapter, she listed a summary of the details she hoped to provide in the chapter.

Next, she began looking through her notes, annotating where each piece of information might best fit into the text. She also took stock of where she was missing information or where she needed to supplement her current information.

As usual, she found her research to be all consuming, and lost track of the time. She was startled to see Mrs. Fraser carrying in her dinner tray. "Is it dinner time already? Where did the time go?" Cate said, hurrying to clear a spot for her tray. "Thank you so much, Mrs. Fraser."

"I hope you're managing to rest amid all that work!"

"It relaxes me, so I'm resting." Cate smiled.

"Well put that restful work aside and eat your dinner. And you, Riley, come with me, I will take you out to do your business."

"Oh, no, Mrs. Fraser, that's too much. I can take him!"

"I'll not have you roaming around the estate in your condition, when you could take ill at any moment."

"I'm not THAT ill, I'm not even sick, honest!"

Mrs. Fraser was already gathering Riley into her arms.

"You just concentrate on eating your dinner and saving your strength." She turned and left the room. Cate heard her talking to Riley as they went. "Now, little pup, I will not take you on any long and luxurious walk like your Mum, but at least you'll get some fresh air and the chance to do your duties. Come along little fellow, let's let Lady Cate have her dinner in peace and I'll give you a nice dinner downstairs." Cate smiled, knowing Riley was in good hands with Mrs. Fraser.

Cate looked at her tray, realizing she was also in very good hands with Mrs. Fraser. She had provided her with another cup of chicken soup, along with a soft-boiled egg on toast. Cate dug in, realizing how hungry she was.

By the time she had finished the last few bites of her meal, Mrs. Fraser was returning with Riley. "Here he is, all walked and fed and happy," she said, as she perused Cate's dishes to ensure that she had eaten everything. "Glad to see you got everything down, protein is what you need."

"Thank you, it was delicious as always. And thank you again for taking care of Riley, I appreciate it."

"My pleasure. Now, we'll stay overnight, that way, we'll be here if you need anything."

"Oh, no, now, Mrs. Fraser, that's where I draw the line. I will not have you staying over night here and putting yourself out, I'm FINE." Cate shook her head adamantly.

"Suppose you get ill again and need something?"

"If I'm that sick, I can call you, I've got your number right here in my phone. I'll keep it right here by my bed all night and call if I need anything."

"Now, I'll not have any of this. Mr. Fraser and myself and young Jack are all staying here. Between your being sick and Jack wondering if there's someone roaming around this place, we're not about to leave you here alone."

Cate gave in. "Thank you, Mrs. Fraser, I appreciate that."

Relief coursed through her knowing that she wouldn't be alone in the castle tonight.

Cate watched her carry the tray out of the room. She meant what she had said. She was incredibly lucky to be surrounded by people who cared so much about her. Or did they? A fleeting concern shot across Cate's mind. Honestly, what did she know of these people? They knew the castle better than she did and had access to her food. Could they have slipped something into it? They could be setting this up. Cate shook her head; she concluded that she was being paranoid. What motive would they have? What would they gain? Nothing was her only answer. She pushed the thoughts from her mind, determined to enjoy her night. She was silly to be worrying herself sick over something that would turn out to have a reasonable explanation. She resolved to enjoy the rest of her evening, deciding to clean up her research and watch a few movies before bed. She concluded that the best idea would be to watch a few comedies. She picked up Riley and settled him next to her on the bed, browsed through a few titles and picked a familiar comedy to stream. Settling back, she turned off her light and prepared to laugh until she cried.

CHAPTER 31

*D*espite the distraction of the movies, as soon as Cate put away her laptop and attempted to sleep, she found her mind preoccupied with the mystery of the timepiece. She tried to distract herself by pondering her connection to the family tree and the questions that remained. She attempted to dwell on the fact that she was not alone in the castle tonight to comfort herself into sleep. Nothing seemed to work. No matter what she did, the mind-boggling mystery ensnared her mind. Where was she when Jack opened that closet door?

Cate grabbed the watch, holding it up above her, staring at it, as she had so many times before. No matter how hard she tried, it wouldn't disclose its secrets. Rising from bed, Cate paced the floor of her room, then found herself settled outside of the large window. She stared out at the moonlit grounds; everything was cast in a white blanket. Nothing seemed to be moving; yet that did nothing to ease Cate's mind.

Standing up again, she paced into her sitting room, sitting on the chaise for a bit, hoping to fall asleep there. Again, her eyes gravitated to the watch. She got to her feet again and headed for the hallway. Looking out, she stared at the doors where Mr. and Mrs. Fraser and Jack were presumably asleep, trying to draw comfort from their presence, knowing they were there if she needed them. If they could see and hear her, anyway.

Cate was about to head back to bed, but impulsively she headed to the room with the closet where she had done her disappearing act earlier. Despite being warned by Jack, the unsolved mystery compelled her to return to search for clues that may help to solve it.

Cate scrutinized every inch of the walls, doorways, doors, and woodwork, any surface that may conceal a mechanism for moving the room or opening a passage. She considered the dimensions of the room; often castles were built with secret passages in them. Though difficult to detect, the room dimensions would reveal the fact that a secret passage existed to a trained eye. Cate found no evidence of that. The dimensions of the room and its closet didn't seem to suggest that there were any hidden spaces.

Cate sat down on the bed, staring at the closet. Her mind wandered through question after question. If she slowed the watch again would she disappear from existence? Would she find her staff asleep in their beds in her altered state? Was she losing her mind?

She didn't have answers to any of these questions and didn't expect she would have them in the near future. She considered slowing the watch just to observe what would happen. Jack's warning echoed in her mind: "until we know what to think, it might be best that you're not fiddling with this watch, we don't want you disappearing for good." He was right, she did not understand what was going on. It might be dangerous to continue to meddle with something she did not comprehend. What if she ended up stuck in the netherworld or wherever she was going?

She quit for the night, heading back to her room. It was almost 2 a.m. when she crawled into bed, sleeping restlessly. She woke up a few hours later in a cold sweat having dreamt of herself disappearing into a spirit realm where no one could see or hear her. She screamed to people who continued about their daily business as though she wasn't there. But no one could hear her, see her or help her.

When she awoke, she had little interest in going back to sleep. The dream, despite not being real, struck terror into her heart and she found herself glad that she had not fiddled with the watch last night. She cuddled Riley closer to her, as though contact with him would hold her in this world.

It was just after 5 a.m. when Cate crawled from her bed and headed to the chaise in her sitting room. She tried not to dwell on her dream but on the fact that the sun would soon rise and daylight would hopefully banish all her fears about disappearing.

She found her mind wandering back to it repeatedly. She flipped on the light to dispel the darkness until sunrise. She blinked a few times as the stark light filled her eyes, blinding her. Changing her mind about the light, she reached over to turn the lamp off and caught sight of Mary's journals on the table. She remembered the entry in the journal on the stuck pages about the timepiece. Picking it up she paged through to find the entry again.

She re-read it piece by piece, trying to glean any information. As I continue these excursions, I can not help but feel the tremendous responsibility to pass along to Gertrude, the entry began. Was Mary's reference to the "excursions" a reference to wherever Cate was going when the watch slowed? She referred to the timepiece, calling it an "awesome object" for which she was a mere caretaker, then discussed an enormous responsibility that she must pass along to Gertrude. None of this pointed to what was happening when Cate disappeared earlier, but they all had to be connected.

Shutting the journal, Cate set it down, frustrated. She was missing something, but she couldn't put her finger on what. Cate went back to her bedroom, finding Riley still sleeping. She reached for her research folder and crept back to the sitting room. Pulling a page out of her notebook, she began jotting things down.

She wrote, to her best recollection, when and where the watch had slowed. She included details such as what she had been doing when it slowed, what happened between the watch slowing and speeding up and anything else relevant that she could remember. She also noted the times she tried to slow the watch, and it had not slowed. Although there wasn't a lot of data on it, she noted the watch only seemed to slow within the castle itself. She also wrote a note to try the watch again outside of the castle; it would not only add to her theory, but it was also the safest place to try since it had never worked outside of the castle so she was in no danger of disappearing.

She noted that, according to Jack, she had "disappeared" the last time she slowed the watch, despite her never having moved, at least not to her knowledge. She also noted that twice before when the watch had been slow, she had seen what she thought to be "people" on the estate. She used the term loosely since she had no evidence that anyone else had been on the estate. And that it seemed these people or what-ever they were, could see and hear her since both of them reacted to either the sight of her or a noise she had made. "Odd," she wrote, "that these 'people' could see and hear me, yet Jack could not see me, nor I him."

Cate reached to the far depths of her mind to determine if there was anything else to include on the note sheet she was creating when a light knock came at the door. If the room hadn't been so quiet, she doubted she would have heard it. "Yes?" she called out.

Her door creaked open a bit and Mrs. Fraser peeked in. "Out of bed already, Lady Cate? Did you sleep? How are you feeling?"

"I feel much better, although I'm afraid I didn't sleep much. Did you and Mr. Fraser sleep well?"

"Aye, we both slept well. Too bad you didn't sleep, I'll have your breakfast up to you soon, you stay here and rest."

"If you don't mind, I'd like to have breakfast with everyone this morning. I'm tired of my own company."

"We'd be glad to have you, Lady Cate."

"Great, I'll be down soon!"

Cate set everything aside and dressed and walked Riley before breakfast. She welcomed the distraction and hoped it would ease some things on her mind for at least a little while.

She met everyone in the kitchen for breakfast just as Mrs. Fraser was setting the table. "Well, good morning again, Lady Cate." Mrs. Fraser said.

"Good morning, everyone! I hope everyone slept well. Thank you all for staying last night." Cate said, smiling.

"Good morning, Lady Cate," Mr. Fraser said.

"Good morning, Lady Cate, I hear you'll be gracing us with your presence this fine morning. Did you sleep well?"

"I didn't sleep very well, but I was glad everyone was here when I couldn't sleep!"

Cate helped Mrs. Fraser finish up with the breakfast and table settings, sitting down to eat with everyone else when everything was ready. Cate did her best to keep the conversation light and flowing through breakfast. She was reluctant for breakfast to end; the distraction was comforting her. But breakfast did end, with Mr. Fraser and Jack preparing to head out for the morning.

Cate remained in the kitchen, helping Mrs. Fraser with some breakfast dishes. She wanted in some small way to thank her for staying the night.

"You don't need to help, Lady Cate, I can do it."

"I'd like to, if you don't mind. I'd like the company."

"Well, if it's company you're after, you don't have to do dishes to get it. Why don't I make you a nice cuppa, you can sip on that and we can chit-chat? Oh." Mrs. Fraser paused. "That would be a cup of tea to you, Lady Cate."

"Oh, I'd appreciate some tea, but I can make it while you take care of those dishes." Cate started to fill the kettle that Mrs. Fraser kept on the stove. "Would you like a cup as well?"

"Yes, please," Mrs. Fraser answered, already readying two cups with tea bags and setting out sugar and cream. She made quick work of the breakfast dishes and was ready to sit down with the tea as soon as the kettle began to boil.

"You timed that well!" Cate said, pouring the steaming water into each cup.

"Usually do," Mrs. Fraser answered, "I never miss my morning cuppa. Couldn't get through a day without it."

Cate smiled at her as she carried the cups over to the table, surprised Mrs. Fraser let her do that much. Mrs. Fraser was busy arranging a plate of cookies from a tin.

"Are these the cookies you sent up for me yesterday? Those were excellent."

"Indeed they are, Lady Cate. Perfect cookie with tea if you want my opinion," she said, dunking a cookie into her tea after mixing some cream into her cup.

"Do you bake often?"

"I do, I find it a good pastime and a tasty one, too." The woman's joke surprised Cate.

"Well, you are good at it, Mrs. Fraser."

"Thank you, Lady Cate."

"I don't bake much myself, I'm not good in the kitchen, once in home ec class, I burned…" Cate began rambling when Mrs. Fraser interrupted her.

"Lady Cate, sorry to interrupt, but I know the reason you want a distraction is that you'd been experiencing some strange things on the estate. As much as I'd like to talk about baking experiences, I'd like to find out why young Jack was so concerned about someone being on the estate."

While Cate hadn't wanted to dwell on it, she appreciated the woman's directness. "Oh, yes," Cate began. "Well, I mentioned to him I've seen a few people around the estate and I think he became concerned that it was more than my mind playing tricks on me."

"People around the estate? You mean that maid?"

"Yes, her and the man working in the back garden. And the other morning, I heard a woman's voice in the hallway before anyone was here."

"I understand you both searched but found nothing yesterday?"

"Yes, we checked everywhere but found no evidence of anyone in the castle."

"The cleaning company has mentioned nothing to me about seeing anything unusual. But you just experienced a major life change. Every place has its own quirks, and the castle is quite large and full of them. Give yourself some time to adjust, Lady Cate."

Cate nodded, then tried to change the subject a bit. "Mrs. Fraser, do you know why this timepiece was so important to Lady MacKenzie? Or if it has any special significance?"

"None that I know of. I recall that she wore it round her neck all the time, never saw her without it. Beyond that I don't know."

"Hmm, I found a passage in Mary MacKenzie's journal,

the one I had to steam to read, it mentioned the timepiece, she called it an 'awesome object' so I was wondering what was so special about it."

Mrs. Fraser thought a moment then answered. "Maybe on account of it being so old? It's my understanding that it's been a family heirloom for generations, dating back to almost the building of the castle, I think."

"Maybe," Cate said, not agreeing, but not wanting to continue the conversation. She finished her tea. "I think I'll take Riley for a nice long walk. Thank you for the tea and conversation, Mrs. Fraser."

"You're most welcome, Lady Cate. Oh, and Lady Cate?"

"Yes?" Cate said, turning back toward her after collecting Riley.

"Try not to worry too much about it, I'm sure it's nothing." Cate smiled at the woman's kind attempt to be reassuring, but deep down she knew it was anything but nothing.

CHAPTER 32

*B*efore heading out the door, Cate grabbed a ball for Riley to play with during the walk. Cate wanted to spend the rest of her morning walking the grounds to keep herself occupied. She hoped the activity would allow her to sort her thoughts. The path Cate chose led them to the loch, Cate tossed the ball and Riley bounded after it then waited for her to catch up and throw it again. Watching Riley play did a great deal to lighten her mood and distract her thoughts.

Even still, her mind couldn't help but return to the mystery every so often. When they arrived at the loch, Cate pocketed the ball and sat down on the edge. Riley collapsed in a heap next to her, ready for a rest after the morning's excitement. Cate stared at the beauty outstretched in front of her, wondering what dark secret it might hide.

She picked up the timepiece that hung around her neck, remembering that she wanted to experiment with it outside of the castle. She had tried the watch twice outside of the castle and it hadn't worked either time. Was that a coincidence or not? Jack's warning rung in her mind, but Cate was sometimes a little too impulsive for her own good. She observed the watch as she rubbed it. Nothing happened. She tried again, just for good measure, still nothing.

The outcome added weight to her theory that the watch only worked within the castle walls, not outside of them. Also, she hadn't disappeared; she determined both were good things.

Lying back in the grass, she gazed at the fluffy white clouds as they rolled by against the blue sky. Her mind wandered over her notes, reminding herself of things to add or going over things she remembered writing. She pondered what to do next. Her mind jumped to the most obvious next step: try the timepiece inside the castle. As afraid as it made her, her curiosity squashed most of the fear. "Curiosity killed the cat," her mother had always warned her as a child. "But, if we didn't try, we'd solve nothing," she had argued back. She had always prided herself on her curiosity; she felt it made her a good researcher.

She relaxed there a few more minutes before sitting up, saying, "Well, Riley, are you ready to go?"

Riley eyed her without lifting his head. "Too tired? Okay, come on, I'll carry you for a bit." Cate lifted him into her arms; he stretched and relaxed, ready for the royal treatment. "Oh boy, Riley, you are getting lazy." Cate laughed as she picked herself up off the ground and brushed herself off. "Castle life suits you."

She started back on the path toward the castle. As she approached the back gardens, she spotted Jack working away at trimming another set of bushes.

"Good morning, again," she said as she approached.

"Good morning, again. And what do we have here? Sir Riley too tired to walk?"

"I'm afraid I tired him out playing ball this morning."

"I'd have thought he'd have you tired out after your sleepless night. For what it's worth, I heard nothing last night."

"Neither did I," Cate began. "I'm not surprised though. I think all those incidents are connected to the watch. I made some notes this morning and if I'm correct, I encountered people on the property when the watch was slow. I tried it again this morning out here by the loch, but it didn't react. So that's the third time that I've tried the watch outside of the castle and it didn't slow. I'd say that means that it only works in the castle itself. What it's doing I don't know, but…"

Jack interrupted her. "You tried it again this morning? I thought we agreed that you wouldn't mess around with that until we learned more about it."

Cate frowned. "How are we going to learn anything about it unless we test it?"

"Cate, this is not a good idea until we determine what's going on, which may never happen. But yesterday you disappeared. You were not there. It's not wise to keep fooling around with something so strange. What if you get trapped somewhere and we can't find you?"

Jack's lecture irritated Cate. He had a point, but she disliked what she perceived as preaching. "Well, I hope we have some answers soon," Cate said, dodging the question.

"Me too," Jack agreed. "Until then, do nothing."

"Well, I better be heading back. I'll talk to you later!" Cate headed toward the castle, glad to leave the conversation behind. Jack's scolding had not convinced her that doing nothing was the right approach. The watch didn't seem to cause any ill effects on anyone else who had worn it through all these generations. Lady MacKenzie wore it last and lived to a ripe old age, dying of an aggressive cancer and stroke, not from disappearing.

Cate convinced herself to experiment with the timepiece, hoping her curiosity was not her undoing. When she reached the castle, she had a bit of time before lunch, so she headed back to her sitting room to add her thoughts and experience from the morning walk to her notes. She read through everything again. While perplexing, her experiences with the timepiece did not seem dangerous.

Cate resolved to explore a theory after lunch. Guilt weighed on her for not telling anyone but she didn't want to go through the argument. She resolved to leave a note in her sitting room. That way, if anything happened and they couldn't find her, everyone would be aware.

Checking the watch, she found it was almost time for lunch. She gathered Riley and headed to the library, her routine spot for lunch. She spent lunch reading a book, or trying to, the task that lay ahead of her preoccupied her thoughts. She spent most of lunch in nervous anticipation. What if something happened to her? Should she call the whole thing off? Would she learn anything or would it cost her more than she was willing to pay? Would the gamble pay off? Cate decided she would risk it. She had to know.

She thanked Mrs. Fraser for lunch when she came to collect the tray then headed back to her sitting room to leave a note, just in case. She left Riley in the library; she hated to do it but she didn't want the worry of losing him again or having him become trapped. She took a deep breath as she looked at him sleeping before closing the doors to the library.

In the sitting room, she took out a sheet of paper and, with a shaky hand, scrawled a note explaining that she had tried to recreate the phenomenon that she and Jack had experienced yesterday. She also told the reader where to find Riley, just in case. She tried to convince herself that her shaky hands were due to the excitement of exploring a mystery, but deep down, she was also nervous.

But she had decided, and she resolved to follow through.

She propped the note against the lamp on the table and stood, steeling her nerves. She strode to the bedroom and entered the closet. With sweaty palms, she picked up the pendant, pausing a moment before continuing. "Here goes nothing," she said, rubbing the watch until she heard the familiar loud ticking and witnessed the second hand slow.

She waited until it slowed to a crawl, and then she unlatched the closet door, peering into the room. This time, she had a plan. She would observe as much as she could to make a record to study later.

At first glance, nothing stood out as different. She pushed her mind to remember every detail of the room. The furniture sat in the same places. Was that the same bedspread? She wasn't positive, but it looked right to her. Was there a lamp missing, she wondered. She wasn't sure. She wondered if Jack or either of the Frasers could see her if they had been in the room. An idea struck her and she approached a mirror. She gazed at her own reflection; she looked the same. She waved to herself in the mirror. At least she still existed somewhere.

Cate pondered for a moment about putting the watch back to normal speed and ending her adventure, but her curiosity got the better of her and she elected to take a quick peek in the hallway. She cracked open the bedroom door and peeked into the hall. She didn't see or hear anything. The hallway didn't appear to be any different from what she remembered. She took a few tentative steps out into it.

She crept down the hallway, her ears straining for any noise. She approached the corner where it led into the next hall with another set of bedrooms. As she approached, she heard voices. She hid herself and peered around the corner to identify the voices. Two women made their way down the hall. Cate ducked back, not wanting to be seen. Since they were still a ways down the hall, Cate risked another glance.

The women appeared to be in maid uniforms. Cate knew the cleaning crew wasn't scheduled to come in today and the women were not wearing the cleaning company's uniforms. The uniforms looked like they came from the 1800s: a long-sleeved black floor-length dress covered by a white apron. Each of them had their hair pulled into a bun.

Cate held her breath, afraid of giving herself away. What was she witnessing? The women laughed as they approached her. One said, "I dare say we better not be late again with her ladyship's tea. She was so cross I thought that vein in her neck would pop."

"I wish all I had to worry about was me teatime," the other woman answered.

"If we're not on time, she might have to spend another second with her own child lest Nanny not take him away fast enough."

The two women giggled. Cate retreated down the hall, sneaking back to the bedroom. She closed the door and pressed her ear against it. Her heart rose to her throat. She listened to the two women chattering away as they passed the door. She breathed a temporary sigh of relief as they passed by without stopping. She was about retreat to the closet and return the watch to its normal speed when a new voice bellowed down the hall.

"EDNA! LORNA! Are we to idle our day away with chitchat and giggling like two schoolgirls? Have we no work to be done?"

Cate heard no response after a short pause. The woman's voice boomed again. "Then we had better get to it, hadn't we?"

Another moment passed, but Cate heard nothing. She figured she might have pressed her luck far enough. She rubbed the watch, intending to return home from wherever she was. Nothing happened.

CHAPTER 33

*P*anic washed over Cate as she witnessed the watch hands still creeping from second to second. Her heart pounded in her chest so loudly she feared it might leap out. Her pulse raced and her breathing quickened. She tried again, and again, nothing. This had never happened before; the watch had always returned to normal speed.

Cate's eyes welled with tears. Jack warned her not to do something reckless yet she had plowed ahead, anyway. How could she have been so irresponsible?

Her thoughts turned to the note she left. She imagined Mrs. Fraser finding it, asking Jack about it. She pictured Jack's reaction, all of them trying to find her but her lost to them, perhaps forever. As she contemplated this, she remembered her notes, also scattered on the same table. She expected to never return to them again.

She pictured poor little Riley, roaming the castle in search of Cate, but never able to find her. Mrs. Fraser doing her best to console the poor little pup, but not succeeding.

Then it struck her. Some of her previous tests of the

watch had not worked on other parts of the estate. Perhaps it didn't work in this area either. Maybe she needed to be in a specific spot. She knew at least one spot where it had always worked in the past.

Hope filled her as she hurried to the closet. She closed the door behind her, closed her eyes, and with a silent prayer, rubbed the watch. Her heart leapt as the second hand sped up. She placed a hand over her clenched stomach, enjoying a measure of relief. Within moments, the second hand ticked normally.

Cate hurried from the closet and down the hall to the library. She opened the doors and scanned the room. Riley was sprawled in the same spot she had left him. Cate rushed over and scooped him up. A startled Riley wriggled before giving Cate a big lick on her face.

"I'm happy to see you too, buddy!" she said as they left the room. She made her way to the lower level, approaching the kitchen. She peered in, inching toward the room, catching sight of Mrs. Fraser still washing lunch dishes. "Mrs. Fraser?" she murmured.

"Oh!" the woman jumped. "Dear Lady Cate, I wish you wouldn't go about startling me so! You creep up so silently I never realize you're there!" the woman said, grabbing her chest. "Now, what do you need?"

Relief washed over Cate. Mrs. Fraser could still see her, she hadn't disappeared; everything appeared to be back to normal. She resisted her urge to fling her arms around the woman in a giant hug.

"Lady Cate? Everything all right? What do you need?" Mrs. Fraser said when Cate did not answer.

"Oh, um, yes." Cate fumbled. She needed nothing; she just wanted to verify that everything had returned to normal. Cate tried to call to mind something she could ask for. "Um, do you have any more cookies? My sweet tooth is bugging me for an after lunch snack."

"Of course!" Mrs. Fraser said, taking the tin down from a shelf. "You should have told me you wanted them when you finished lunch and I could have brought them up to you."

"Oh, well, I just got the craving now," Cate fibbed. "I wasn't thinking about it after lunch."

"Well, that's rather fast. You just finished your lunch a few minutes ago!"

"What?" Cate responded. She knew more than a few minutes had passed since lunch.

"I say I just saw you a few minutes ago, your cravings come fast."

"Really? Has it only been a few minutes?" This time, Cate was confused. It must have been longer than that. She calculated the timeline in her head. Between checking on Riley, writing the note, traveling to the bedroom closet, spending at least fifteen to twenty minutes wherever she went, it must have been over a few moments. She checked her watch, it read a few minutes past the time it had been when she slowed the watch.

"Yes, girl, it's only been a few minutes. Do you want some milk or tea with them?" Mrs. Fraser handed her a plate with four cookies on it.

"No, thanks. Just these, thank you, again!"

Confused, Cate took the cookies and Riley back up to her sitting room. There the note sat, undisturbed. She picked it up, remembering writing it with a shaky hand and crumpled it up. Cate picked up her note sheet and began adding to the information already there. She tried to be as detailed as possible, writing everything she witnessed.

She wrote a few tentative conclusions and additional questions. Thus far, the watch always worked in the closet. It also worked in a few other places in the castle. Did other places exist where it always worked? Those she encountered did not look like they lived in this era.

The new information that she collected from her daring experiment satisfied her. She figured that was enough excitement for one day though, so she didn't plan to do it again despite the remaining unanswered questions. She marked today as a win.

Checking the time when she finished her notes and her cookies, she discovered that it was a little past two. She still had plenty of time before dinner to work on her book research.

Retrieving all her materials and her laptop, she spread everything out around her in the sitting room, pushing a coffee table aside and planting herself cross-legged on the area rug. Riley ventured over, excited to spot Cate on his level and climbed into the space between her legs to curl up for another nap.

Cate picked up where she had left off before dinner the day before, continuing to fill in information on potential chapters, raise new questions and pinpoint where she needed to fill in additional material. Cate concluded that she had accomplished enough after working two hours and took a now restless Riley out for another walk before dinner.

Gathering her cookie plate, she planned to return it to the kitchen before heading out. She dropped the plate off and thanked Mrs. Fraser again for the delicious cookies.

"Heading out for a walk with Riley?" Mrs. Fraser asked her.

"Yes, just a quick one before dinner."

"Have fun, Riley! And you too, Lady Cate. Oh, Lady Cate, before you go, would you like us to stay the night again? It seems like you're feeling better but if you don't feel quite at home yet and want someone around at night, we're happy to stay. I just want to make the arrangements."

Cate no longer felt afraid of disappearing and she didn't believe there were any grifters hiding on the estate. Although she couldn't be certain about what was going on, she didn't feel as though it would bring her any harm. Perhaps she was viewing a window into a spirit realm and if this were the case, she didn't believe spirits could do her any physical harm. They didn't seem to have harmed any of her ancestors. No matter what the explanation was, after her post-lunch adventure, she sensed she was likely safe unless she herself used the watch again. "I'll be fine, Mrs. Fraser, but thank you so much for offering."

"My pleasure, Lady Cate."

Cate felt like she had been a little curt, so she added, "Oh, if it's ever easier for you to stay the night, Mrs. Fraser, please do so. You are welcome anytime, you need not ask, just let me know you'll be staying so no one is startled in the middle of the night."

"Thank you, Lady Cate. I shall do that if we find it easier to stay, perhaps in bad weather or the like."

"Great!"

Cate headed out the door for a walk with Riley, spending most of her time before dinner enjoying the outdoors with him. She spotted Jack and Mr. Fraser finishing up some work before the end of the day. While she wanted to share her afternoon romp with Jack, she decided against it since he was with Mr. Fraser and also, because she didn't want to hear any lectures about using the watch again. Instead, she just waved and continued on.

During her dinner, which she took in the library while watching a few episodes of a favorite program on her laptop, she got a text from Jack: *u ok? Mrs. F said you didn't need us to stay, r u sure?*

Cate answered: *I'm sure. I don't think anyone is on the property, I should be fine! Thanks!*

Jack returned the text with: *Ok, if you're sure. Text if you need anything.*

Cate answered a simple "will do" and continued on with her meal. As night approached though, Cate second-guessed her choice in sending everyone home. The castle could be spooky at night, but she decided that she was fine and it would just take time for her to become accustomed to it.

Cate headed to her sitting room early, content to settle there with Riley before bed and watch a movie. As she relaxed on the chaise, her mind focused on the day's events and on the watch. Despite the movie playing on her laptop, she couldn't help but wonder about the watch and the scene she had watched unfold after she had slowed it. What did it all mean?

Cate stared at the watch, wondering if she should try it again. She had presumed once was enough for the day, but now, alone in the castle, with her mind wandering from notion to notion, she considered trying it again.

Impulsively, she rubbed it. Nothing happened. Cate sighed; it didn't appear to work in this room either. The closet was the only place she was certain it worked. She realized that it also had worked a few times in her bedroom.

Leaving her laptop, with the movie still running on the chaise next to a sleeping Riley, she tiptoed to her bedroom. Perched on the edge of the bed, Cate considered what she was about to do. She wondered if she should leave another note just in case or perhaps wait until daytime when others were on the estate.

She decided not to wait and rubbed the watch. She watched it as it began to slow down. Taking a deep breath, she looked around. Again, nothing seemed different. She considered bringing the watch back to normal speed since she had proven her point that it worked in the bedroom but her inquisitive nature pushed her to take at least a brief look around. As she related to Jack, if she didn't explore and experiment she would never discover what was occurring.

She headed for the sitting room. Two major differences in this room struck her. Both Riley and her laptop were missing. Wherever she was, Riley was not. A momentary pang of panic settled on her. Not knowing where her little friend may be in relation to her was upsetting, but she remembered that once before she had "lost" Riley but found him to be just fine after the watch returned to normal speed.

She considered returning, wanting to be sure she was right about Riley, but instead, she pressed on to do more investigating.

She left the bedroom, creeping down the hall, trying to note any differences, but failing to notice any. Wary of who or what she might encounter, she snuck around the castle. Reluctant to meet anyone since she didn't know where she was, she did not want to try to explain who she was.

She didn't see or hear much until she crept down the main staircase. She was taking a chance using that staircase, but it was broad enough that she could spy anyone on it before stepping out of the hall and exposing herself to the main entryway.

Cate crept down each step. More than any other noise she made, she thought her pounding heart may give her away to anyone close to her. She reached the bottom with no trouble. Voices came from the nearby sitting room. She crept toward the doors, which were ajar, and peered in.

Inside she saw several people, some sitting, some standing near the massive fireplace. They all wore some form of evening-wear and chatted over drinks. The clothing looked out of place; seeming to come from another era. Despite having a limited view, Cate judged them to be fashions popular in the 1920s. Odd, Cate reflected, this didn't match at all what she had seen earlier.

The scene intrigued Cate and would have loved a longer look and listen, but was as nervous as a long-tailed cat in a roomful of rockers and decided that it was best to head back to her bedroom and try to return home and back to Riley.

She turned and snuck toward the stairs. As she climbed, she reflected on what it all meant. Why where these people dressed so differently from the ones she had seen this afternoon. Who were they and where was she?

Halfway up the staircase a loud voice interrupted her thoughts. "Oi, what do you think you're doing there, miss? Who are you?"

Fear struck deep into Cate, she swallowed hard, turning to face the voice. Cate acquired an answer to one question, and it stared her right in the face. Wherever she was, the people could see her. An obvious fact given the man staring straight at her with a stern look on his face. Cate identified him as a servant, a butler or a footman, by his dress.

He approached from the far side of the entryway, making his way toward the stairs. Cate hesitated, two choices faced her. She could stay and explain or make a run for it. While he was still at a distance, Cate chose the latter, leaping up the stairs two at a time rather than face him. She cursed her impulsiveness as she ran down the hallway toward her room. She heard heavy footfalls coming behind her and the man shouting for help from anyone within earshot.

Racing down the hall, Cate made it to the doorway of her sitting room and ducked inside, shutting and locking the doors behind her. Out of breath, she hurried to the bedroom, not bothering to shut the doors this time. She hoped the first set of doors bought her enough time to get home. She rubbed the watch and witnessed it start to pick up speed. Men shouted in the hallway and doors were opened and closed. They approached her bedroom. She closed her eyes and held tight to the pendant.

CHAPTER 34

*C*ate listened to the voices coming closer and closer to her room. She wondered how she would explain who she was if they found her here. With her eyes still closed, she strained to listen to the noises of the nearby rooms being searched.

In an instant, the voices changed. They were no longer shouting and Cate heard no more doors being opened. Instead, Cate's ears picked up two very different voices. They emanated from somewhere much closer than the hallway. Startled, Cate opened her eyes, searching for a place to hide.

Something seemed familiar about these voices, Cate realized as her eyes darted around the room for a hiding spot. Finding nowhere obvious, Cate figured it might be possible to squeeze under the bed to hide. She dashed for the bed, kneeling on the floor when she realized whom the voices belonged to.

Relief struck her and Cate sunk her head into her hands. Cate, you silly girl, she chided. The voices belonged to two famous actors arguing on-screen about who would do the dishes. In her panic, she had forgotten that the romantic comedy was still playing on her laptop.

Confident that she was safe and alone in the castle, Cate got up and headed for the bedroom doors. There she spied her laptop sitting where she left it and little Riley lying next to it, fast asleep as though she never left him. She stared at the pup for a few moments as her heart slowed and her limbs stopped feeling like jelly.

After taking a few moments to recover, Cate made her way back to the chaise, cuddling Riley into her arms and letting him settle back to sleep on her lap.

She left the movie playing, finding it a comforting background noise as she annotated her note sheet regarding her latest adventure. She noted that this time the people wore clothing from a different era than in her previous experience with the phenomenon. Also, one of them interacted with her, reprimanding her and eventually following her when she did not respond.

After jotting down everything that she remembered, exhaustion set in. The burst of adrenaline after being caught and the run through the castle had left her spent. She called it a night and headed to bed. She hoped to fall asleep right away while her energy was drained and before her mind started churning about everything she had experienced throughout the day.

Fortune smiled on Cate; moments after her head hit the pillow she fell asleep, drifting off to a deep sleep for the entire night. When she awoke the next morning, Cate wondered if she dreamt it all. Lying in bed for a few extra minutes, Cate tried to recall all the details from her evening experience. In her first waking moments, they had been hazy, and she almost concluded it never happened. But upon climbing out of bed and gathering her notes from the side table of the chaise lounge, Cate found the experience detailed in them. She wasn't dreaming when she wrote the notes nor was she detailing a dream.

Looking over her notes from the two incidents from the previous day, she noted again that the people she encountered in her first experience wore clothing from around 1850, however, the second group she came across more closely matched fashions from the 1920s. Why the inconsistency, she wondered. What differences existed between the two incidents? Two sprung to mind: the time of day and the room location. She reviewed her notes again when a new idea occurred to her. Before she put them down to begin her morning routine she wrote two words at the bottom of the page in bold letters: TIME TRAVEL???!!!

CHAPTER 35

ime travel: those two words rattled around in Cate's head all morning. Was she experiencing time travel? Was that even possible? That would explain the people dressed in clothes from a different era. At first she conjectured she was seeing a spirit realm, where ghosts of the past still carried out their daily duties. But with the discovery of seeing several people from yet another time period, she no longer supposed that explanation made sense. Cate's thoughts on the subject ranged from a small measure of certainty that this explained the various things that she had been experiencing to sheer disbelief that she was even considering this.

Even if she was correct, unanswered questions and unexplainable things abounded. She could barely count this as an explanation. Cate's mind was abuzz with so many queries and thoughts that she couldn't concentrate on any research during the morning.

The questions rattled around her brain, driving her almost batty. Not able to contain the information, she let her thoughts spill out to Riley, as she often did. "What do you say, Riley? Is time travel even possible?"

The little dog cocked his head as though considering the inquiry. "You aren't giving much feedback, are you?" Cate said. "I might have to enlist the help of someone else on this one. What do you say, little guy? Should I tell Jack or not? Do you expect he'll have me committed?"

At the mention of Jack's name, Riley sprang to his feet and raced to Cate, tail wagging intensely. "I have my answer. You trust him, don't you, Riley? Well, that's good enough for me! I'll tell him!"

Cate opted for another long walk to the loch with Riley to gather her thoughts and with the hope of running into Jack. After only a few steps down the path, she ran into him. "Got a minute?" she asked. Despite her worry of sounding crazy, she trusted Jack and wanted to run her theory past him. She hoped to tell him the theory in such a way as to minimize sounding like a complete nutcase.

"I always have a minute for Lady Cate and Sir Riley," Jack answered.

"Mind taking a walk with us?" Cate asked, imagining it might be better to have a little distance from the castle when she dropped the bombshell. Plus it felt easier to talk while walking than to make eye contact when admitting to someone that you think you may be traveling through time.

"Sure," Jack said. "Everything okay, Cate?"

"Yes, everything is okay. I... Well..." Cate stammered, not sure where to begin.

Jack stopped walking. "Cate, what is it?"

"Well," Cate began again, looking at the ground, kicking the gravel around.

"Yeah, I got that part," Jack joked to lighten the mood.

"The thing is..." Cate danced around the subject, second-guessing her decision to share the information. After a pause, she said, "I used the watch again, twice. I have a theory. A crazy theory but still a theory. And I'm not positive, but…"

"What? Twice? Cate, you promised." Jack looked disappointed.

"We won't get any information if we don't look for any."

"I can ask my grandfather when he gets back, he might have some information, he's worked here a long time."

"But if he can't help, we have nothing."

"What if something happens to you while you're experimenting with this? Then we've really got nothing and no Cate either."

Cate frowned at the last statement, but let it go, opting instead to remind him that she had an idea about what the watch was doing. "But that's just it, I think I know what the watch is doing."

He sighed, not pleased, but at least willing to continue the conversation. "Okay, I'll bite, what do you think it's doing?"

"Two words," Cate exclaimed, "time travel!"

"Time travel… time travel? Cate, are you being serious?"

"Yes, I'm being serious, it sounds crazy but just listen to what happened when I tried it yesterday," Cate said, knowing how crazy she sounded but also feeling disappointed that he wasn't taking her seriously.

Jack seemed intrigued. "Okay, I'm not okay with you trying this out, but since you already did, I'd like to hear why you presume you are time traveling."

"Okay," Cate said, eager to explain. "Well, yesterday afternoon, after lunch, I decided that I would try the watch. I was responsible and left a note, just in case," she said, shooting him a look. "So I went to the closet, the one I disappeared from and I rubbed the watch and it slowed down. I started by looking around the closet and bedroom; nothing looked different to me. So, I ventured into the hallway. I made my way to where the hall branches off and spotted two women walking down the hall, talking. They were dressed like chambermaids, but not like present-day maids. From what I glimpsed of them, I'd put their clothes around the 1850s, give or take a little."

Cate continued rambling about her experience at lightning speed, "I didn't want them to see me, so I snuck back to the bedroom and waited 'til they passed by. Then I heard someone else talking to them, I caught their names, and I wrote them down in my notes. I can check the records to see if they worked here in the past. Anyway, I didn't stick around after that. Well, I did, only because I forgot that the watch only works in certain areas and I tried to come back from the bedroom and it didn't work. Boy, was I panicked. But then I remembered it worked in the closet, so I went back there and voila! It worked, I was back and only a few minutes had passed. Mrs. Fraser said she saw me only minutes before I tried it!"

"I tried it last night and..." she continued.

Jack interrupted her. "Whoa, whoa, Cate, slow down. I need a moment to process what you've told me. You think you saw maids from the 1850s walking around the castle, then you couldn't get 'back' but then you did. My head is spinning."

"No," Cate said, feeling hurt, "I don't THINK I saw them, I SAW them Jack, plain as I see you standing in front of me."

Jack frowned.

"You think I'm crazy," Cate said, noticing his expression and lack of response.

"I don't know what to think, Cate," he said pausing. "But, no, I don't think you're crazy."

Relief washed over Cate. "I did see them," she reiterated, "and they weren't mists or vapors or random shapes, they were plain as day people walking and talking."

"And you tried again last night? Did you see the same people?"

"No! That's where things gets interesting. I remembered that the watch always slowed down for me in the bedroom. So I tried it there. No one was in the bedroom or sitting room, but my laptop and Riley were both gone. I took a walk around the castle to investigate and…"

"You took a walk around the castle to investigate? Cate! You do not know where or when or whatever you are and you're gallivanting around like you're at the local fair."

"I was careful, for the most part." She shrugged.

"What's that mean?"

"I heard people in the sitting room. I peeked in, several people were there. But they weren't dressed like they were from the 1850s, they were dressed like they were from the 1920s!"

"Now you're in the 1920s? With different people."

"Yes, they were different people and yes, I'd put the year somewhere in the twenties based on the clothes they were wearing. Who says being a history professor never paid off, right?"

"Funny, yes, seems right handy to identify the era you're time traveling to."

"Well, anyway, I didn't stick around, you know, to be safe and all. So I was heading back up to the bedroom, but someone spotted me, a footman, I think. I raced to the bedroom and set the watch back to normal speed, and there I was, back in my bedroom in this time."

"You got caught?"

"No, I didn't get caught, I ran away and escaped," Cate corrected.

"Oh, right, my mistake, someone spied you, somewhere in some time, but you ran away and escaped, sorry. I'm just envisioning the next time when maybe you can't run away."

Cate scowled. "Well, let's hope that doesn't happen. Anyway,…"

"So there will be a next time?"

"Well…" Cate wasn't sure how to answer the question. It was true they didn't have solid information and were only working from theories. But theories needed testing. Even if it wasn't only a theory, Cate ruminated, she'd still want to investigate. Immersing herself in the past would be an appealing proposition for any historian. What better way to discover the past? It would be akin to doing an immersion when mastering a new language. "Yes, I guess is the long and short answer," she admitted.

"Oh, Cate, I know I must sound like a broken record, but I don't think you should mess around with this stuff until we know what's going on, and maybe not even then. What if you get caught or stuck or whatever can happen when you play with that watch? You're a nice lassie, Cate. I don't want anything to happen to you."

"I appreciate that, I do, but…"

"But you've no intention on listening?"

"If I'm really time traveling how exciting is that? It's an opportunity you can't pass up, right?"

"That's a big if, Cate. You're talking as though you're sure that's what's happening."

"Okay, point taken, we're not sure. But, I strongly suspect I'm right, nothing else makes sense. I mean, at first, I hypothesized seeing a spirit world or something, but two different spirit worlds? That theory doesn't fit anymore."

"Yeah, time travel makes way more sense than spirit worlds, although, I missed the part where time travel made any sense."

"Funny," Cate groaned. They had reached the loch some time ago and sat on its bank. Cate stared out over the scenery. It seemed their conversation had ended. Neither of them able to make any further conjecture and both of them at opposite ends about whether Cate should test the watch.

They sat in silence for a few moments, each lost in their own thoughts. Breaking the silence, Jack said, "My grandfather is coming back at the end of the week. Can you at least not experiment anymore with that until we can talk to him?"

Cate considered it. It was only two days. While she was anxious to learn more, maybe she should wait. Her encounter with the footman last night was still unsettling; perhaps she shouldn't be taking any more chances at the moment. Still, she knew herself well, if she promised she'd regret it. She didn't want to break a promise. "If you just saw how it worked, I think you'd..." she began.

"I'm not sure I want to see how it works, it's bizarre even if your explanation is correct. It's downright scary if you ask me."

"But, I think if you tried it you'd see that it's..." she started again.

"Cate."

"I just think..."

"Caaaate."

She wrinkled her nose, crossing her arms. "This could be the greatest discovery of all mankind and you don't want to even discover how it works!"

"We don't know WHAT it is and can't you wait two short days?"

"It's possible your grandfather will not know anything!"

"Or if he'll have us fitted for straitjackets!"

"Just let me show you once how it works and you can decide how dangerous it is for yourself."

"I feel like if I don't agree you're just going to do it on your own, anyway."

Cate reflected for a moment. "Probably."

"As much as I don't want to do this, I'd rather not have you do it alone."

"So you'll do it?" Cate clasped her hands together under her chin, anticipating a positive answer.

"Well, Lady Cate, since you're twisting my arm, I suppose I will."

Cate grinned. "Meet me in the library after lunch."

CHAPTER 36

The morning dragged by for Cate. After Jack had left, she spent a good bit of time with Riley, playing and enjoying the morning before heading back to the castle. With two hours still left before lunch, Cate tried to fill her time with research, but found her mind too distracted.

After what seemed an eternity, Mrs. Fraser appeared in the library with lunch. Cate had little appetite but forced most of her lunch down. Mrs. Fraser's excellent cooking made the chore easier.

Mrs. Fraser came to collect her tray and within a few minutes of her departure, a knock sounded at the library door. "Come in!" Cate yelled.

Jack pushed the door open. "Reporting for duty!" he said as he came through the door, saluting.

"You will NOT be disappointed. Come on!" Cate exclaimed, hurrying out. "Well, at least I hope not," she added as she left the room.

"I hope I'm still around not to be."

Cate shot him a glance over her shoulder as she hurried to the stairs.

"Sorry, bad joke," he said. "Just making sure you really want to do this!"

She laughed. "Out of the two of us, I don't expect it's ME who doesn't want to do it."

"Okay, I'll admit this is not the greatest idea I've ever heard, but I'd rather you not mess around with this stuff alone."

They arrived at the bedroom door, Cate burst through. "Come on!" She headed straight for the closet. "Close the door," she instructed. "Okay, here we go!" She held the timepiece and rubbed it. Taking a deep breath, she waited for it to slow. Smiling, she looked up at Jack, starting to speak to him. Before she could, he disappeared right in front of her eyes.

"Jack?" she called out. "Jack?" It was no use; he was gone. The timepiece had completed its circuit and was now scarcely ticking. She speculated that he must have stayed in their own time. She rubbed the pendant again and followed the second hand as it speeded up.

When it approached its normal speed, Jack reappeared in front of her.

"Cate!"

"Jack! Sorry, I'm not sure what I was thinking; I lost you when the watch slowed. I don't know why I assumed we'd just both go. Perhaps we both need to touch the watch? Let's try that." Cate looked up to behold Jack's face with a mix of confusion and near horror.

"Cate, you just disappeared in front of my eyes. One minute you were here, the next you were gone. Sorry, I need a minute. I mean I realize you disappeared once before, but not right in front of my eyes! That was... weird."

Undeterred, Cate responded, "Here, try holding on to the watch with me, maybe then I won't disappear!"

Jack placed a shaky hand on the timepiece with Cate's, wrapping her hand in his. "Okay, now rub it," Cate said, following her own instructions. He followed suit, and the second hand began to slow. Within seconds, the timepiece was hardly ticking at all, slowed to almost a stop. "You made it!" Cate joked, this time, looking straight at Jack who still stood in the closet with her.

"I did, I guess," he said, pressing his hands on his body in a few places as if checking to make sure it was still there.

"Wanna look around?" Cate said, grinning.

"Uh, well, do I have a choice?"

"Nope, come on, we won't stay long, but see if you notice anything different."

Cate inched open the closet door, peeking out to make sure no one was in the outer bedroom. Spotting no one, she pushed the door all the way open. "I didn't recognize much as different in this room. Only that the lamps were missing, which makes sense if we are in the 1800s."

Jack nodded in agreement without vocalizing a response. "Okay, let's check the hall." Cate pressed her ear to the door for a moment. Satisfied, she unlatched it and nudged it open. She glanced up and down the hall, seeing no one she tiptoed into the hallway, motioning Jack to follow her. "Let's head toward the front stairs," she whispered.

Jack nodded, and they crept down the hallway. They rounded the corner; Cate whispered that she had seen the maids here the day before. She was about to take another step down the hall when Jack grabbed her arm, pulling her back around the corner. He pressed a finger to his lips motioning her to be quiet.

Cate, confused at first, soon understood when she over-heard voices approaching down the hall. She peered around the corner, seeing three women coming down the hall. Two of them were the maids she came across yesterday; the third woman was not a maid. Cate guessed by her dress and keys dangling around her waist she was the housekeeper.

Cate ducked back around the corner and signaled Jack to look, too. He glanced around the corner then nodded back to Cate to demonstrate that he saw them. He motioned to her to signal they should return to the bedroom. She nodded in agreement and they crept down the hall and back into the bedroom. Jack eased the door shut as the voices continued to approach their location.

Cate and Jack froze, standing still right inside the doorway listening as the group of women turned the corner and passed their door. The staff seemed to be discussing a cleaning schedule while the owners were away visiting relatives in London. They passed by the bedroom, continuing down the hall, with the housekeeper giving a long list of orders.

The voices faded down the hall, Jack breathed a sigh of relief. "Should we head back?" Cate asked.

"Yes, please, that's enough excitement for one day," he whispered.

Cate started to head to the closet, then stopped without warning and turned toward him, saying, "This is where I was yesterday when I couldn't get the watch to work..."

Jack interrupted, "Let's talk about this after we're back."

"Oh, right, okay." Cate went to the closet, closing the door behind them. She held the timepiece up and Jack put his hand over hers, rubbing the face with their thumbs together. They stared at the second hand as it returned to normal ticking. Once the speed was normal, Cate said, "Okay, that should be it. I told you! Those people are real. Do you believe me now?"

"I witnessed it with my own eyes but I still can't say I believe it."

"Amazing, isn't it? Encountering people who shaped the history of this castle. It's every historian's dream to go back in history."

"I'm not sure I would call it a dream."

"There isn't a historian alive who wouldn't give anything for five minutes in a room with some of the biggest influencers in history."

"There must be a reason no one knows about this, Cate. I don't think we should use this thing or tell anyone about it. Maybe my grandfather will have some information."

"Okay, okay, I promise not to use it. I feel better knowing someone else experienced this. Now I'm sure I'm not crazy."

"Oh, I experienced it, all right. You're not crazy. Or if you are, so am I."

"Mass hysteria?" Cate joked. "I don't think that's the case here."

"How are you so excited about this? That's enough excitement for me for the day. Time for me to put my own shape on the castle starting with those bushes."

"Okay, yes, you're right. And I've got to document that experience."

"Okay, Cate. And you promise, no more 'trips', right?"

"This time I promise." Cate flashed a smile. "Scouts honor!" she said, holding up three fingers. "Oh, wait, while you're here, would you mind carrying this box of papers to my room? It's kind of heavy, I never got the chance to finish looking through it and I'd like to."

Jack picked up the box, and they left the closet and headed for the hallway. They stepped out together, startling Mrs. Fraser as they almost barreled into her.

"Oh, excuse me," she said eyeing them and raising an eyebrow. "Ahh, putting the strapping young man to work are we, Lady Cate?"

"Yes, this box has a lot of great information for my book, but it was a little too heavy for me to carry."

"I'll just drop it off there and be on my way," Jack said,

beginning down the hall toward Cate's bedroom. "Any special place you want it?"

"No, anywhere near the chaise would be fine, thanks!"

"Quite an asset, he is," Mrs. Fraser said, smiling at Cate. "You know for as long as anyone can remember there's been a Reid on this estate. The estate couldn't run without them!"

"Yes, that's what Jack's grandfather told me. Seems they are as much a part of Dunhaven Castle as the MacKenzies are."

"That they seem to be. Well it seems you're in the middle of your research so I won't keep you."

"Yes, yes, I was," Cate said, judging that it wasn't a lie, "thanks, Mrs. Fraser."

CHAPTER 37

*T*he rest of the week dragged by as Cate waited for Jack's grandfather to return from his trip. She had so many questions she hoped to have answered. One of the most frustrating parts of waiting was the uncertainty. She wasn't sure if Mr. Reid could answer any of her questions when they had a chance to speak with him. Cate tried to fill her days with research, but often daydreamed of visiting the past or wondering if her theory was correct.

During her research, she tracked down old family records in an office room including some employment records and wage sheets. After some tedious searching, she found maids named Lorna and Edna who worked on the estate during the 1850s. She concluded this offered further proof of her theory and added to her growing set of notes on the phenomenon.

After what seemed like an eternity, Saturday made its debut. Cate awoke to a rainy, miserable day. The weather was cool and damp when she took Riley out for his morning constitutional, so Cate decided the day was perfect to stay in and curl up with a good movie. Planning on spending the day wrapped in a blanket on her chaise, she readied her laptop with a few movies and stretched out to relax when her phone chirped to life.

Checking the lock screen, she saw a text from Jack: *My grandfather is home, meet for dinner?*

Cate's mind buzzed with excitement; perhaps now she would get some answers. She texted back: *Sure... where?*

Jack answered: *He said at the castle if that's ok*

Cate considered it for a moment. Given the weather, she had given Mrs. Fraser the rest of the day off, figuring she could fend for herself for dinner. She regretted the choice now if she was having company for dinner; she was a horrible cook. But she wanted answers, and she was willing to cook a dinner to get them if she had to. She answered, ending with an emoticon of a tongue sticking out: *Yes, that will work. No promises on dinner... I'm a terrible cook :P*

Jack answered: *See you around 4? I can cook... you two can talk*

Cate would not complain about that. She answered: *Deal... I'd politely decline and cook myself but no one wants to eat my cooking*

Jack answered with an emoticon of a tongue sticking out. Cate settled back in the chaise; she still had a few hours to kill before they met so she played a few of the movies she had selected. She hoped they would make the time go faster. She couldn't wait to see what Mr. Reid had to say. She cautioned herself not to get too excited; it was likely that he would have no information. But the hope that she might have answers to her questions overwhelmed her mind, and she found herself a ball of nerves all day, checking the time every five minutes. A few times, Cate wondered if she had accidentally slowed the timepiece, because time seemed to be standing still.

After what felt like an eternity, her clock read 3:30 p.m. Cate had enough time for a quick walk with Riley. She arrived back at the castle a few minutes before Jack and his grandfather arrived. She was still shaking off her soaked raincoat and removing Riley's sodden jacket when there was a knock on the heavy brass door knocker that hung on the front door.

Cate pulled the heavy door open. "Lady Cate!" Jack bowed theatrically. He held a bag of groceries in his hands.

"Come in and get dry!" Cate said. "Good to see you again, Mr. Reid, and thank you for coming!"

"It sure is wet out there, how are you enjoying our lovely weather, Sir Riley?" Jack asked, bending over to give the small dog a scratch under his chin.

"He doesn't mind the rain so much, he's all boy. At least not when it's not thundering, he hates that."

"Shall we head to the kitchen?" Jack asked.

"Sure, oh and thank you again for offering to cook."

"I was worried you'd cook cereal for dinner," Jack teased her.

"Oh, come on, I'm not THAT bad. I'd have opted for peanut butter and jelly at least!"

"Oh boy, I wish I hadn't offered, we missed out, Pap!"

Mr. Reid chimed in, "I'd have taken anything this pretty lassie fed me, I'm not picky."

"Thank you!" Cate said. "How was your trip?" she asked as they walked to the kitchen.

"Great, nice to get away."

Cate asked where he had traveled and some general questions about his trip as they made their way downstairs. Once they arrived in the kitchen, Mr. Reid took a spot at the table while Jack made his way around the kitchen gathering materials for his meal like a professional. Cate offered to help, but he refused saying he didn't need any help, instead, suggesting she plow right into the interview with his grandfather.

Cate sat down at the table opposite Mr. Reid. "Well thanks for coming. I'm not sure if Jack mentioned it but I'm putting together materials to write a book about the castle's history and I figured you might be a good source of information. So I'd like to ask you a few questions if you don't mind," Cate began.

"Aww, come on, Cate, skip to the juicy stuff. Ask him about the theory you have about that watch of yours."

Cate shot Jack a glance. "I wasn't going to lead with that, but, okay. I guess the real reason I wanted to talk to you, not that the other reason isn't legit, it is, but, well, I mentioned to you before that the watch was slowing down. You looked at it and told me nothing was wrong with it, and I now agree, because I deduced the watch should operate that way." Cate stammered around, trying to find the words to make her theory sound less crazy.

Mr. Reid continued to stare at her as she spoke, without offering much response, which made Cate more nervous. She continued to babble. "Well, what I mean to say is, Jack mentioned to you that I hypothesized friction induced it because I developed a habit, a tic, no pun intended." She laughed nervously. "Of rubbing it and I postulated that maybe somehow that messed with the internal workings. But now my theory is it's not just some random event, but that it's the watch's purpose…"

"Oh, for heaven's sake, Cate," Jack interrupted her, "she presumes she's time traveling by slowing the watch down, Pap. Ever heard of anything like that?"

Cate blushed. "Yes, that's what I concluded. That's my theory, nothing else made sense, but I kept seeing random people dressed in old-fashioned clothing when the watch was slow. Am I just going crazy?"

Mr. Reid chuckled. "So you figured it out, young lassie? Good for you. Lady MacKenzie didn't know if you'd be bright enough to catch on to it. She didn't leave you with many clues, wondered if the secret might be best left to die with her since she couldn't tell you herself. Said if you were clever, you'd figure out the secret. She had faith that if anyone could solve it a MacKenzie could."

Cate's mouth dropped open. She wasn't sure if she felt relieved or not. Her theory was correct, but hearing that was more of a shock than she had prepared for.

"Wait a minute," Jack said, coming over to the table, "she's RIGHT?"

Cate snapped back to reality. "HEY!" She countered, "You saw it, too, you agreed with my theory!"

"Well, it's a shock to hear that we were actually time traveling."

"We?" Jack's grandfather raised an eyebrow. "Well, you're off to a right start, I'd say."

"Yes," Cate answered, "we tried it together. Well, after a total fail when I disappeared for a few seconds without him."

"Like I said, you're off to a good start, you figured out quite a lot young Cate." Mr. Reid nodded his head at Cate.

"I'm just shocked that I was right. I mean I was convinced of my theory, but how has this been such a well-kept secret?"

"Ah, good question, the family never speaks of this secret to anyone outside of themselves. And whatever Reid is working on the estate."

Jack's grandfather continued, "Long ago, when the castle was built, the new owners detected what they called anomalies. This led to the rumors of the castle being haunted. And the builder, Douglas MacKenzie, you've no doubt come across his name during your research, was the curious sort. He, along with his construction manager and later estate manager, Jamie Reid, my ancestor, spent countless hours studying these anomalies. Almost drove them crazy, but after some work, Douglas devised a mechanism that could interact with what he termed 'rips' in the 'fabric of time'. He, along with Jamie, built the watch with this mechanism and used their invention as an instrument to control these rips.

"The secret has been passed from generation to generation. Always passed verbally, never written. You understand, if the wrong person discovered it, it could lead to disaster. The preceding caretaker always passed the secret to their heir. This time was different, no one knew what you'd be like and no one could find you before Lady MacKenzie passed. She tasked me with guarding the secret until we were sure you'd be able to take on the responsibility."

"So," Cate began. "Wow, I'm sorry, I need a minute. I have so many questions! I just… I can't believe it. I mean I've done it, I've time traveled, but I still can't believe it."

Jack continued making dinner, but chimed in from across the kitchen. "You and me both. It's still surprising even after experiencing the phenomenon for myself."

"Lady MacKenzie knew, did her mother, Mary, also know?"

"Aye, lassie. I worked on the estate when Lord MacKenzie passed and left the responsibility to Lady Mary since Lady Gertrude was too young."

Cate nodded, that explained the journals. Mary's adventures weren't parties that she hosted, they were events at the castle in different eras. It also explained why pages were missing from the journals. Anything Mary wrote regarding the watch had to be destroyed so the secret was not recorded anywhere.

"You mentioned not knowing if I'd be suitable to take on the responsibility? Then the secret could have died with Gertrude?"

"Aye, as I mentioned, it's quite a responsibility and Gertrude would have rather seen the secret die with her than fall into the wrong hands. Not that she doubted you, but never having met you and not knowing anything about you, well, I guess she erred on the side of caution. You can imagine the repercussions if this fell into the hands of someone who would exploit it for their own gain."

Cate reflected for a moment. "Yes, I can see your point. I found some journals Mary kept from when she had inherited the watch and, while they were redacted, she describes the secret in the same way: as a responsibility. I see it as a gift, what historian wouldn't love to immerse themselves in an era not theirs. The learning potential is unlimited."

"You're eager, I see, but you must temper your eagerness with caution. You must be careful with this 'gift,' Cate, you don't always understand the repercussions of changing too much in the past. You must follow the rules that have been passed through the generations. Striking a balance and following those rules are the responsibility that both Mary and Gertrude spoke of."

"I see your point, again. I guess my enthusiasm got ahead of me."

"Aye, it can be exciting, but you have to be careful. Got to consider what you're doing before you start changing things. Caution like that requires a cool head and a steady hand," Mr. Reid cautioned her.

Silence fell over them for a moment while Cate collected her thoughts. "Do you know how many 'rips' exist?"

"I'm not sure if we ever had an exact count. The rips exist in different places throughout the castle. Different rips connect to different times. Lady Gertrude disliked traveling, unlike her mother. If I remember, Lady Mary identified at least four spots."

"Do you remember where these spots exist?"

"Aye, one of them in the bedroom Lady Gertrude stayed in, one of them in the bedroom down the hall, another in the downstairs office, that's a tricky one, never know who might be in there, and the fourth she found exists in another bedroom, the one they call the Blue Room."

Cate fell silent for a moment, mulling over her questions.

"May be more, those were the ones she identified. Her husband took ill and passed her the watch and the secret with little information. Oh, that reminds me there's a hallway that seems to work in any time to return, handy to remember in case of an emergency. It's the one that looks out on the back garden."

Now things were adding up for Cate. She was correct in her assumption that only certain locations worked to trigger the watch. Each location triggered a different time.

"The secret is passed down in BOTH the MacKenzie and Reid families?" Cate asked.

"Yes. The Reids' duty is always to protect this secret right along with the MacKenzies. It was a pact made between Douglas and Jamie."

"So, you helped Mary and Gertrude protect the secret?"

"Aye, lassie. Took many a trip with Lady Mary back in my younger days. As I said, Lady Gertrude was not a fan of traveling as much as her mother." He turned to Jack who was seasoning a pot of whatever steamed on the stove. "Now, I'm officially passing the mantle to you, lad. The secret is now yours and Cate's and it's up to you to protect it and Cate."

"Thanks, Pap, I have my work cut out with this one," he said, nodding toward Cate.

Cate laughed, "Hey, I'm not THAT bad. He's been doing a good job so far," she said to Mr. Reid. "So, only the three of us know?"

"That's right, lassie."

"Mr. and Mrs. Fraser?"

"Charlie and Emily? Nay. I dare say she might faint dead away if she found out."

Cate laughed at this joke, although she agreed that might be the exact reaction from Mrs. Fraser.

"That reminds me," Cate said, "once I 'traveled' back and when I came back, Mrs. Fraser said she'd just seen me. But I was gone for at least fifteen to twenty minutes. Does that make sense?"

"Aye, and a good observation on your part. When you travel, the time where you're from almost stands still. That's why the watch is slow. The watch keeps time from YOUR time. Now, I said ALMOST. We calculated the ratio to be about fifteen minutes in the past to one minute here. Tempting as it may be to spend a lot of time in the past, you must remember that you can't go disappearing from your own time for too long. People will wonder."

"Always keep an eye on YOUR time. It's the inscription on the watch and it was in Lady Gertrude's note. NOW it makes sense!"

"Aye, lassie, that's right. The warning from Douglas MacKenzie himself. Had the phrase engraved on that watch to remind everyone."

Cate's thoughts absorbed her for a few moments, as she tried to piece together the puzzle when another query struck her.

"On a different note, do you know why my family branch became estranged? I found a family bible with an ink blot over my branch of the family. As you mentioned, I wasn't easy to find. I found evidence that Gertrude visited my parents before my birth, but then it seems like all contact was cut off and our side was blotted out in the family bible."

"I cannae help you there, lassie. Lady Gertrude never mentioned it, never discussed your side. She knew your family, but not where to find you. I got the impression that your grandparents moved and changed their names around when a spot of trouble cropped up. The castle's secret almost being discovered. Perhaps they moved to protect your family from being sought by any undesirable people. My guess is Lady Gertrude stayed away after your birth, just to keep your family safe."

"That makes sense and seems reasonable. This is a lot to digest, but thank you for the information. This is incredible."

"I'm sure you're still reeling. No doubt you'll have more questions. When you do, I'll be here to help you as best I can," Mr. Reid said smiling at her.

Jack delivered full bowls of what he called his "famous stew." Cate had to admit the meal smelled delicious. "Well, there you have it, Lady Cate. Your theory was right, mystery solved! Now you can relax!"

"Relax? My mind is whirling with the possibilities! Do you like history, Jack?" Cate asked.

"Oh, boy," Jack groaned. "You sure you don't want your old job back, Pap?" he joked.

"Oh, come on, Jack, the adventures are just beginning," she said with a gleam of mischief in her eye.

Made in the USA
Monee, IL
28 March 2021